"Secret Legacy kept me spellbound from page one to the very last word! The tension and relationships are beautifully written and will keep readers coming back for more. I got chills up my spine more than once. I can't wait to see what happens next."

— JJ KING, USAT BESTSELLING AUTHOR

"A whimsical tale that will transport you from the first page."

— CARLYLE LABUSCHAGNE, USAT BESTSELLING AUTHOR

"This book is packed full of awesomeness! Supernatural academy? Check. A girl who feels like she doesn't belong? Check. Sexy, mysterious boy? Check. And alllll the secrets, twists, and turns to keep you flipping pages. You don't want to miss this one!"

— LIZA STREET, USAT BESTSELLING AUTHOR

Original Copyright © 2020 Carissa Andrews

Published in 2020 by Carissa Andrews

Cover Design © Carissa Andrews

All rights reserved.

ISBN-13: 978-1-953304-03-2

HAUNTED LEGACY

Book 3 of the Windhaven Witches

CARISSA ANDREWS

AUTHOR
REVOLUTION

CHAPTER 1
DEATH IS MY CURSE

is time has come...

H Abigail's cryptic words have lingered with me all summer. No matter how hard I've tried to shake them, they've settled underneath my skin, making a home just beneath the surface.

As much as I want to forget them, it's an impossible task.

To make matters worse, after all the energy Abigail must have expelled fighting Cat's Fetch, I've only managed to catch glimpses of her. They're fleeting and nowhere near enough time to question her on what those words meant. It's maddening.

I shudder, unable to stay warm any longer. The brisk chill of being on the cusp of fall has crept into the evening air. I pull my sweatshirt in tighter, letting the shiver roll through me. Despite the change in temps, I can't be bothered to go inside just yet.

My gaze flits from the glittering water to the setting sun hanging low above the pond. Deep-gold tendrils soak in the magenta ribbons of the sky, as if the added color somehow feeds it. Closing my eyes, I breathe in deeply through my nose, wishing the clean air could wash away the worry buried in my soul.

Even if Abigail's warning weren't enough—every time I look at Wade I see something else. Something that wasn't there before. As much as I love him, as much as I want to be with him... I can't shake this intense dread that his father was right.

Death follows me wherever I go.

It's like I'm stuck inside an episode of "Buffy." Only, death isn't my gift. It's my *curse.*

I don't want to be the reason Wade loses his one chance at being human. Of experiencing all this one and only life has to offer... I don't want to be the reason he dies an early death and has to forfeit it all. I wouldn't be able to live with myself.

My breath hitches in my throat and I blink away the liquid terror escaping from my eyes.

Wade has tried so hard to keep up the status quo. I know he wants this to work desperately, but...

My chin quivers. Despite trying to find an answer, I know what has to be done—what I've always needed to do. I've just been too scared to think it, or say it out loud.

Not that I've had anyone I could say it to other than him.

I've had no one to talk to. Cat and Colton are gone. Evidently, thanks to Colton's stunt last year, they've been transferred to another academy closer to the psychic Diana Hawthorne so she can keep an eye on them. Granted, it was probably a wise move, but still. Without Cat at least, their absence has created a vacuum for all of my thoughts to spiral around inside my head whenever I find myself alone...which seems to be happening more and more.

Maybe it's my destiny?

Look at my mom and dad... Abigail...

The landscape is changing now with school starting back up, and I can't help but think now's the time. Wade could still find someone new. Someone who isn't bad news for him.

Someone his Angel of Death father will approve of...

Someone *normal*.

Instantly, my mind conjures up images of Chelsea, Wade's strawberry-blond, green-eyed landlady. She's funny, pretty, and...uncomplicated. She's practically me, but the *light* version.

My insides twist and my heart constricts in on itself. The impulse to gag tugs at the back of my throat, but something in the recesses of my mind resonates with the idea.

He'd be better off with her.

"Hey there, beautiful. I thought I might find you out here," Wade says, making my insides try to jump outside. I hadn't even heard his footsteps coming up behind me.

Wiping quickly at my face to hide the tears, I shoot him a halfhearted smile and attempt to stand up.

"No, no... sit," he says, dropping down beside me on the dock.

I sit back down, unsure how to handle this moment. I wasn't expecting it to come so soon. Panic claws at my insides and I blink back the emotions still washing over me.

Swallowing hard, I turn to him. "So, what brings you here? Everything okay?"

Glancing at me, his silver eyes sparkle mischievously. There's an air of anxious energy in the way he holds himself. He doesn't say anything, so I narrow my gaze, trying to figure out what he's up to.

Finally, he chuckles. "Oh, don't look at me like that. Everything's fine. What about you? You seem a little..."

"I'm fine," I say, brushing off his observation by swiping my hand in the air. Guilt instantly jabs me in the ribs, but I ignore it. "Just wanted to sit outside and enjoy the end of summer. It'll be too cold to sit out here soon."

"You're not kidding. It's freezing already," he says, cramming his hands under his armpits and shivering.

The cool breeze ruffles his dark hair. With the sun's low light, it highlights the strands of red woven through the black, making it look like flames flickering against the royal blue sky.

"Did you want to head inside?" I say, pointing back toward the manor.

"Only if you want to. I don't want to cut your relaxation short," he says shaking his head.

"I haven't eaten yet. We could head inside to grab a bite," I offer, trying to buy myself some time.

"That might be nice, actually," he says, grinning again. He stands up quickly, practically bouncing off the dock with enthusiasm. Bending back down, he extends a hand to me.

Taking his offering, I pull myself up to a stand. "Thanks."

Wade lifts his arm, twirling me in a circle on the spot. "You are most welcome, Ms. Blackwood."

Unable to help myself, a small smile lifts the corner of my lips.

Wade locks eyes with me long enough to make me squirm under his silver scrutiny.

Without batting an eye, his features soften and he whispers, "God, you're so beautiful. I love the way the sunlight ignites your hair. It's like the sun is setting in those strands." Grinning broadly, he twirls a finger through one of my unruly auburn curls.

I run a hand across my collar bone, wishing like hell I could find a way to change what we are. "Wade, I have something—"

He holds up a finger, pressing it to my lips. "Eh, eh... nope. Me first." Removing his finger, he shrugs sheepishly. "I mean, I know it should usually be ladies first, but you'll just have to deal this time, Dru." He winks at me, sending a wave of anguish cascading through my entire being.

My lips tighten and my mouth goes dry. Nodding, I raise a hand, allowing him to proceed.

"Actually, you'll need to come with me," he says, his eyes once again sparkling. He takes my hand, leading the way off the dock.

Confusion rolls through me but I can't seem to muster enough energy to formulate a reason for his near-giddy excitement. Instead, I fight the bile rising in the back of my throat and the unrelenting nervous energy. I know if I don't act soon, I'll lose my nerve altogether. Instead, I'll want to stay in his arms and ignore the pain and suffering being together will inevitably bring.

As we walk through the courtyard hand-in-hand, he plucks one of the red roses from the garden and hands it to me. "But he, who dares not grasp the thorn, should never crave the rose."

Pressing the stem between my fingertips, I tip my head in acknowledgment. "Anne Brontë."

"Indeed," he beams. "One of my favorite poems."

"Hmmm," I say, staring at the shimmering petals, wondering if he can somehow sense what's on my mind.

Leaning in, he kisses the side of my cheek. His scent teases my senses, lulling me into a safe space.

Maybe it's not as bad as I think... What if I'm wrong about all of this?

Inhaling deeply, my resolve slips.

Removing my hand from his, I place it along his jawline, drawing his lips to mine. For the first time in a long time, I close my eyes, letting the feel of his skin guide my reactions, rather than relying on my troubled mind.

Placing both hands along my neck, he inhales sharply, pulling me in close. His lips bear down on mine, kissing me as if his life depends on this single exchange of passion.

As he pulls back, my head swirls, but my worries sink into deeper waters.

"Come on, let's get that bite to eat. I still have something for you..." he says, grabbing hold of my hand and pulling me toward the kitchen's entrance.

When we get inside, the manor is quiet—as it has been all summer. Dad's been in and out, only here for the briefest of moments before having to flit off again. There's barely enough time to connect, let alone ask him how he's been or where he's been going.

Most of the time, it's not so bad, but I can't help but wonder if I'm driving him away, too.

"What would you like, my dearest Dru? Pasta?

Chicken? Tacos with ice cream?" Wade asks, opening the fridge and freezer at the same time.

I chuckle. "What would you like?"

"I'm not fussy. I'll cook whatever the lady of the house would appreciate."

I shoot him an uncertain smile, dropping my gaze to the floor. "Something simple, I guess."

Wade's dark eyebrows rise to the sky, and he closes the fridge door. "Pizza it is." He reaches in, grabbing a cheese pizza and plunking it on the counter.

Shaking my head, I turn to the stove and set the preheat temp.

"Would you like plain and simple? Or a culinary explosion in your mouth?"

My eyes widen. "A what?"

Wade laughs. "Cheese pizza or something with a bit more pizazz?"

I narrow one eye. "What would pizazz consist of?"

"Whatever you like. Ham and pineapple. Mushrooms and cilantro. Tabasco sauce and nacho chips..." he says with a flourish of his hands.

"Let's go with just cheese. Less to go wrong," I say, grabbing a couple of plates.

"Ye have little faith in my culinary expertise. But, alas, I will bow to the wishes of my mistress," he says, folding an arm over his midsection and bowing slightly.

He dislodges the pizza from its box, placing it on the pizza stone and looking at it longingly.

"You could always go hog wild on half of it. Then, if it's horrifying, we still have a few salvageable slices," I suggest, shrugging.

He claps like a toddler and spins back to the refrigerator. A moment later, half of the pizza is piled with mushrooms, onions, ham, and something green. I'm not entirely certain it's edible, but if it makes him happy, so be it.

"So, I have some news..." Wade says, wiping his hands on his jeans after he places the pizza in the oven.

"Is this the surprise?" I say, turning to him.

"Oh, lord, no. That will come soon enough," he says, waving his hands out in front of him. "No, this is just news-related news. Small talk, if you will."

"Ah," I say, nodding. "Carry on."

"Thank you," he says, tipping his head. "As I was saying... I have some news. You know how I was going to struggle with swinging tuition after this next semester?"

I narrow my gaze. "Yes?"

"Well, I've just landed a gig," he says, grinning.

My eyebrows rise. "You have? That's great. What is it?"

"It's another PCA job. Chelsea introduced me," he says, leaning against the counter.

The mention of Chelsea's name twists the knife still buried inside me. I inhale sharply through my nose. "Oh...yeah?"

"Yeah, there's a lady in my building who needs a little help. She's getting older and doesn't have any family around here. Chelsea's been worried she might have to transfer her to a nursing home or contact the county... but when I told her I used to be a PCA, she did a little digging and helped get everything in place," he says.

"That's great—" I say, trying to muster as much excitement about it as I can.

"It's not a be-all, end-all or anything. But at least it buys me some time. Especially since my dad isn't likely to change his mind anytime soon," Wade says, rolling his eyes.

"What do you mean?" I say, walking to the oven and clicking on the light. I bend in to take a look at the pizza's progress. So far, my half looks nearly done, but the other half looks like it needs another twenty minutes to heat through.

"You know, our assets," Wade says, shrugging nonchalantly.

I stand up, unable to disentangle my eyebrows from one another. "Huh?"

Wade rolls his eyes, as if this is the last thing he wanted to be thinking about. "Just family money and stuff."

The timer on the oven beeps and he steps up, ushering me to step aside.

My mind whirls, taking in this new information. When we were back in the catacombs, I remember the two of them talking about the family assets... but I thought his dad meant their powers.

Wade slices up the pizza, spreading the pieces out evenly on the plates. "Dinner is served," he says, with a hand flourish.

I blink from him to the plates, absently grabbing one for myself. "I thought... I thought you didn't have any inheritance. I'm confused."

Grabbing his own plate, Wade holds out his other arm in an offering for me to grab it.

I blink hard, but interlock my arm in his.

"It's complicated. The inheritance is magically bound. When my grandpa died, as next in line I should have been given access to our assets. But..." his voice trails off as he leads me from the kitchen. We loop through the main entrance and down the hallway to my bedroom.

"But...he's denying you," I say, beginning to understand the full scope of things, "*because of me.*"

Wade shrugs as if it doesn't bother him in the least. "It's just money."

"But—what about your tuition? Your life? You've been so worried about finances...why would you turn that away?" I sputter.

"I can't believe you're even asking me that," he says indignantly.

I shake my head, trying to understand why he'd turn down an easier life—one without financial struggles—just to be with me. It's ludicrous.

He deserves so much more. I can't let him give up his entire inheritance just to be with me.

We reach my bedroom door and Wade drops my arm to reach for the handle.

"Wade," I whisper, unable to look him in the eye. I stare at my plate, tears welling up behind my lids. "I think we should break up."

I look up just in time to see his bright face falter. His hand drops from the door handle in slow motion and as it creaks open, I turn to face the room. Red roses or their petals cover every conceivable surface of my bedroom. Red candles flicker romantically, sending a powerful surge of regret through me.

"Happy"—his voice is barely a whisper as he swallows hard, trying to recover—"one-year anniversary."

CHAPTER 2
WHAT'S FATE GOT TO DO
WITH IT?

Everything is upside down.

I hadn't anticipated this empty, horrible hole that's settled inside my torso. I thought I was doing the right thing, but I can't escape the memory of utter despair on Wade's face. His sad, silver eyes are burned into my mind, and no matter what I do, I can't erase his expression. From the moment I broke things off with him, all I wanted was to take it back. To rewind time and erase the whole thing. But I couldn't make my brain align with my heart. I need to protect him...I need for him to forget about me.

Hell, I need to find a way to forget about him.

Yet, everywhere I go... he's there.

My eyes flit to the edge of his gorgeous face, just two seats up in the row beside me. The sunlight cascades through the window and highlights the edges of his face. It illuminates the tips of his dark eyelashes, drawing my attention back with every blink.

If I thought starting the new school year would give us

the opportunity for space, I certainly hadn't considered just how much our paths are intertwined. He's in every single one of my classes, with the exception of one—*Resurrection Theory*.

It's a daily kind of torture, and one of my own making.

Glancing down at my notebook, I scribble in circles, not taking in a thing Mrs. Clement is telling the class. Her voice drones on in the background, but as fascinating as life and death entities should be, I can't muster the focus to listen about guardians, Lemures, the Four Horsemen, or fate.

Fate can suck it, if you ask me.

Without warning, the person behind me kicks my chair, making me jump. I look up to find a classroom full of expectant eyes all trained on me.

"I, uh—" I stutter, shifting my gaze around the room. Briefly, I stop at Wade, but as soon as our eyes connect, my insides flip and the room spins. Quickly, I return my gaze to the teacher. "What was the question?"

"Ms. Blackwood, I know it's early in the semester, but I'd sure appreciate it if you'd pay a bit more attention," Mrs. Clement says, raising a white eyebrow over the rim of her red-framed glasses. Her piercing, ice-blue eyes slice right through me and I sit up a bit straighter. "There's a lot to cover and you, of all people, would do well to learn the lessons coming through for you. Remember, this isn't just generic fluff. While I might look like I'm up here spouting off about a single random topic, each and every one of you is getting tailored insights that will illuminate the way for you. While much of it overlaps, I mean, you wouldn't be in this class if it didn't...you still need to perk your ears and have a listen. Yeah?"

With my cheeks flaming, I nod and drop my gaze to my notebook. "Sorry," I mumble.

"Now, then... As I was saying, learning how to spot a harbinger of the veil can play a critical role in not only preparedness for how to deal with it, but also protection. When our gifts are tied to life and death, not everything that finds us will be all rainbows and butterflies, if you know what I mean. Sometimes, things go very, very wrong. When they do, the cost could be your life—or the life of someone you love. Do you understand?" Mrs. Clement's eyes again fall to me, and I nod, showing her I was paying attention.

Her words rest with me as validation.

"What causes some of these entities to be formed?" Wade asks. Hearing his voice slices right through me.

Mrs. Clement walks around to the front of her desk and leans against it. "Good question, Mr. Hoffman. Some are ancient ones, formed with the early magic summoned out of creation. They're almost woven into its very fabric. Others are created due to their circumstances."

Wade leans back in his chair, crossing his arms over his body, a telltale sign he's not impressed with the answer.

"I understand that's not the most descriptive of answers, but until you know what you're dealing with, it's hard to give a straight answer. Do you have something specific in mind?" Mrs. Clement asks, tilting her head to the side.

It takes him a moment to answer, but when he does he shakes his head. "Not exactly. I'm just thinking about the things I've come up against already. It seems each thing has its own set of rules and none of them jibe with one another."

"I think I see where you're going. This rule separation could be because each entity group is much like a society in and of itself. Just like with people in general, there are no hard and fast rules. We have to work within the confines we're given," she says, tapping the edge of her desk. "Does that help?"

"Sort of. Thank you," Wade says, nodding.

I narrow my gaze, wondering what exactly he was getting at because his tone says something totally different.

"All right, time for the groans to begin," Mrs. Clement says, rubbing her hands together and grinning broadly. "For this week's first lesson, each of you will be given a Life and Death Entity to research. However, there's a caveat. You'll be paired up with a partner who has a divergent set of magical aptitudes so you can view your entity from different perspectives. Together, you'll do some digging to uncover not only their origins and why they exist, but also some of the more mysterious aspects of your choosing. After all, these are magical beings by nature, so there should be some interesting tidbits you could unearth. Then, you and your partner will deliver a presentation next Friday on what you discover."

Then, as expected, the sea of lamentation erupts from the class. Mrs. Clement raises her palms upward, nodding in evident approval.

Leaning back in my chair, I sweep my gaze over the class. Maybe it won't be so bad. There are plenty of people in here that I've never even seen before, let alone spoken to. Maybe this is just the start Wade and I need in order to move on.

"Here's how this is going to work... I've paired you up

with a partner. When you have your assignment, I'd like for you to find each other and introduce yourselves, if introductions are necessary," Mrs. Clement says, grabbing a stack of papers from her desk. "I know this probably seems very old-school in this modern era of texting and Snapchatting, but I can't help it. I do love me a bit of antiquity." She winks, clucking her tongue and jabbing her pointer finger out like a gun. "Besides, magical boundaries notwithstanding, I want to look each of you in the eye so you can't tell me you didn't receive your assignment." She turns her gaze directly at me, as if she's already sussed out I'm the problem child in class.

Wonderful.

I grin back at her, trying to present myself as attentive as humanly possible. The last thing I need is to begin this year with a teacher on my back. Starting at the front of the class and working her way down each aisle with a cheerful grin on her face, she passes a sheet of paper to each student. She even whistles a bit of a tune as she hands them out.

As she passes a sheet to Wade, I hold my breath, waiting to see who he's partnered with. Half of me hopes it's a girl, while the other half is screaming that it better not be a damn girl. Placing the paper on the desk in front of him, he sits very still. His right hand covers the sheet of paper, as if he needs to build up the strength to turn it over.

Biting the side of my cheek, I blink away from him as Mrs. Clement thrusts out my sheet of paper.

"It's a bit like a sorting hat, isn't it?" she says happily. Then, she moves on, doling out the next batch of torment to the student in front of me.

Suddenly, the burden of knowing who my chosen partner is becomes heavier than I anticipated. My heartbeat thumps awkwardly in my chest, threatening to bring me down if I don't give in and turn the paper over.

Mrs. Clement settles herself behind her large wooden desk. All around me, people get up, finding their partners and grouping their seats closer together. I inhale sharply and my eyes flit to Wade. His paper is held out in front of him as if he's pondering his fate. However, he abruptly stands up and walks to Mrs. Clement's desk.

All at once, sheer panic flashes through me. What if he's my partner? Is he asking to be reassigned? Would he do that?

I bounce between anxiety and humiliation.

Surely Mrs. Clement wouldn't have put us together? I mean, out of twenty-five or more students, what are the chances? It has to be pretty low, right?

The urge to know drives me to flip the paper over. I have to know why he's talking to Mrs. Clement.

Taking another deep breath, I stare down at the name and assignment in an odd sense of relief and disappointment.

Assignment: Lemures
   Partner: Colton Gilbert

On the upside, it's not Wade. But on the other hand, it looks like I'll be doing this assignment alone. So much for meeting someone new.

While my wariness is alleviated somewhat, I can't help

but be a little surprised. Doesn't the school know Colt and Cat are gone? Surely Diana Hawthorne would have made sure things were done properly before taking the two of them down to Georgia?

Gathering up my things, I throw my backpack over my right shoulder and walk to the front of the room. I pass Wade, who has returned to his seat. His hand flies across a small notebook as he scribbles something down, but as soon as I walk by, he stops. His dark lashes flutter as our eyes connect briefly. I shoot him a quick, awkward smile, then turn to face the teacher.

As I step up to the desk, I hand Mrs. Clement my paper. "I think there's a bit of a mix-up, Mrs. Clement. Colton Gilbert is gone this year. He and his sister are learning at an academy down south for the year. I'm not sure that they'll be back, to be honest."

Mrs. Clement takes my paper, adjusting her red rims on her nose. She eyes the document with sudden suspicion. After a moment, she slams it down. "Goddamn administrative staff. They never tell me this stuff. They know it can affect the outcomes of my class. I swear, Ms. Cain does this shit just to screw with me. Damn masochistic wench."

My eyebrows flutter upward in surprise but I stifle a bit of a laugh. I've never heard a teacher be quite so brutally down-to-earth and honest. I have a few choice words about Ms. Cain, too, but I'd never say any of them out loud. Especially not inside the walls of Windhaven Academy. I know how some of the magical elements of this facility work.

Sighing heavily, she tugs over another sheet of paper,

eyeing the two of them side-by-side. I bend forward, trying to get a better view.

"Well, Ms. Blackwood, it's not ideal, but looks we all have to make sacrifices this year" she says, scribbling out Colton's name and the assignment. She writes new ones down and thrusts the sheet of paper back to me. "Forget Lemures, they're not as exciting."

I flip it over to get a better look. Scrawled across the page in big bold letter is: The Three Fates.

Underneath, my eyes flit to the name.

Adrenaline courses through my veins as my heart sinks.

Of course, it is.

I glance over my shoulder just as Mrs. Clement calls out, "Congratulations, Mr. Hoffman. Looks like you'll have a partner after all."

CHAPTER 3

OPEN WOUNDS

Space. Just a little bit of freaking space would have been nice. But instead, it's like the universe just wants to meddle in my life, making things as hard as humanly possible. Life, death... *relationships*.

I want to do the right thing—but it's impossible to tell what's right anymore. Especially when I can't even get away from the one person I desperately want to be with but know I can't. Or at least *shouldn't*.

My gaze softens as I stare at the walls of the resurrection chamber, wishing the stillness of this space could permeate the rest of my life. Instead, things are about to get very complicated. I'd hoped to communicate with Abigail, but she's still as difficult as ever to connect with. Between my dad's trips and Abigail being MIA, this house is the epitome of silence. Yet, inside my head, it's never been louder. I check my watch and stand up. It's about that time.

Taking a deep breath to calm my nerves, I turn to face the way out. Light from the small window illuminates the edges of the staircase wall, beckoning me upward. Dropping my shoulders, I make my way to the staircase.

Fate.

I roll my eyes at the word as I ascend the stairs from the resurrection chamber. Even my teacher is taunting me with this ridiculous assignment. If only she knew just how difficult this was going to be. A part of me wishes like hell Cat and Colton were still here. While doing this assignment with Colton wouldn't have been ideal either, it wouldn't be quite this cruel. At least for me.

Guilt rolls through my midsection. Not thinking about Colton's feelings is part of the reason they're not here in the first place.

Shaking my head, I close the door behind me and gather up my laptop and notebook. The last thing I want to do is come back here.

I close my bedroom door behind me, just in time to hear the doorbell ring. The hairs on the back of my neck rise, ushering a shiver straight through me.

"Here goes nothing, Autumn," I whisper to myself as I walk down the expansive hallway toward the front entry.

As I reach the main staircase, a rush of cold air thrusts past me, making me pull up short. Clutching my laptop to my chest, I spin around. "Abigail?" I call out.

The frigid air remains, making my breath billow out like it's the middle of January.

Again the doorbell rings, making me jump. Shuddering away the chill, I rush to the door and fling it open.

"Hey," Wade says. He runs a hand across the back of his neck, then crams his hands into his jeans pockets.

"Hey. Come on in," I say, stepping aside and opening the door wider for him.

He tips his head and steps inside. "So, this is..."

"Yeah," I say, nodding.

"Well, did you want to stay here? Or go someplace a little less..."

"Nah," I say, swiping my hand in the air and hoping I pull off a bit of nonchalance. "It's all good. Wanna go to the dining room? Or the study?"

"Which place would make you feel more comfortable?" he asks, shifting his gaze to the dining area.

"Let's go down to the study. The Wi-Fi is better," I say, tipping my head toward the staircase and nodding for him to follow me.

I walk up the grand staircase and push open the double doors directly in front of the landing. A large table with cushy red leather chairs rest directly opposite us. Beyond, the wall of windows overlooks the courtyard and pond, with a view of the glittering water that's only rivaled by sitting on the dock. The trees haven't quite begun their descent into fall, but you can tell by the hint of fog lingering on the water's surface that it's just around the corner.

Entering the study, I flip on the switch and all around the room small lamps ignite, casting a warm glow. The dark-red mahogany built-ins, along with the desk to the left, look very impressive, even to me.

Wade enters the room, his eyes wide as he takes in the space. He walks over to the right wall, letting his fingertips grace the spines of many books adorning the dark mahogany shelves. He stops at a framed picture of me as a small child. I'm outside the house in the courtyard and my mom is just off to the side, smiling like she doesn't have a care in the world.

"This room is...something else," he says, turning his chilling gaze to me.

Everything about him screams unbearably sexy and I breathe in deeply, trying to focus on staying centered. I nod, placing my laptop on the table. "Yeah, I don't usually come up here, but since Dad's not home, I figured it was a good place to study. I mean, it's even in the name of the room, you know?"

Wade chuckles, his gaze falling to the floor as a hint of a smile graces his lips.

"So, fate, huh?" I say, trying to bring us around to why we're here.

Wade's silver eyes flit upward to me and his lips press in tight. "*Fates*, actually." He walks over, standing behind one of the leather chairs and looking out over the water. After a moment, he takes a seat and turns to face me.

I quirk an eyebrow. "Have you been researching without me, Mr. Hoffman?"

His dark eyebrows tug inward. "Well, I..." he stammers.

I chuckle. "I'm teasing. It's fine. Okay, so what do you know?" I pull out my pen from the notebook ring and poise it, ready to take notes.

Inhaling deeply through his nose, he shrugs. "Not much. Just that the idea of fate isn't as simple as it seems. Like we didn't know that already..."

I look up, feeling the weight of his stare. "Wade," I say, tilting my head to the side.

"Nevermind." He lifts his left shoulder and tips his head. "All right, so fate isn't a single entity. There are actually three sisters who manage the destinies of everyone."

My eyebrows fly upward and I lean back in my chair. "Oh?"

"Right?" Wade nods. "Well, if you believe in this sorta thing, anyway. I mean, who knows if it's true...but since we're researching *entities*, I figured there must be a kernel in there somewhere."

"Fair point," I say, nodding, and scrawling the information down. "Okay, so, anything else?"

"Not really. That was as far as I got before I realized you'd probably want to do the research together." Wade's eyebrows intertwine, and he shakes his head. "I mean, not that you wanted to actually do the research with me in the first place, but..."

I sigh. "Wade..."

As if I didn't feel like absolute crap as it is, his persistent jabs aren't helping.

"Forget it. Anyway, the point is, I'm here to work on things as a team. You know, because that's what partners do. Work on things. *Together*." He lifts his gaze, again locking eyes with me.

His words are pointed and they do exactly what he intended they do—cut deep.

Yes, as it turns out, I'm horrible at relationships. Not just romantic ones, either. I haven't called my mom in ages. I barely see my dad. Hell, lately, I've talked more with James, the housekeeper, than anyone else. Living or dead.

"Yeah, well...we better get a move on, then. I don't have all night," I say more tersely than I intended. Trying to ignore his digs are difficult, but if it's part of what I have to endure to protect him, then so be it.

"Autumn, I didn't mean..." Wade says, remorse splashing across his features.

I raise a hand between us, cutting him off. "Look, it doesn't matter. It is what it is."

"Yeah, but I don't even get what *this* is. It's like you've taken the one good thing we both had going for us and decided to bin the whole thing. I don't get why..." Wade says, ditching any pretense of learning more about our assignment.

I look back at my laptop longingly, wishing we could just focus on that instead of the emotionally charged conversation he seems hell-bent on pulling me into.

Leaning back in the chair, I pull my feet up and use my legs as a barrier between us. "Maybe you don't have to understand everything. Have you ever thought of that?"

His eyebrows lower and he leans in. "I beg to differ. You owe me. At least with this and after everything we've been through. Dru—"

My heart skips a beat and before I can think things through, I hear myself say, "Don't call me that."

The reaction is instantaneous. Wade's wounded expression resurfaces and shreds any ounce of self-reserve I have left. He pushes the chair back, standing up and backing away.

I drop my legs, standing up, too. "I didn't mean to—" I begin.

"Wow," he says, dropping his gaze to the floor as his eyebrows fly upward. "I mean, okay... I knew things were dire. I knew you were going through something here and needed some space, but I didn't know we'd reached *this* place."

"Wade, we can't be together..." I say, fighting back tears.

"Why? Because *you* decided?" he demands.

I roll my head back, staring at the ceiling. A single, stupid tear trickles down my cheek and I swipe at it. "No, because I'm not right for you. Because things would never work. Because we're so different..."

"And what?" he says, stepping forward and towering over me. Sandalwood and soap circle around me, tugging at every raw emotion left dangling.

My chin quivers, but I manage to say, "Your dad said that we..."

"Who the hell cares what my dad said? He had his one life and he fucked it up. I'm not going to let him dictate the one that I have, too. Don't you get that?" he spits back. His eyes penetrate mine, pleading with me to understand.

"You deserve someone better than me," I whisper.

He snorts indignantly. "Are you kidding me? Nah, you've *gotta* be kidding me... Who are you to decide whether or not there's someone better for me out there? You don't get that responsibility. My dad, as much as he wishes it weren't the case...doesn't get that responsibility. It's mine. Do you hear me? *Mine*."

As if to punctuate his statement, all of the lightbulbs in the room burst. Instinctively, I hunch forward and cover my head.

"It wasn't me—" Wade cries out, reaching for me.

I drop my hands, surveying the room. Shards of broken bulbs are everywhere, and the only light cascading into the room comes from the far-off sunset that's about to extinguish itself.

Wade's eyes are wide as he backs up and turns in circles with his hands raised.

Suddenly, the same intense cold from earlier sweeps through the room. Wrapping my arms around myself, I turn around, hunting for its source.

"Do you feel that?" Wade whispers, shivering as his breath bursts out in small clouds. "It's like the room just plunged by forty degrees."

"Yeah, I feel it," I say, shifting myself closer to him as I continue to monitor the space.

"Is Abigail pissed or something?" he says, reaching out and pulling me into his arms.

I blink hard, unsure whether or not to allow myself the pleasure of staying there or not. His strong arms and warm body are a safe place and I feel anything but safe...

I place a hand on his chest, but gently push myself away, giving us both a little space. "I'm not sure. I haven't really seen much of her since..."

"Maybe we should, um, go somewhere else to study?" Wade offers, tugging at my sleeve as he backs toward the door.

I nod, taking a step toward the table to grab my things. "Yeah, that might be—"

Behind me, a gurgling sound erupts, making me spin on the spot. Wade's eyes are large silver circles of sheer panic as he drops to his knees and gropes at his throat.

CHAPTER 4
HAUNTING

Racing over to Wade, I drop down beside him. "Wade," I cry out, reaching for him and trying to process what's happening.

There's nothing in sight, but the room is utterly frigid —like all warmth has been ejected. My fingertips freeze against his skin as I try to pull back whatever is there, but there's nothing.

"Where is it? What is it?" Panic wells up inside me as I realize I have no idea what to do or how to help. My worst nightmare is coming true right before my eyes.

Wade continues to struggle, fighting off the unseen force. His face transitions from a bright red to a muted shade of gray.

"Stop—stop this!" I scream, throwing my arms down like a petulant child.

All at once, the room spins and I find myself flat on my back on the floor as if a blast just went off. Wade drops his arms as he slumps over, landing hard on his right side next to me. He gasps for air, then goes completely silent as his

CARISSA ANDREWS

beautiful eyes flutter closed. I push myself up to my knees, scrambling over to him and pulling him into my lap.

"Wade, Wade, please..." I murmur, running my hands over his hair and the side of his face. Bending down, I place my head against his chest. The faint thump of his heartbeat greets me, settling my own out-of-control pulse slightly. "Oh, thank god."

I watch his eyelashes flutter like he's deep in a dream and I sit there, holding him and brushing my fingertips against his forehead.

The room slowly warms up, releasing some of its foreboding vibe. The sun has set and the only light penetrating the room cascades in from the chandelier in the entryway. It adds an eerie glow on the top of his head, like he's adorned with a halo, and it pulls me back to reality.

That was close...*too close.*

I don't know what happened, or why. If it was a ghost, I don't understand why I couldn't see it.

Some postmortem medium I am.

Suddenly, Wade's eyes flicker open and he abruptly sits up. His left hand rises, resting at his clavicle as he turns his perplexed gaze to me.

"What was that?" he says, his voice barely a scratchy whisper.

I bite my lip and tug my eyebrows in. "I don't know. I couldn't see anything. I wish I..."

Swallowing hard, Wade places a hand on my shoulder, pushing himself to an unsteady stand.

"You should be careful. You don't have to rush," I begin.

Wade shakes his head. "No, I need to get outta here. I need air—"

Undeserved disappointment rolls through me, but I nod and stand up, too.

"You should come with me," he says, his eyes wide. Backing out of the study, he studies the doorway as if it's the gateway to hell.

"I can't, Wade," I say softly. "This doesn't change anything..."

"Please," Wade pleads, grabbing hold of my hands. "You're—it's not safe here. There's something in this house and it's not happy."

"Then I need to get to the bottom of it," I say, straightening my shoulders. "Right now, I'm the only one who can. I'll summon Abigail and get her to help me. Besides, technically, I don't know that it's here. You could have brought it with you. I've been learning..."

"But—"

I drop his hands and walk out into the landing. "No buts. Go home and get some rest. Keep the phone next to you and call for help at the slightest sign of anything." I bite my lip as I turn around to face him. "Maybe ask Chelsea to keep an eye on you."

Wade's eyes narrow and his jaw sets.

"Come on, let me help you to your car," I say, bending an elbow for him to grab hold of.

Instead, his eyelashes flutter, and he steps around me, reaching for the handrail. His footsteps are deliberate and slow, but when he reaches the front door, he grabs hold of the handle to open it, then pauses.

A long, awkward silence floods the otherwise-expansive entryway and I hold my breath, waiting.

Finally, he turns around. "Autumn, it's not me I'm

worried about. You need to be very, very careful. Please, reconsider and come with me."

I tilt my head to the side, shooting him a lopsided grin. "You know I can't do that."

"Then please, call someone—*anyone*. Call James and have him stay with you until your dad gets back. You shouldn't be alone in this house right now," he says, concern plastered over his features.

"Okay, I'll think about it," I say, walking up and taking hold of the front door. Opening it wide, I stand aside. "Are you sure you're good to drive?"

Wade's jaw sharpens and he nods. "Yeah, I can handle it." He shoots me a sideways glance and drops his gaze to the ground as he walks out the door and down the front steps. As he reaches the driver's-side door, he stops as if he's going to say something, but thinks better of it. With a click, he opens the door and hops inside.

Conflicting feelings twist and churn inside my chest as I watch his taillights fade down to the end of the driveway. Am I doing the right thing letting him leave? Is he right? Should I have gone with him? As much as I would have loved to do that, this event only put things into sharp perspective for me.

I lied to him earlier. Whatever happened didn't come with him; it was here before he arrived. I felt its presence and didn't know what it was.

Now, it's time to figure it out.

I close the door and spin around on my heel. "Abigail," I call out, letting my voice echo all through the house. "I know you can hear me. Where are you?"

Dead air permeates the space around me and I let out an exasperated sigh. Where in the hell is she?

All of a sudden, movement on the upper landing catches my eye. It's too fast to see exactly what it is, but I race up the grand staircase after it.

"Abigail? Is that you?" I say, stepping out on the upper landing.

I turn to the right, surveying the hallway. All movement has ceased and there's no evidence of anyone, living or dead, within eyeshot. To my left, the study doors are still splayed open wide, but it's so dark out now, all I can see is my reflection on the glass staring back at me. Stepping forward, I grab each door hand and tug the doors shut.

I'll need to find some consecrated water, salt, and a boatload of sage tomorrow to clear its energy.

As I release the handles, a strange, subtle clicking sound echoes down the hallway. The sound isn't like anything I've ever heard and the hairs on the back of my neck stand on end.

Suddenly, staying home alone doesn't feel like it was the wisest decision. Swallowing hard, I pull my phone from my pocket and clutch it close. Peering into the darkness of the hallway, I take a few tentative steps forward.

The clicking sound comes and goes, stopping at odd intervals that make it impossible to track. Especially as the thrumming of my heartbeat pounds inside my ears.

"Hello?" I call out. My voice wavers, and rather than being clear or forceful, it's barely louder than a whisper. "Who's there?"

I continue to creep forward, edging farther from the entry's light and into the darkness of the hallway. Holding my breath, I eye the light switch where the corner bends, and I debate whether it's better to make a run for it or continue slowly to avoid startling it.

Slow and steady wins out as I tiptoe down the hallway. The crackling sound skitters across the space, as if crawling the walls beside me, then directly behind me. Goosebumps flash all over my body as I spin around, trying to get a clear view of whatever it is.

I catch a glimpse of a figure, but it phases in and out like an old television show that's lost its reception. The clicking circles around me until it vanishes down the hall and around the corner. Picking up speed, I chase it, almost forgetting to flick on the switch as I get to the corner.

Stopping, I turn back, flicking the light switch. The archaic sconces along the hallway ignite, casting an amber glow into the hallway, but I don't know if it has made the space any less foreboding.

Closing my eyes, I try to calm my heartbeat and center myself. If there's one thing I've learned over the past year, it's that things can go sideways fast when you're not in control. With my eyes still closed, the crackling starts again, this time directly beside my right ear.

Refusing to even breathe, I wait for it to pass before opening my eyes. As I do, the apparition flickers again in front of me. Its features are part human, part something else, but it all happens so fast, I can't quite latch onto it. When it reappears, it's farther down the hallway, and it vanishes into a room opposite my dad's bedroom.

I've never been in most of these rooms, let alone know what they were being used for. However, I do know that the last time I was led by a ghost, it brought me to answers. Walking forward slowly, I choose to follow the specter, hoping this time, it will be the same.

When I reach the doorway, I listen intently. The clicking sound has ceased, but the menacing undercurrent remains. I can't explain it, but something about all of this feels so familiar...

The lights in the hallway flicker, diverting my attention to them. Suddenly, the chill creeps in again, evaporating the warmth in an instant. It removes any feelings of security and happiness, replacing them with an empty dread. I shiver it away, refusing to let it deter me even if my heart rate is at an all-time high.

This is my house, dammit.

With my phone still clutched in my left hand, I reach out and fling the door open. The room is dark, so I straighten my shoulders and take a deep breath. Stepping inside, I flip on the light switch and soft, white light bursts from the ceiling, casting deep shadows across the furniture in the room. Each piece is covered with large, off-white sheets, making it look as though stereotypical ghosts crowd the space. But I know better.

Narrowing my gaze, I take another small step into the room, eyeing each piece of furniture with suspicion. I pause, half anticipating one of the sheets to move or race toward me. I've watched enough horror movies to expect that much. However, once inside the room, the cold dissipates and the despairing sensation vanishes with it, leaving me confused.

Why would it lead me here? Was there a reason? Or was it just to scare the hell out of me?

One way to find out.

I reach out, tugging off the sheet closest to me. As it drops to the floor, it reveals a large, burgundy wing-backed chair. Flashes of a distant memory play at the back of my mind, but I can't quite place whether they're real or not.

Yanking off the next one, it reveals a floor lamp with stained glass covering the lightbulb. The next one is a bookshelf piled high with books that overflow its capacity. As I pull the next sheet back, I drop it and stare, mouth agape, at a large table covered with paints, paintbrushes, and a canvas. I stare into the depths of the eyes of a woman in a still-unfinished portrait. Even without being completed, I'd know that face anywhere.

Swallowing hard and backing away, my mother's familiar features stare back at me.

CHAPTER 5

MESSED UP

I stare at the painting, unable to close my mouth.

Who painted this? Was it my dad? Why was it covered up? More importantly, why was I led here in such a weird, spooky way?

Fumbling for my phone, I tug it out of my front pocket and hit Mom's number. My heart drums a beat of anxiety in my ear as I press the phone close.

"Hi, sweetie. Is everything okay?" Mom asks, her voice edging on wary.

I exhale audibly, dropping my shoulders in relief. "I was about to ask you the same thing."

She laughs softly, "Why wouldn't it be? It's eight-thirty on a Tuesday night. It's not like Mistwood is the epicenter for craziness, you know?"

Smiling, I say, "Yeah, I know. I don't know, I guess I just..." I stop, unsure how much I want to tell her. I know how she hates anything supernatural. The last thing she'd want to know is I was guided by a ghost to a painting of her. It would freak her out for days.

"You just...?" Mom presses, alarm beginning to paint her words.

"I guess I just miss your voice," I mutter, staring into her acrylic eyes in the painting.

"Awww, I miss you, too, sweetheart. We haven't had a whole lot of time to chat since you started...*school* last year," she says, skirting around the obvious.

"I know, I'm sorry. It's been really busy," I say, dropping my gaze to the floor. I swallow hard and back out of the room, flicking off the light and shutting the door. "How have you been? What's new there?"

"Not a whole lot. The neighbors are still crazy and work is keeping me busy. On the upside, I love seeing Mr. Larsen's eye twitch every time I mow the lawn with a push mower instead of a rider. That's pretty much the highlight of existence out here. What about you? Is...are you adjusting?"

I stare at the closed door in front of me for a moment, letting all the weird adjustments I've been through these past few months wash over me. I wish I could talk to her—tell her more than just the surface-level stuff.

"Yeah, things are going good," I say, trying to convince myself.

"Good, good. And how's the boyfriend? Wade, right? He sure is a cutie."

A quick jab to the chest stops my words in my throat. Before I know it, tears are welling in my eyes and I croak out, "We broke up."

"Oh, Autumn, honey. I'm so sorry. He seems like such a nice guy. What happened?" she asks.

Turning down the hallway, I clutch the phone with

both hands as I swap ears. "I don't know. Things just got...*complicated*."

"Oh, I know how that goes."

Her words are pregnant with hidden meaning and I bite my lip. "Mom, I know you don't like to talk about it, but...what happened between you and Dad? Why would you leave all of this? I mean, he seems like a nice guy."

A long pause stretches between us and I open my mouth to ask if she's still there.

"He is a nice guy and I'm sure there's a lot you've been uncovering. I wish... I just..." she says, clearly having trouble putting her thoughts into words.

Taking a seat at the top stop of the grand staircase, I hold my breath, waiting for her to continue.

"You need to know we never meant to hurt you," Mom whispers.

"What do you mean? By breaking up? Or—?"

"I meant by not telling you what you were. Autumn, we knew very early on you inherited gifts from your father's side of the family. You have to understand, I haven't always hated the supernatural. I know it seems like it to you, but I used to be different. Just like you, I was once enamored by the idea of having powers outside of sheer humanity. When we realized you could see and talk to ghosts, at first we both thought it was a gift. But the older you got..." Her voice drifts off, and I can hear her get up from wherever she was sitting.

"Wait...you knew?" I say, unable to stop the rising resentment from building inside me. My entire childhood, she made it seem like the supernatural community was a bunch of miscreants who needed to be controlled.

Mom's heavy sigh doesn't make me feel any better.

"When we lived at Blackwood Manor, you would often tell us about the *friends* you'd see in the house and on the grounds. We knew right away what was really going on. But when you went missing..." her voice chokes off.

I press my fingertips to my lips to keep them from quivering.

Her voice is a little more solid when she continues. "Autumn, I swore when we found you on that dock after weeks of being missing that I would do anything and everything in my power to protect you. The Blackwood family has trodden the line between life and death for centuries, and I wasn't going to let you fall prey to its legacy, if I could help it. That's why your father and I parted. We knew being in that house would only heighten your gifts and one day...if we weren't careful, it would claim you, too."

The oppression from this revelation is almost too much, and the air in this wide-open entry closes in around me.

"So, you're telling me *I'm* the reason you and Dad broke up?" I squeak.

"Honey, it's not like that. We wanted to keep you safe..."

"I, uh...Mom, I love you. But this is..." I say, blinking back tears as I stand up. "I gotta go."

Without giving her a chance to respond, I click the phone off and cram it back into my pocket.

Not only did my mom know what kind of supernatural gifts I had all along—they're the reason my parents aren't together.

The longer I'm in this world of the supernatural, the

more I understand my mother's despise of it. Then again, maybe it's me who's the problem?

If I had any other ability, being with Wade wouldn't be a problem.

I always thought having powers would make me special, or open the world up to me. Not close it in and make it impossible for those around me to have any kind of a relationship—whether with me or not.

I thought having powers would be a blessing. Not a curse.

The entryway feels far too big and oppressive as I sit here all alone. Taking the stairs two at a time, I race down the hallway to my bedroom. Before I even reach my bedroom door, I can feel my phone buzzing in my pocket. It's likely my mom trying to call me back or Wade calling to check in on me. Either way, I can't take any more draining conversations. I need some time to process.

I'm still no closer to understanding what's happening in this house. Why a ghost attacked Wade and why I couldn't even see it... or why I was led to the painting of my mother.

On one hand, it feels as though my gifts are getting stronger, but on the other... Just when I think I have a good grasp on what I'm capable of, the rules change.

As I walk into my open bedroom, I flick on the light switch and move straight to the large picture window. The landscape is a sea of dark blues and blacks, and I drop the blinds, needing to pull into my space, wrapping it around me like a safety blanket.

For the briefest of moments, I consider trying to Skype Cat, but think better of it. My laptop is still upstairs and the study is the last place I want to go until it's daylight. While I could call her from my phone, it just doesn't feel the same.

Eyeing the clock, I see it's barely 9:00 p.m. While it might be a Tuesday, it's still awfully early. Resigning myself to an early night of solitude, I head across the hall to run myself a bath. I need to calm down and if there's one thing the big tub is good for, it's relaxing. After grabbing a handful of lavender and sage bath salts, I hold my hand out, letting the running water release them from my grip. Instantly, the scent calms my nerves and I pick up the lighter from the top drawer of the vanity and light the candles around the room.

After an uneventful, candlelit bath, I wrap myself in towels and plod across the hall with my hairbrush and dirty clothes in hand. Dropping the brush on my desk and the clothes in my hamper, I take a seat on the edge of my bed, eyeing the doorway to the resurrection chamber.

How did things get so messed up?

Rolling my eyes, I walk over to my desk so I can brush my hair. I pull up short as I reach for a brush that's not there.

"What the hell?" I say, staring at the desk like it's going to magically appear.

Shaking it off, I walk over to the hamper and dig through the dirty clothes. Not there, either.

Confused, I walk out of the room and back into the bathroom. It's not there, either.

I did grab it, right?

My brain is a swirl of bewilderment, but I pull open the drawer with my extra combs and picks. They're not ideal for brushing out my unruly red locks, but when needs must. I'll hunt for the brush tomorrow when my brain is clearer.

Dressing in my night shirt and underwear, I hop into bed and stare the ceiling for what feels like forever.

Eventually, my eyelids flutter closed and darkness consumes me.

The cool autumn breeze ruffles the back of my hair. It's not quite cold enough to induce a shiver, but it's enough for me to tug the collar of my shirt up.

Walking through the dense trees, I make my way to the altar space, unsure if I will be successful this time. Things have been getting worse, and if I can't find a way around this curse, people will die. People I love.

Kneeling down at the edge of the pentacle, I light the first of five red candles. Bowing my head, I utter the incantation, and move on to the next one, until each are lit.

My heart pounds in my chest, threatening to break the confines of my ribcage as I enter the circle's sacred space. Blinking back the terror rising within me, I reach into a small pouch dangling at my side. This time, I believe I have everything I need to do this properly. With my right hand, I let the salt trickle out. It cascades downward, catching the sun's light and making it appear like gold streaming from my palm. Slowly, I walk clockwise to seal the circle's energy.

Turning to the center, I light the large, white pillar candle. When it flickers to life, I bow my head, stealing a moment to calm myself. Despite my best efforts, my pulse continues to race.

Should this go wrong, I've made assurances. My legacy will live on. Yet, I still hope for the best.

Digging into my left pocket, I hold out my hand above the

candle's flame until the skin aches from the heat. Should this be my last act, I want to at least remember what it feels like to be alive. Bowing my head, I whisper the words meant to call the Moirai to me.

If this works, it will go one of two ways. They'll either forgive this transgression, or I will be dead before I can speak my piece. There's only one way to know for sure.

Opening my palm, I allow the handful of frayed red threads to fall into the flames.

I wake up in a cold sweat, unable to move or even breathe. The dream was so real, but so far away. As if I was watching someone else—not me—do the actions.

Something big is coming and whatever it is, I'm totally unprepared for it.

If I can't get Abigail to come to me, there's really only one person I can turn to for clear answers.

Tomorrow, come hell or high water, I will find a way to track down my dad.

CHAPTER 6
ONE REASON

As it turns out, tracking down a man without a cell phone is more or less impossible. Over the next two days, I've tried just about everything imaginable. Just shy of calling my mom and asking if she would know, I finally resign myself to scribbling a note on the kitchen counter for James.

I still have no idea when he comes and goes. He's almost as elusive as one of the ghosts. But if there's anyone who would have details, it would likely be him. Even if he wants to pretend he doesn't.

Tomorrow, Wade and I have to do our presentation on the Fates and we've barely even scratched the surface on research. After what happened last time, it's safe to say neither one of us wants to study at my house. But I'll be damned if we study at his. So, the Academy library it is.

With my dad still MIA and the study session lingering over my head, the entire school day drags on and on. As interesting as it is to learn about psychic drawing, spirit crossings, and truth hidden in myths, it's not until I get to Malevolent Spirits 101 that I actually perk an ear.

"As we've been discussing, malevolent spirits aren't always easy to distinguish. Oftentimes, they come across very benign," Professor Lambert says, sweeping his light-brown eyes over the entire class. His expression is tight, as only a tenth of us seem to be paying any particular attention. The entire back row appears to be in varying degrees of grogginess.

To be fair, it's hard to concentrate in his class. It's the last one of the day and by this point, even with the cooler autumn air, the room is stiflingly hot. Add on top his slightly monotone speech and you have yourself a recipe for glazed eyes and nodding heads.

"So, with this in mind, what is the number one way to know if a spirit you encounter is benevolent?" he continues. Professor Lambert catches my gaze long enough to realize I'm awake and he says, "You there, Ms. Blackwood. Any thoughts?"

I sit up a little straighter. "Not exactly. But I can tell you from experience, when they're angry, you'll know it."

The professor quirks a gray eyebrow. "You've encountered a malevolent spirit?"

I nod, scratching at the side of my head. "Oh, yeah."

"Do you feel safe?" he asks, sudden interest blossoming in his tone.

I squirm a bit in my seat but tip my head. "Yeah, it's no big deal. It's only been the one time."

He holds my gaze for a moment but returns to his air of academia. "You see, the manner in which a human dies plays a vital role in its ability to cross over. Not every soul becomes a ghost, and not every ghost deteriorates into malevolence."

I raise my hand.

"Yes, Ms. Blackwood?" he asks when he notices.

"Is there any reason a ghost would go unseen?"

He narrows his eyes. "How do you mean?"

"Well, I already know I can see ghosts. But the one... the malevolent spirit—I can't see it. I was wondering if you knew why?" I say.

Tipping his head in contemplation, he says, "Could be any number of things. Appearing corporeal takes energy. If the spirit is fairly new, it might not have mastered that ability. Did you say it was angry? Did it do something?"

My eyebrows knit together, and I nod. "Yes, it attacked a friend."

Professor Lambert paces in front of his desk and rubs at his chin. "All right, so it could be that it needed to muster enough energy to physically interact. When we're alive, we take all the physical interactions we have for granted. But when you're a spirit, each interaction is depleting. The more energy it needs for one form or another, the less it has for a different form. Does that make sense?"

"I think so," I say. "Basically, if the malevolent spirit wants to, say, choke someone or blow out lightbulbs, it can't also muster the energy to be seen?"

"Precisely," he says with a curt nod.

"Ah, gotcha."

My mind is a cyclone of thoughts, each vying for a moment's attention. I barely hear the rest of the class as I contemplate who—or what—is now in my house and how I can get rid of it. Even if it's never attacked me, the energy has certainly turned more hostile, and the last thing I want to do is live in a haunted house. Well, more haunted than usual, anyway.

When class is over, I make my way down the hall as people everywhere disperse from the building and head home. Wade is already waiting for me at a back table when I enter the library.

"Hey," he says, flashing me a tentative smile.

"Hi," I say, sliding into the seat across from him. I drop my backpack to the floor and pull out my laptop.

"So..." he says, scrunching his face.

"So," I repeat, locking eyes with him.

"How have you been? We haven't really touched base much since the whole conjuring reenactment," Wade says, smirking.

"I should be asking you that, actually," I say, pointing to him. "Are you okay?"

He shrugs nonchalantly. "Fit as a fiddle. But definitely glad to be studying here." His silver eyes catch mine and I can see the wheels in his mind turning. "Anything else happen? I mean, have you been—"

"Yeah, nothing really all that strange since. It's weird, though... Since I can't see it, I don't know who or what it could be. I mean, I know it's not Abigail, even if she's been a bit MIA. I can still sense her around me. It's like she's just, I don't know, busy or something. But this—"

"Yeah, I don't think it's Abigail either. When I was disembodied, I got a good sense of her. She means well and definitely has an air of benevolence. Whatever attacked me..."—his eyes go distant—"it wasn't her."

"What did it feel like?" I ask, narrowing my gaze. "When it attacked you."

"Like something was pressing on my throat and I couldn't get any air," he says, shuddering. "But first...there was just an extreme sense of oppression. Anger. Fury, even."

"I'm so sorry, Wade. I didn't mean for—" I begin.

Wade raises a hand and cuts me off. "It's not your fault, Autumn. I've felt something there before, but I couldn't put my finger on it. It comes and goes. But...for whatever reason, it's growing. Getting angrier."

My forehead creases and I lean back. "You've felt something at the manor? When? You never told me that before."

Wade's gaze drops to the table in front of us and he winces. "Yeah, I guess... I figured you knew. I mean, there are a lot of energies. But it seems like they all kind of like their space."

Surprise and irritation flare inside me and I bite down on my lip to keep from saying something I'll regret. As much as I thought I knew Wade—and as much as I love him—secrets seem to shroud around him like a blanket.

Not just any secrets, either; big, terrible, life-altering secrets. Like the fact that my house is full of ghosts I've never even realized were there.

Like he's next in line to be a freakin' *Angel of Death*. Oh, and he's not supposed to have anything to do with necromancers like me.

So, there's that.

"I know that look," Wade says warily. "What's on your mind?"

I sigh. "It's nothing."

"Come on. Don't do that. Don't shut me out," Wade whispers, his eyes pleading with me.

"You hold a lot back from me. I thought we were both on the same level...but there's so much I didn't know about you. Or what you can do. Or hell, what I'm dealing with," I say reluctantly. "For all I know, you even got a read on who it is. Or maybe your dad has? Surely the Angel of Death can do that, right?"

Wade's eyes widen, but he shakes his head. "Angels of Death are bound to take the souls ready to cross planes. They don't focus on the ones who wish to stay behind. I guess you could say there's too much to do and not enough time to do it. There's no point in focusing on the energies that don't want help." He quirks his lips to the side and continues. "But to answer your question, no. I don't know who it is. I don't have any powers. Not really. I only get vague impressions of energy right now. Good, bad. Happy, not so happy. I suppose you could call it empathic, but I don't even know if it's as potent as that. And truth be told, I never even thought to ask my dad. He wouldn't overly approve the request, if you know what I mean."

"Yeah, I know what you mean," I whisper, tucking my hands under my thighs. "He's not a fan."

Wade's eyebrows tug in and he leans forward. "Autumn, he doesn't know you. He only knows what necromancers do to the status quo. He doesn't know *you*."

"I know," I say softly. He doesn't overly want to get to know me either and a part of me can't even blame him. I didn't know I was a necromancer for most of my life, but one thing's for sure, I'm not even sure I want to be one. It's done nothing but cause problems.

"Look, if you want help figuring out what it is"—Wade reaches across the table—"I want to help. I know I can't cast them out or cross them over, but I can at least try to guide you with the stuff I do know."

"I'm a big girl, Wade. I can handle it on my own," I say, shaking my head.

His face tightens and he says, "I'm perfectly aware of how strong you are. That's not what I was implying at all."

"I know. It's just..." I swallow hard. "It's hard enough having to work with you on this presentation."

Wade snorts. "Is it actually that bad to work with me?"

"You know what I mean," I retort.

"Do I?" he says.

"Wade I don't like this any more than you do. None of this is my choice. I'm just—"

"Not your choice? Autumn, this is *all* your choice," Wade says, slamming a hand down on the table. "It's certainly not mine. I want to be with you. There's nowhere on this whole fuckin' planet I'd rather be. Don't you get that? I *love* you..."

My breath hitches and I blink back the emotions threatening to consume me.

"I—" I stutter, unable to form words.

"I don't know what your deal is or why you keep pushing me away. But I'm not going anywhere. I'm going to help you get to the bottom of this. Whatever is going on in your goddamn house could be really bad. Maybe it hasn't attacked you yet, but it could. I'll be damned if I let that happen. We'll figure it out together," he spits. His jaw clenches tight and his nostrils flare, but he doesn't back down.

I know better than to fight this. As much as I want to protest, I know it will only make him dig his heels in deeper. "Fine. You can help me, but that's all. Nothing else has changed. I can't risk—"

"*You* can't risk? This is all about your risk, is it? Autumn, I'm willing to risk *everything* to be with you. My whole life, I've wandered from place to place, searching for the one thing that would bind me to this human form. Because honestly, so far, things have kinda sucked. All I was looking for was that one reason to stay. Did you know that when my grandpa passed, I planned to end my own life?"

His silver eyes bore into mine and my heart stops.

"*What?*" I sputter.

He swallows hard and nods absently. "I had nothing left. No parents, no friends. And when Grandpa was gone, no family at all. They were all on the other side. Why would I want to stay when I could ascend early? I could begin fulfilling my true purpose and have all the powers that come with it."

"But you only get one life to live. And it could have changed. You have so many years ahead of you. You could travel and see the world. You could have met..."

"And I *did*," he says, cutting me off. "I met the one woman who has made all this torment worth it. She was my *one reason to stay*."

His words linger between us—heavy, potent things that could crumble realities and break down barriers. My gaze falls to the table as I contemplate their meaning.

Inhaling sharply, my eyelashes flutter. "Does that mean...? You wouldn't—"

Wade's face is suddenly the epitome of calm. "No option is off the table."

CHAPTER 7
THE THREAD OF LIFE

I look up, meeting Wade's expectant gaze. "You can't be serious?"

"It's not ideal, obviously. But I'm not ruling it out, either. Granted, I do have a few more cards up my sleeves as I try to get into some good graces," Wade says, grinning and clearly trying to lighten the mood.

"No, you can't do that," I say, shaking my head. "You think you can drop that kind of a bomb on me and then change the subject? Nope. No, sir."

Wade's expression is thoughtful as he says, "Autumn, you and I view life very differently. I love that about you. But for someone like me, it's just a pit stop on the way to my full-time gig. I know what's waiting for me on the other side of this. Most people—you included—don't. That's why it seems so scary."

My stomach churns and I feel utterly sick. Even if he's right—even if this life means little to him because he knows what the rest of eternity looks like, I can't imagine a time when he'd consider just...opting out.

"Yeah, but you should want to protect this chance. Don't you think? Not waste it?"

"It's a lot easier to put things into perspective when you know one lifetime is all you get." He flashes me a quick smile and leans back. "I mean, I know most people believe that, or at least worry about it, but they're so disillusioned. They don't think in terms of a whole lifetime anyway. They just see what's happening right now. When things go wrong, they think it's the end of everything."

"What do you mean?"

"Like, when they can't afford something, or they lose a job..."

"Or a girl," I add, shooting him a pointed glance.

He ignores me and continues. "But for me... I don't care about all the stupid stuff—money or jobs..." He catches my eye and holds it for a beat. "...Or *rules*."

I narrow my gaze, but I can't think of anything to say to that. There's a certain amount of sense hidden in those words and I could feel them taking seed in the back of my mind, if I'm not careful.

"Sometimes rules keep us safe," I say breathlessly.

"Not when they don't make sense," he responds. "That's when I make my own rules."

"And on that note..." My gaze floats to my laptop and I tap the top of it with my fingertips. "We should really get this assignment done."

"All right," he says, smirking slightly. "Let's bring on the Fates, then. Maybe they'll back me up here."

With the tip of my head, I lift open my laptop and pull my notebook out of my backpack. This afternoon's conversation has my mind spinning in a thousand directions, and none of them are focused on this research project.

Wade stands up, pulling his chair over to my side and setting it down inches from mine.

I shoot him a look of surprise, but he sits down, holding his hands up innocently. "I need to see the screen, too. No laptop over here."

Nodding softly, I turn back to the laptop and type 'the fates' into Google. It brings us to a page on the Moirai. For some reason, this name rings a bell, but I can't quite put my finger on why. I'm fairly certain I've never heard the name before and we didn't even get this far when Wade had come over.

I lean forward and scan the result. "It says here they control the thread of life for every mortal from birth to death. One sister is the 'spinner,' another the 'allotter,' and the last is the 'inevitable.' I suppose that means death?" I say, chancing a sideways glance. Wade's close proximity makes my pulse race and his scent does absolutely nothing to clear my head. If anything, it cracks my resolve and makes me question what in the hell I'm thinking.

"Well, it might mean the one who calls upon death, but she wouldn't be death itself. We know that already," he says with a tip of his chin.

"Good point," I nod, turning back to the screen. "Ah, it says here she merely chooses the *manner* of a person's death and the time frame it happens in."

Wade tips his head, reading. "So, while the other sisters create and maintain the thread of life, this last one—Aisa —she cuts the string with some sort of *magical shears.*" He leans back a bit, his eyebrows furrowed.

"I know that look. What is it?" I ask.

"I dunno. It just kinda seems a bit ludicrous, doesn't it? I mean, who writes these things? A thread? Shears?" He chuckles. "It's like someone asked a kid to explain the ways of the universe and then just wrote down what they said."

"I take it this doesn't jibe with what you know?"

"Not exactly. But then, who am I? Sure, I have access to this school for now, but I won't unlock any of my family's gifts until much later. So everything I know could be bunk. But this...it sounds like a fairy tale gone wrong. Don't you think?" he asks, meeting my gaze. "I mean, if it were really that simple, why hasn't someone tracked down the Moirai and stolen those damn shears? Hypothetically, it could mean they'd live forever, right?"

"Well, maybe it has nothing to do with the shears *per se*, but more about the entity wielding them? For all you know, *any* shears she holds becomes magical," I say, playing devil's advocate. "Heck, maybe she could even bite the damn thread and it would end a life? As long as the cord is cut, that's the end of that, so to speak."

Wade shrugs. "A fair point."

"You don't look convinced?" I say, lowering my eyebrows.

"It's not that."

"What then?" I ask.

"It seems like an awful lot of fuss for each mortal life. You know? Three larger-than-life entities, all working to balance the lifespans of humans. I mean, as the population grows, so do the number of Angels of Death, for example. How in the hell could three sisters manage all of that?" Wade says, scrunching his face.

I shake my head. "Don't look at me. Until last year, the strangest things on my mind revolved around whether or not forensic scientists could really figure out a death by blood spatter."

Wade snickers. "Yeah, things have gotten significantly more outlandish."

"Well, regardless, we need to learn what we can so we can pass this presentation. Then, whether or not they exist becomes irrelevant, I suppose," I laugh.

"Yeah, unless one comes knocking on your door," he says, leaning over and bumping his shoulder into mine.

"Let's hope not. At least, not for a very long time," I say, shuddering.

We spend the next two and a half hours digging through all of the known history archived at the Windhaven Academy on the Moirai. By the time we're done, I have more questions than answers in terms of who the Fates are and whether or not they're even real or simply a metaphor. Separating fact from fiction is certainly difficult, to say the least. For some reason, none of the documentation at Windhaven Academy seems to separate out where the stories began or if there have ever been any true sightings.

On the upside, the discussion in class should be entertaining, if nothing else. Especially if Wade has anything to do with it. I can already see him opening up a discussion on how the Hellmouth is more plausible.

Wade leans forward, thumping his head onto the table beside me. "I tap out. I can't research this anymore."

I chuckle. "Yeah, me either. I think we have enough to at least sound like we know what we're talking about. Don't you?"

"God, let's hope so," he says, his voice muffled by the tabletop.

Reaching down, I grab my backpack. "All right then, it looks like we can head out."

Still leaning forward, Wade tips his head up, leaving his chin on the table. "Wanna get a bite to eat? I mean, it's almost 7:00 p.m. and I don't know about you, but I'm starving."

"Wade... I don't know if that's such a good idea," I warn.

"Come on, Autumn. It's just food. Please?" he asks, sitting all the way up and pressing his hands together in prayer position. "Don't make me eat alone."

I stare at him for a moment, then exhale in defeat. "Fine."

"Excellent," he says, suddenly hopping off of his chair and reaching for the back of mine.

"I got it," I say, shooting him a sideways glance.

"As you wish," he says, backing away genially.

"Where would you like to go?"

"The usual, of course. It's not like there are many options in this teeny tiny town," he says, grabbing his backpack off the floor.

I snicker under my breath. He's certainly not wrong.

"Okay, so I'll meet you at the Bourbon Room?" I say, shoving my laptop in my backpack.

"How about we ride together? It's just down the road. I'll drive," Wade offers.

I hesitate, wondering if I should insist we drive separately. Against my better judgment I say, "Yeah, okay."

Ten minutes later, we're sliding into a booth on the far end of the restaurant. It overlooks a small lake, which glitters in the setting sun.

"So, I've been thinking..." Wade says, scrunching his face as he sets his hands down on the table between us.

"Okay?" I say, narrowing my eyes.

"Have you ever seen other ghosts in your house?" he asks.

I give it a moment's thought and shake my head. "No, I don't think so. Just Abigail."

"Does your house have any wards or anything that would have kept them out? Or only let the nice ones in?"

My eyebrows rise, but I shake my head. "I honestly have no idea. I'm hoping to track down my dad. If I get the chance, I'll ask him."

Wade nods, but doesn't say anything at first. His expression twists into one of contemplation. Then, after a moment, he says, "Why do you think it's been so hard to contact Abigail?"

I shrug. "I don't know? I guess I sorta just thought it was because of what happened back at the catacombs. Dealing with the Fetch and then inhabiting my body—it took a lot out of her."

"Yeah, but it's been almost five months. How long does it take a ghost to recharge?"

I snicker. "Your guess is as good as mine."

The server walks up, her tablet computer in her hand. "The usual?"

"Yeah, sounds great," Wade says, nodding.

She starts to spin away, clearly believing Wade spoke for both of us.

Instead, I raise a hand and say, "Actually, I think I'd like something different."

Wade quirks an eyebrow and leans back.

"Okay, honey. What will it be?" she asks, eyeing me with curiosity.

"Can I look at a menu?"

"A menu?" She says, almost incredulously. "The two of you have been in here at least a dozen times a month for the past year."

"Please?" I say, smiling serenely.

She rolls her eyes, grabbing a tattered copy from her apron and handing it to me.

I splay it on the table and take a good look. Nothing sounds as good as the usual mushroom and Swiss burger, but I'll be damned if I eat the same thing as always.

"I think I'll go with the fish tacos," I finally reply, closing the menu and handing it back to her.

"Mkay," she says, snatching it back and whirling around.

When I face Wade again, his eyebrow is arched high and a smirk graces his lips.

"What?" I retort.

"Nothing. That was just..." he says, shrugging. "I think you hurt her feelings."

"Oh, shut up," I say, swatting at his hand. "I just felt like something different."

"Interesting."

I scrunch my face. "There's no hidden meaning in there."

"If you say so," he laughs, raising his hands like he's about to be arrested.

"Anyway..." I say, watching him from the side of my eye.

"Anyway," he repeats.

We both sit there in a moment of awkward silence and I clear my throat. "Where were we?"

"Oh, yeah..." Wade says, dropping his chin and nodding to himself. "Uh—I was thinking about Abigail. Do you think she knows the house is being haunted?"

"What do you mean?"

"Like, is she being suppressed by the other energy? Or"—he eyes me intensely and raises a hand to the ceiling —"is she allowing it to happen?"

My eyebrows tug in and I sit back. Surely she wouldn't allow a malevolent energy to invade the home. She's never seemed like that kind of ghost.

Granted, my experience with them has still been limited, but it feels right.

But the question does pique my curiosity.

With the new entity in the house, why hasn't she been around? Could she be in trouble? Or worse...even if she's not the one haunting the house in a creepy way, could Abigail be letting it happen? And if so, to what end?

CHAPTER 8
LUCKY TO HAVE FOUND YOU

As I park Blue in the circular drive, my thoughts are a swarm of frustration, worry, and suspicion. But as I walk up to the front door, the darkness ignites a new concern—one that says I still haven't pinpointed the source of the new hauntings and I'm not entirely certain how safe it is inside.

Taking a deep breath, I unlock, then push open the front door. It creaks loudly, echoing into the main entryway, announcing my arrival.

Surprisingly, light filters into the entryway before I even flip the light switch. Setting down my backpack next to the staircase, I walk into the dining room, following the light.

"Hello?" I call out.

I wasn't expecting anyone, but Dad could be home, for all I know. That would be a relief.

As I enter the kitchen, James looks up from the stove. "Ah, Ms. Blackwood. I was hoping I'd catch you this evening."

"I—uh, I was kinda hoping I'd run into you, too," I say, smiling.

"Yes, your note. You'll be pleased to know I've been in contact with your father and he plans on returning tomorrow," James says, stirring some ground meat in a pan.

"That's fantastic. I have a few...uh, questions I really need to ask him," I say, trying to sound nonchalant. "Whatcha making?" I hop on the counter beside him, wrapping my hands around the edge of the granite countertop.

"Breakfast burritos. Your father said you used to be fond of them as a child, so I thought I would whip up a batch to put in the freezer for you. They're far healthier than those toaster tarts and Red Bull," he says, shooting me a sideways glance. His soft brown eyes sparkle with a certain knowing that only wisdom in age brings.

"You're not wrong," I say, grinning.

It's actually nice to have someone else in the house—someone who doesn't bring any baggage. I didn't realize how off I've been, being here all alone.

"Everything all right, Ms. Blackwood?" James asks, quirking an eyebrow.

I blink away, realizing I must have been staring. "Yeah, sorry. I was just thinking..."

"Anything I can be of service with?"

I think on that question for a moment, then hop down. "Well, maybe, actually. You haven't... Do you ever sense something odd in this house?"

His eyes meet mine with a surprising level of guardedness and I chew on my lower lip. "How do you mean?"

It occurs to me, he may have no idea about the Blackwood family abilities, let alone the haunted nature of this house.

My eyebrows knit together. "Do you ever feel like there's something here? Like a presence?"

James shuts off the burner and turns on another one. He walks to the refrigerator and pulls out the eggs. "Every now and again, I do get the distinct impression we are not alone inside Blackwood Manor. But from what I understand, that is to be expected."

"You mean Abigail?" I say, narrowing my gaze.

He nods curtly.

"Yeah, I don't mean her, actually," I say, scrunching my face.

James turns to me, his eyes clouded with concern. "Would this have anything to do with the mess in the study?"

My mouth pops open and I nod. "Oh, I'm so sorry. I should have told you—"

He waves a hand dismissively. "It's quite all right."

"I was going to clean it up this weekend. I've just had so much on my mind."

"It is all taken care of," he says turning back to the stove and cracking a number of eggs into the pan. "But to answer your question, yes, I have felt at times the energy of the manor take on a more...ominous vibe. I had hoped your father could explain it to me but we seem to be missing one another in person as of late. You know, when your father hired me a number of years ago, I was under the impression it would be him and I as the only living souls wandering these halls. It's been ever so pleasant to have you here," James says, reaching out and patting my leg.

"Thank you," I say. "I just wish he'd be here more often, too."

"Oh, I do agree with you on that," he chuckles, adding in some cut up sausages into the egg mixture. "He's always been very busy. Trying to occupy his time and keep his mind away from his worries."

"He was lucky to have found you," I say. "Where did you two meet?"

James looks up, his eyes distant for a moment. "Well, I've known your father for a very long time. In fact, your grandfather and I were childhood friends."

"Really?" I say, surprised I hadn't thought to learn more about James sooner.

"Oh, indeed," he says, nodding. "Charles and I got into plenty of mischief. Granted, he more than I."

I drop my gaze to my knees and grin.

"It's always a bit strange to be the mundane human in the mix of very gifted individuals. But your grandfather never made me feel *less-than*. I suppose, this was passed down to your father," he says shutting off the burner and readying the tortilla shells. "When my wife Beverly died, I was at a bit of a loss. Your father gave me purpose again. Even if it was only merging our loneliness so neither were truly alone. Besides, once you're taken in by the mystery of Blackwood Manor, any chance to come back is a second chance at unraveling it."

"I guess I can attest to that," I say, nodding. I pause for a moment, thinking about his life and how it must have been for him, being friends with my grandpa, being around this world, but not having any special powers of your own. "Well, I need to get some homework done. Thank you for doing this and talking with me. We should do it more often."

"No trouble at all. Have a lovely evening, Ms. Blackwood."

I hop off the counter and walk to the door, but turn back and say, "Call me Autumn."

James smiles in return. "Goodnight, Autumn."

Smiling to myself, I walk out into the hallway. When I get into the main entry, I walk past the large staircase and down the hallway that leads to my bedroom.

If James has felt the energy of the manor shift, too, then it must be more of a problem than I thought. There's a good chance when Dad gets home, we'll have to perform a banishing or summoning to learn why it's here and what it wants.

In the meantime, maybe I can get Abigail to communicate with me.

As I reach my bedroom door, the hallway is flooded with a strange chill. Spinning around, I search the space, but nothing is evident.

Once inside my bedroom, I pull up short. There, on my bed, is my backpack.

The memory of setting it by the staircase rushes back to me and the hairs on the back of my neck stand on end. Whoever, or whatever, must have moved it.

"Abigail?" I call out, my voice quivering.

Without waiting for an answer, I run over to the small door leading to the resurrection chamber and throw it open. Racing down the stairs, I close my eyes and summon the torches to ignite.

"Abigail, are you here?" I demand, my heart pounding.

She doesn't answer, but I can feel her presence all

around me.

I'm suddenly consumed with a vision of something outside of myself—something not my own.

As if stepping into an augmented reality, I'm in this same space, but I'm no longer alone.

Along the outer edge of the resurrection chamber, a man—Warren, my great-great-grandfather—walks the circle in a counterclockwise fashion, saying something I can't hear or make out. Yet, without a question, there's a knowing inside of me. It's almost like a cellular memory. He's attempting a resurrection.

Peering around the space, I search for the source of his attempt, trying to understand why it's him and not Abigail who is casting this spell. In the corner of the room, a pile of sheets rests on the floor, bound in the shape of a woman.

Swallowing hard, I continue to watch as Warren kneels down, still muttering to himself. He takes out a small bottle and pours it into the center of the pentacle.

Setting the bottle aside, he takes out a small dagger, barely larger than six inches, and he slices open his left hand. As the blood runs free and uninhibited from his palm, it mixes with the blood already making its way to the outer edges of the internal pentagon. As it swirls and spirals together, a blast of energy releases, blasting Warren and all of the contents—candles, sand, salt, blood—across the room. All light is extinguished, and we're suddenly plunged into darkness.

I hold my breath, unsure what it is I've just witnessed —*and why*.

As expected, knowing what I know about him, it didn't work the way it should have.

However, slowly, from the corner of the room, light arises out of the pile of white sheets. Warren scrambles over to it, ripping away its bindings and unfurling Abigail's body. He clutches her form close to his chest, tears streaming down his face as he rocks back and forth on his knees.

I don't know how long she'd been dead at this point, but the bloating and distortion to her otherwise-beautiful features is startling. The stench released from unwrapping her enclosure reaches even to me, and I throw my elbow over my face to stop myself from gagging.

The light continues to grow, first emanating from Abigail's abdomen, then expanding outward across her skin, until she's nothing but a glowing orb of bright white-blue light.

"Abigail, my darling, my love. Please, tell me thou art with me? I am here—" Warren murmurs, groping at her arms.

Silence greets him, growing ever louder as the light pulls from her body and thrusts itself outside. The ghostly echo of the woman herself hovers inches above her body, then rights itself.

"Warren... What have you done?" Her words reverberate off the stone walls, an accusation hidden in their depths.

Scrambling to his feet, Warren's face is contorted in anguish.

"Why are you displaced, my love? I followed the ritual, as you have done."

Recognition flashes across her face and she sighs. She places a spectral hand alongside his jaw, her eyebrows tugging in.

"Warren, you know this magic is beyond you. Your gifts—they are very different from my own. You should not be meddling with such things." She drops her hand, her gaze drifting to her still body.

"But you are here now. You can help me to—"

Abigail's eyebrows knit together and her lips slowly tug downward.

Reaching for her, Warren's hands go through her arms, and he stumbles slightly.

"What is it, darling? What are you not telling me?" he asks. "Why are you not re-inhabiting your body?"

If ghosts could shed tears, Abigail looks as though she might actually cry. "Do you remember the first time I realized my calling?"

"Of course, how could I not?" he says, eyeing her every movement.

She drops her hands to her sides and turns from him. "I knew the power I beheld must not be taken lightly. It was magic with devastating power," she whispers.

Warren shakes his head, "I do not understand."

"Wielding the power of life and death...it is but pulling the strings meant for the gods. When one string is pulled out of its sequence, the universe will respond in kind. A life for a life..."

Her words yield their own power and sense of caution —yet I can already tell there's more she's not telling him. And he knows it.

"Darling," he repeats softly.

"You should not have dabbled in magic you do not have the power to wield, my love."

"I do not understand," he says, practically pleading.

"You are here. You are with me. Why will you not simply re-inhabit—"

"Because I cannot," she whispers.

He stares at her indignantly. "What do you mean you cannot? You are here; your body is there." He points to her corpse, as if it's simply a vehicle she needs to step into.

The apparition of Abigail kneels beside her body. Her ghostly hand runs along her semi-bloated arm, and she slowly shakes her head.

"It has been too long. Even for an experienced necromancer, the time has come and gone."

"But," he begins, dropping down by her side, "I cannot lose you. You cannot leave me here alone." Tears emerge and he blinks them away, wildly clawing at his cheeks. "We were meant to carry on our legacy together."

"It appears being without me is a concern you will no longer be tormented with," she whispers, forcing a smile.

Confusion blossoms across his features and Abigail ignores it. Instead, she points at the body before her. "You must find a way to get my body into the catacombs. Once inside, I will walk you through my entombment."

He blinks away the tears still falling. "But if I am to bury you, how will you be able to—"

Rage suddenly blossoms in her essence and she quivers violently. "I will never return. Do you not see? I have been damned, Warren. Cursed, by you, to remain as I am before you. Now, do as I ask, or we shall suffer a worse fate."

The vision ends abruptly, and I bend over, gasping for air.

Why did she show me this? Is she trying to tell me she's losing control? That she is the entity going rogue?

If so, what in the hell am I meant to do about it?

CHAPTER 9
SEEKING ANSWERS

After last night's revelations, I barely manage to pay attention to classes. Even the presentation with Wade goes by in sort of a blur. Until now, it never really occurred to me to wonder if Abigail should still be here. Once I got past the initial disruption of her being a part of this house in the first place, it all just sorta felt...normal. It didn't even cross my mind that maybe she never got the chance to cross over. Or that she might still want to.

I vaguely remember her saying something to me when I first entered the resurrection chamber. She wanted my help releasing some sort of binding, but I couldn't deal at the time. Everything was too new.

Could she be growing restless because I haven't helped her yet?

"Well, that went considerably better than I expected," Wade says, sliding his backpack over his shoulder and walking over to me.

I blink up at him. "Huh?"

"You know, the presentation we just did not more than fifteen minutes ago. On the Fates..." he says, chuckling. "Ring any bells?"

"Oh, yeah. Right?" I say, nodding and scooting out from my desk. "Sorry, I was just so relieved to be done, I kinda zoned out the rest."

That part is true. At least now my forced togetherness with him has come to a close. Maybe now I can spend some time trying to sort out my brain.

"Funnily enough, I did notice you were off in another land." He grins, then winks in one of his trademark moves that still sends my heart racing. "Where were you just now, anyway?"

I sigh heavily, walking out of the classroom with him in tow. "I don't know. Home stuff, I guess."

"Everything okay? You haven't had any more ghost attacks or anything, have you?" he says, alarm flushing his features.

"No, not really..."

He arches an eyebrow.

"Well, I mean, my backpack did a disappearing act last night. Then reappeared in my bedroom. So, I guess there's that," I say, making a face.

"Nothing else, though? No more explosions or..."

I shake my head. "No, nothing like that."

"Good," he says, exhaling loudly.

"It's just been...*tense*. My dad's supposed to be back sometime today, though. So, I'm going to drill him about what's been going on. With any luck, I'll finally get some answers."

"Need any backup?" Wade says, his eyebrows knitting together.

I shoot him a sideways glance as we turn down the hallway leading to the commons area. "No, I'm pretty sure I can handle my dad."

With everything going on, part of me wishes I could just give in to what he wants and say screw it all. As much as I love him, and I really do—I don't want him throwing his life away for me.

Walking up to one of the large, plush chairs, I set my backpack down and take a seat.

"I bet it will be a relief to finally get some answers," Wade says, dropping into the chair beside me.

I scratch at my temple. "It all depends on how many answers I can actually get out of him."

"Good point. Well, the offer still stands. I know how intimidating it can be to talk to a dad," Wade says, smirking sheepishly. "Plus, I'd still love to finally get to meet the guy."

My eyebrows flick upward and my lips tug down. "Oh, right. You never got to meet him..."

Instantly, my heart constricts and a wave of guilt rolls through me. For as many times as Wade's been at the manor, my dad's been MIA. While it would have been nice to introduce them, now it just sorta feels...awkward.

Wade shoots me a sideways grin. "So, what do ya say?"

I scrunch my face. "I dunno..."

"Come on, Autumn. You can just introduce me as a friend," he says, frowning. His eyes reflect that aura of hurt just bubbling under the surface, but he holds it together pretty well. "I mean, that's what's holding you back, right?"

"Wade..." I begin, trying to sound reasonable.

He swipes away my comment with a stroke of his hand. "Nah, it is what it is right now. I get it."

I chew on the side of my cheek. He gives me the puppy dog pout and I can't help but crack. "Fine. But just for a little while. Okay?"

He tips his head. "Deal. Wanna head out now and see if he's there?"

I shrug. "I suppose."

"Okay, go home and check. If he's there, text me and I'll meet ya. I'm gonna swing by my place and change quick."

My gaze follows the length of his body. He's wearing ripped up jeans, a black Pink Floyd t-shirt and his leather jacket. Nothing too crazy.

"Why do you need to change?" I ask, quirking an eyebrow.

His dark eyebrows furrow and his silver eyes glimmer. "You let me worry about all that. I'm not gonna show up looking like a ragtag misfit or something."

"He's not gonna care—"

"Shhhh. Just go with it and let me do my thing," he says, holding a hand out in front of him.

I snicker to myself and stand up. "If you say so."

He grins broadly. "See ya in about an hour?"

I tip my head, hiking my backpack up over my shoulder. "If he's there, yes." I turn around and walk out, not wanting him to see the panic welling up inside me.

Butterflies tussle around in my stomach and I can't help but curse myself under my breath. I should have said no. I should have stood my ground to keep my distance. Every time we have to get together it makes it harder to remember why we should be apart in the first place.

Why can't I just say no to him?

The entire drive home is an escapade in testing my resolve.

I wonder whether or not I should I text Wade back, saying my dad isn't there. Would he come over anyway? Surely he wouldn't... Then again, would it be so wrong to have Dad meet someone who's been a big part of my life? Besides, Wade's sort of right. I could use another set of ears when I ask Dad about the house, the hauntings, and Abigail.

By the time I reach the manor, I've settled on letting Wade come over...as long as Dad is home. Nothing could go wrong there, right? Especially if I stick to the plan and get him out of the house after we find some answers.

When I open the front door, there's nothing immediately evident, pointing me toward whether or not he's home. The house remains as calm as ever.

"Dad?" I call out, glancing around the entryway. The large grandfather clock ticks loudly, punctuating the seconds that pass in silence.

Sighing to myself, I walk past the staircase and turn left, heading to my bedroom to drop off my backpack.

Just as I reach the door, I hear a voice call out, "Autumn? Is that you?"

I set my backpack on the floor inside the doorway and lean out into the hallway. "Dad?"

"Hey, sweetie. I thought I heard you," Dad says, walking down the hallway from where I just came. "How have things been?"

"Thank god, you're home," I say, breathing a sigh of relief. "I was beginning to worry."

"Why? Is everything okay?" he asks, his light eyes

clouding with worry. For the first time, I notice just how tired he looks. Wherever he's been has certainly taken a toll on him. There are deep bags under his eyes, like he hasn't slept well in a while.

"I'm—uh, are you okay? You don't look so well," I say, stepping toward him.

He takes a step back, shaking his head and rubbing at his eyes. "Oh, yeah. Just a little jet-lagged. I have to adjust back to our time."

"Where have you been? I mean, one day you were here, then you were gone for weeks. James said you were called away, but he didn't know much else," I say, tilting my head to the side.

"Yeah, that happens sometimes. I wish I could tell you more about it, but I'm not really allowed to..." he says, his gaze falling to the ground.

I chuckle softly. "Why? Do you work for the CIA or something?"

Dad's eyes widen, but he takes a step back and laughs. "Definitely something. What are you up to now? Did you want to catch up a bit?" He nods back toward the entryway.

"Actually, I'd love to. Let me just put all of my school stuff away quick."

"All right. Meet you in the sitting room. I love the light this time of day," he says, grinning.

"Sounds good. I'll be right there." I nod.

Walking into my bedroom, I pull my phone from my pocket and stare at the blacked-out screen. Despite my hesitation, I tap on the screen, unlock the phone, and type Wade a quick message.

. . .

Dad's home. We'll be in the sitting room up front, so ring the doorbell when you're here.

Shoving my phone back into my pocket, I walk out of my bedroom. When I reach the sitting room, Dad's sitting on one of the couches, staring out at the front yard. From the large picture window, the most prominent feature is the large oak tree just outside. Near the ground, though, is a garden full of shrubbery, with flowers that have clearly passed their prime as fall approaches.

"I love this time of the year," Dad grins, still staring out the window.

"I do, too. Fall's my favorite." I sit down on the love seat opposite him. Watching him for a moment, I can't help but wonder if he's doing okay. Something about him just seems a bit forlorn, but I'm not sure if we have the kind of relationship where I could call him on it.

"Dad," I say, looking down at my hands. "Could I ask you something?"

His gaze drifts over to me. "What is it?"

I watch him for a moment, weighing what it is I really want to ask him. After a moment of internal debate, I say, "Has Abigail ever lashed out before?"

His eyebrows furrow and his expression softens. "How do you mean?"

"Like, has she ever broken a room full of lightbulbs..." I say, letting my voice drift off. "Or tried to hurt anyone?"

Surprise flashes through his eyes, but he recovers quickly. "Well, no...not that I can think of. But, then again, she's never interacted with me much. I've never been able to truly communicate with her before."

I nod absently. "That's right, you can't see her. But you sense her, right? Has she ever attacked you?"

Dad's eyes narrow as he thinks. "Now that you mention it, there have been a few times where I felt constrained by a presence. Almost as if I was being bound or tied down. It usually happens right before I wake up, though, so I've always attributed it to a sleep paralysis. But, perhaps that was her?"

"Hmmm..." I say, biting my lower lip. "Do you think there are any other entities in this house? Anything that could want to do harm?"

"Has something happened?" Dad asks, standing up and taking a seat beside me.

I nod. "Well, yeah, actually. When you were gone, a friend of mine was attacked. He couldn't breathe. It was like someone, or something, was choking him. And the lights in your study—they all blew out at the same time. It felt very hostile, but I couldn't see anyone. So, I can't be one hundred percent that it was Abigail, you know? But after being here for a year, I sorta feel like I've grown to know her..."

"Have you tried asking her?" Dad asks, narrowing his gaze.

"Sort of. She's been really hard to reach lately. I'm not sure why."

"Hmmm...that does seem a bit fishy then, doesn't it? What are your instincts telling you?" he says, nodding and rubbing at his chin.

"Truthfully, I don't know. I'm only starting to understand my gifts. My exposure to ghosts has been pretty limited. It's all so new still, to be honest."

"Well, keep an eye on it. If it happens again, let me know," he says, reaching out and patting my leg.

I shiver from the coolness of his touch, but smile. It's not often he's shown any signs of affection. The movement actually reminds me of how Mom used to do the same thing when she was trying to console me.

Suddenly, the doorbell rings, startling us both. Dad pulls his hand back with a start.

"Who's that?" he blurts out with a hint of annoyance.

I rise from the love seat and smile. "It's okay, Dad. It's just my friend. The one who was attacked, actually. Wade—"

Dad bolts upright, his face flushing with an irate sense of fury. "Send him away. I don't want him here."

CHAPTER 10

SACRED SPACES

"What on earth are you talking about?" I sputter, unable to process the abrupt change in direction.

Dad shakes his head, recovering some of his calmness. "Sorry, Autumn, but I just got back. It's been a stressful few—I don't even know how long. I just want a little peace and quiet."

He walks out of the sitting room, leaving me in the cloud of confusion left in his wake.

With my mouth open wide and my head spinning, I fumble forward, making my way to the front door. I pull it back, unsurprised to find Wade standing there waiting.

"That took awhile," he says, grinning. The smile fades from his face when he catches the look on mine. "What's wrong?"

"I—" I begin. "I have no idea what just happened."

Wade bends forward, taking my hand in his. "What is it? What happened?"

"My dad and I were having a conversation—a good

one, actually. But he freaked out when you rang the doorbell," I say.

Wade's face crumples. "He really doesn't want to meet me, does he?"

"I don't think it has anything to do with you. He said something about just getting back and needing some time to relax," I say. "He seems so—stressed. I don't know what he's been working on, but he had bags under his eyes..."

"Well, don't read too much into it, then. I know how irritable I get when I'm dog-tired. It's probably best to give him some space to unwind," Wade offers with a shrug. "Well, I guess I should be going, then." He jabs a thumb back toward his Impala in the drive.

"Do you..." I say, chewing on my lower lip. If Cat were here, I'd ask her to come over, but since I'm left with few options, I look up to Wade's expectant gaze. "Can you come in for a bit? I don't really want to be alone right now."

Wade's eyes widen, but he nods. "Of course."

I back up, letting him walk past me and into the house. Taking a deep breath, I close the door.

My insides constrict. While my brain is saying one thing, my heart is saying another and I can't seem to get both on the same page. Either way, I just need to feel some sense of normalcy.

"Come on," I say, tipping my head toward the hallway. We make our way to my bedroom in silence, but the thoughts inside my head are anything but quiet. It's like the angel and devil on my shoulder have suited up and gone to battle.

When we reach my bedroom, Wade stands awkwardly, waiting for me to usher him inside.

"Go in," I say, thrusting my hand out and shooting him a tense smile.

When he's inside my room, I cast a tentative glance down the hallway and close the door. Turning around, Wade stands in the middle of the room, waiting patiently with his hands clasped behind his back.

I smirk, surprised by his stiff demeanor. For as long as I've known him, he's been the most easygoing person I've ever met.

I flick on the light switch beside the door and my bedside lamps both flicker to life. The late-afternoon sun is setting, drawing deep shadows in the trees outside and into the corners of my bedroom.

"You can sit, you know," I say, pointing to the window seat and walking over to it myself.

Wade follows me, watching me with curious eyes.

I sigh loudly and take a seat. "Thanks for coming in here. I just—without Cat, I don't really have anyone to talk to. And things have just been...weird."

"Tell me about it," Wade agrees, sitting down on the bench beside me. His knee bumps mine, and he leaves it there.

Rather than shifting away, I stay there, letting the closeness of him burn at my senses. Things have gotten so confusing around here, at least I know it's one thing that's still real.

Clearing my throat, I say, "Despite all the weirdness back there, Dad and I did talk a bit about the haunting. Not a lot...but enough."

"Okay?" Wade says.

"I told him about your attack. He thinks it could be

Abigail," I say, casting my gaze out over the courtyard. Without looking at him, I can feel the weight of his stare.

"Really? I thought we decided it wasn't her. The vibe isn't right," Wade counters.

I nod, turning to face him. "I know. But then I remembered something Abigail said to me really early on. She told me she was bound or there was a binding she wanted my help with. She said I was the only one who could help. At the time, I didn't know what that meant, but then I saw how she became a ghost."

Wade's silver eyes expand. "You did?"

"Yeah," I say, narrowing my gaze as I remember the vision. "It was like she was reminding me of her request—or like it was the only way she could get through to me. Either way, it left me thinking I should have been asking more questions. Like, how do we help her? It never really occurred to me that she might not want to be a ghost."

"Did she ask you to help her cross over?" Wade asks.

"Not in so many words. But it's the feeling I got. Any ideas on how to make that work?"

He shrugs. "I understand the straightforward crossings, but ones like hers aren't really my area of expertise just yet. I could find out, though."

"Would your dad answer any questions if he knew it was for my family?" I frown.

"There's only one way to find out for sure," he says, smirking. Reaching out, he places his hand on my knee, and holds it there a moment.

The gesture is small, but it's enough to make my pulse race. I wish things were different. I wish there wasn't this distance between us, even though I'm the one who put it there. I wish I could release it all and just be with him. I wish...

Without warning, the lights on my nightstands begin to flicker.

"Shit, not again," Wade says, suddenly standing up. His face is apprehensive as he spins around, looking for something neither of us can see. "Is she here?"

I stand up, trying to sense Abigail. "I don't know. I can't tell."

A cold, suffocating energy invades the room, closing in on me. I shiver, trying to release its grasp.

"Do you feel that?" Wade says, clenching his jaw. "It's like all the warmth from the room is being squeezed out."

I nod. "Yeah, I feel it—"

With a soft pop, the two lights on the nightstands go out and the room goes dark. The light from the picture window cascades a dark blue across the space, giving me enough light to walk over to the bed. I pull the chain on the lamp, hoping the light will turn back on, but of course, nothing happens.

"I think we should get outta here. Come with me to my place," Wade says, suddenly at my side.

I shake my head. "If this is Abigail, I need to know why she's doing this."

The hairs on the back of my neck rise as if a hand brushed along them. The next thing I know, a strange, scratching sound permeates the stillness. It starts off low and quiet.

Holding my breath, I spin around as the sound moves from wall to wall, rising upward and falling down toward the floor.

"Where is it?" Wade asks, trying to stand between me and the unseen specter.

"I don't know," I breathe. For the second time in a fortnight, I'm afraid to be in my own house. "Abigail—is that you?"

The scratching sound abruptly stops, and I reach out for Wade, grabbing hold of his hand. Before I can make contact with him, I'm slapped across the face. The motion of it makes my head snap back and stars blossom across my vision.

"What in the hell just happened? Are you okay, Autumn?" Wade says, reaching out and pulling me into his protective embrace.

Despite myself, my body trembles as I reach my hand up, covering my cheek. "It slapped me—she slapped me."

"What in the hell? We need to go..." Wade says, steering me toward the door.

"No, I need to talk to her. We need to figure out why she's doing this," I cry out, twisting toward the middle of the room. "She won't stop until we know why."

"It's not safe in here. Who knows what could happen next. We need to think and come up with a better plan."

"Then, let's go to the resurrection chamber. It's a sacred space. She wouldn't hurt us down there," I say, twisting in his arms.

The scratching noise resumes, echoing all around us in no particular order. It's like it's all around us, and this time, it's punctuated with a deep knocking sound, like someone dropping something heavy on the floor.

"*Get out...*" a voice whispers, sending icy chills coursing down my spine.

Wade's voice rises an octave as he says, "Won't hurt us? How do you know that? She seems pretty pissed off."

"She must be confused—or hurting. I don't think she means to be doing any of this," I say, releasing myself from his embrace to make my way to the door. "But there's one way to find out for sure. Let's go."

Wade snickers, muttering under his breath. "Just trying to scare us... Yeah, I'd say she's doing a bang-up job of managing that. Especially after last time."

"Come on," I say, grabbing his hand.

Wade clutches my hand tightly but follows right behind me. The closer we get to the doorway leading to the resurrection chamber, the louder the scratching along the walls becomes. Out of the corner of my eye, a shadow moves in the darker recesses of my room, making me freeze.

"Did you see that?" Wade says, twisting toward the shadow.

"Yeah, and I don't wanna stick around to see how it manifests." I twist the door handle, opening it and taking the first few steps with Wade in tow. The ordinarily cool air of the basement level rushes up at me, but it's warmer than my bedroom right now.

Trying to calm my nerves, I reach out to the sacred space of the resurrection chamber, summoning the magical torches on the walls to ignite. However, they refuse to heed my calling.

"Do you have your phone? I can't get the torches to light," I say, turning back to Wade.

"Yeah, I think so." He reaches into his pocket, fumbling with his phone. It drops from his hand, tumbling down a number of steps before sliding between the stairs, presumably landing on the dirt floor below. "Dammit. Sorry, Autumn."

"It's okay, I'll grab it," I say, dropping his hand and racing down a few stairs.

"Wait. Did you hear that?" Wade reverses his direction, stepping out of the stairway, and back into my bedroom. "Hang on. Someone's calling your name. I think it's your dad."

Turning back around, I walk up a couple of stairs. My heart is racing, and I know we need to summon Abigail in a safer space. "Don't worry about it. I don't want to bring him into—"

All at once, the large picture window in my bedroom shatters into the room. It peppers Wade as he hunches over, shielding himself from the debris.

"Wade—" I cry out, racing back up the steps. Just as I reach the door, it slams shut, separating the two of us and plunging me into darkness.

CHAPTER 11

PANIC ROOM

"Autumn!" Wade yells. I can hear him clawing at the other side of the wooden slab separating us. "I can't—the door handle is missing!"

"What the—?" I sputter, dropping my gaze and reaching for my side of the handle. The light is practically nonexistent from the glass block window on the outer wall, but he's right. It's gone. It's as if it has been magically erased from existence. I spin on the spot, my hands raking through my hair. "Think, Autumn, *think*..."

"Stand back," Wade says. "I'll kick it down."

"No," I say, twisting back to the door. "It opens inward, remember? You kicking it won't help. Let me try."

Spreading my hands out to either side of the stairwell for more stability, I lift my left leg and aim it at the door's lock. With as much leverage and might as I can muster, I land my kick squarely on the weakest point, but it doesn't even budge. I try again, with the same result.

"Dammit," I curse. "It won't budge. I don't think I have enough leverage from the stairs."

"There has to be something..." Wade begins.

Something crashes in my bedroom and the pieces tinkle like wind chimes as they hit the floor. Suddenly, the sound of furniture twisting on the hardwood floor makes me freeze.

"Wade, what's happening? Are you okay?" I call out. My upper body begins to tremble in the silence that greets me. "Wade—"

"I'm okay," he says, breathlessly. "Shit, she's seriously pissed. She's tipping the room upside down. How do we get you out? Is there any other way?"

"No, this is the only door in or out," I mutter, sliding down the door and taking a seat on the first step. I bury my face in my hands, trying to block out the terror rising up inside me.

What do I do? What do we do? Why in the hell is any of this happening?

"Abigail," I yell. "Abigail, stop this right now. I get it. You want help and I haven't been listening. But I'm listening now. What can I do to help?"

Maniacal laughter echoes up from the resurrection chamber, making the hairs all over my body stand on end. It doesn't even sound like a person, let alone Abigail.

There's a loud thump on the other side of the door and Wade screams out in pain. A muffled scraping sound follows.

Springing to my feet, I scream, "Wade? Are you okay?" I bang on the door with the side of my fist, trying to beat it into submission.

From farther away, Wade calls out, "She's getting stronger. She dragged me clear across the room. Autumn, we need to get out of this house. *Now*."

"I don't know how," I say, casting my gaze around the stairway. What little light I had from the glass-block window has faded and it's gotten darker. My gaze lingers on the blocks, but even if we managed to find a way to bust eight inches of glass block, I don't know if I'd be able to fit through the small opening. "Wade, you need to find my dad. Run and get help."

"On it," Wade calls out.

My heartbeat thrums loudly in my ears, making it impossible to hear anything but my own panicked state. How did things get this messed up?

I rub at my forehead, trying to calm my thoughts so I can think clearly.

I gotta do something...gotta help somehow. How do I make things right when Abigail won't even talk to me?

What on earth have I done to warrant this?

"God, I hope Dad can help," I whisper to myself.

With shaky legs, I walk down the stairs. I feel completely helpless.

So much for this gift of being a postmortem medium. I can't even seem to control the ghosts in my own damn house. What good is this stupid ability if I can't even keep myself or the ones I love safe?

If there's nothing else I can do, I'm damn well going to at least retrieve Wade's phone. Each step I take is deliberate and slow, just in case Abigail decides to throw anything else at us. Upstairs, everything seems quiet, but the oppressive energy is still lingering in the air. There's no way I'm going to be lulled into a false sense of security. Not here—not in this house.

When I reach the final stair, I take a deep, cleansing breath and close my eyes. It may be pitch black, but I'm lucky enough to have other senses I can tap into that make moving around in the darkness much easier.

I let the panic and fear wash away as I tap into something deeper and more powerful. Behind my lids, the room takes shape in bright florescent outlines as the corners and edges of the room become evident. This extrasensory ability doesn't bring back any alarming entities, so I take another breath and walk out into the resurrection chamber and around to the back of the stairs.

With my second sight, the phone comes into view, and I bend down to pick it up. Keeping my eyes closed, I cram it into my pocket rather than mess with the flashlight. It will only destroy my night vision, and who knows how much battery power is left? I need to conserve it, just in case.

There's still no more movement upstairs, and I pray that Wade's able to locate my dad...and that he can help.

Without warning, Abigail's form rushes into my extrasensory view. Her hair is wild and her eyes are wide with fury—but I can't hear her. She stops mere feet from me, her arms flailing wildly.

"Abigail, I can't understand you. You're too quiet. What's going on? Why are you so angry?" I blurt out in one big blob. I try to keep my voice calm, but I'm not sure I pull it off.

Her face contorts angrily, and her arms only flail harder. Still, I can't hear a word she says as she opens her mouth wide and silently screams in my face. Every cell in my body crackles with an energy that makes goosebumps flash across my skin.

"You need to stop this—" I demand, taking a step toward her with more courage than I actually feel.

There's a loud crash right above our heads, making me jump. Then, at the top of the stairs, something heavy slams against the door. I turn my attention toward the sound, unsure if Abigail is trying to cause more destruction or if Wade found my dad. The thud is followed immediately by a strange crackling sound, like flames licking at firewood. Stumbling backward, my heart races, threatening to burst from my chest.

If Wade's hurt...

I turn my attention back to Abigail, but she's gone. I can't see or sense her at all, regardless of which senses I use.

"Dammit," I curse, racing back to the staircase. "Wade? Is that you?"

The door continues to crackle and groan until the faceplate springs apart. Then the entire latch system bursts, sending pieces of metal flying down the stairs. Wade flings the door open, jamming a foot against the door and thrusting out a hand.

"I couldn't find your dad, but found this," he says, holding up a pry bar.

My eyes widen as I race up the stairs and out the door. "Where in the world did you find that?"

"One of the rooms your dad's been fixing up. Abigail tried to throw it at me," he says, grabbing my hand and pulling me from the room. "Come on, we need to get the hell outta here."

Blood trickles down his face, evidence some of the chaos caught up with him. "You're hurt," I say, reaching out and hovering my fingertips above the wound.

"Yeah, picture frame. You wouldn't think those damn

things could hurt so much," he mutters, rubbing at his head. "Anyway, doesn't matter. I'll live."

Swallowing hard, I drop my hand and exit the stairwell. My bedroom looks like a bomb has exploded. The window is completely gone, and my curtain rail hangs at an odd angle as the remnants of the curtain flutter lazily in the breeze. Glass covers the floor and every footstep I take crunches ominously, like I'm walking on the bones of the dead. My bed is tipped on its side and every single drawer on my dresser is open to some degree. Nothing is where it should be. Books, lampshades, my laptop—everything is scattered across the room like someone picked it up and shook the contents.

"Holy shit," I mutter, unable to stop looking.

"Yeah, it's not the worst of it. We need to go—" Wade says, dragging me out of the room.

I follow him out into the hallway on some sort of dazed autopilot, but my awareness catches up with me when I see one of the large family pictures of my dad on the floor. He's younger, barely sixteen, I'd guess, as he stands beside an older man and woman—my grandparents, I'd gather. Though I've never met either of them.

"Oh my god, my dad—" I sputter, suddenly dragging my feet. "We need to find him. He needs to get out of here, too."

Wade shakes his head, turning around and placing both hands on my shoulder in the middle of the hallway. "I've looked everywhere, Autumn. If he's in this house, he's doing a helluva job hiding. Maybe he has a panic room or something for situations like this. He's obviously a grown man who knows to take care of himself during something like this. We need to go…"

The walls begin to rattle, but everywhere I look, things are knocked over or broken. Picture frames, knickknacks, items I haven't even given a second thought to—like the grandfather clock—are already strewn across the floor.

"Why is she doing this?" I cry out, covering my mouth.

"I don't know, but we can figure it out later." Wade takes off down the hallway, carefully jumping over items on the floor.

I follow him, treading gingerly so I don't do any more damage. So many family heirlooms are shattered into pieces, and I have no idea if they'll ever be restored. My heart breaks for my dad. This house is everything to him... He's going to be so upset.

When we reach the main entryway, I pull up short and cover the cry of surprise springing from my lips. The grand staircase dangles from the upper landing as if it was twisted in two different directions.

"How in the hell?" I sputter.

Wade shakes his head. "I don't know. I was trying to find your dad. When I ran up the stairs, it was like they were trying to buck me off."

"I should go up there. Maybe my dad's—"

Wade grabs my hand and pulls me toward the door. "It's not safe. Not the stairs and definitely not this house. Your dad can handle himself."

A strange, eerie chuckle echoes through the entryway. Suddenly, the temperature of the space drops by at least twenty degrees.

"We're leaving, *now*," Wade asserts definitively. Without letting me even attempt the hunt for my dad, he practically drags me from the house kicking and screaming.

The door groans, giving him some trouble at first, but he somehow manages to get it open. The second we're outside, the cool, fall breeze ruffles my hair, lightening the pressure against my chest. I hadn't noticed just how heavy the energy was in there, but it was almost suffocating.

Wade races down the front steps two at a time, reaching his Impala and opening the passenger-side door.

"Get in," he demands.

I do as he says, taking a seat without question. Closing the door, I stare at the dashboard, unable to divert my gaze from it to look at the manor. Everything has been turned, literally, on its head and I have no idea what I'm going to do.

Wade hops into the driver's seat and tears out of the driveway like we're being chased by hellhounds. And maybe we are.

My heart clenches, and in the pit of my stomach a new kind of terror emerges.

What if Wade's wrong? What if my dad's not safe?

What if after all of that, Abigail's hurt him...*or worse*?

Tears well up in my eyes, and I'm suddenly consumed by this fresh terror as it washes over me.

My dad and I have hardly had any time together. I've barely even scratched the surface of who he is, or our family history.

I haven't heard anything from him. What if he's hurt or dying inside and I'm leaving him there to die alone?

CHAPTER 12
THE SPACE BETWEEN US

"Come on, Autumn. We need to get inside and regroup," Wade says, standing beside me with the passenger door wide open.

I blink up at his outstretched hand. I don't remember the drive or arriving at his apartment. Hell, I don't even remember him parking the car and getting out. Reaching for his hand, I allow him to pull me out of the car. My legs don't feel like they're attached to my body, as I practically drop to the ground.

"Whoa, I gotcha," he says, wrapping his warm arms around me and holding me close. "It's okay, it's—we'll figure this out. I promise."

I place my face against his broad chest, listening to his heartbeat as he slowly rubs the palm of his hand over the back of my head.

Suddenly, my chin quivers and tears spill over the edges of my eyelids. "What if my dad..."

"Shhhh..." Wade murmurs. "I'm sure he's fine. We can call the house and if nothing else, go back there in the morning. Things seem worse in there after the sun goes down. Let's just ride this out and we'll do what we can in the morning."

"What about the police? Shouldn't we call them?" I say, lifting my head and staring deeply into his silver eyes.

Wade's eyebrows rise and he shrugs. "We can, if you think that'll help. I don't know what they'll be able to do, though. It's not like they're ghostbusters. They're just cops."

I run my hand over my mouth, backing away from him. He's right. I know he's right, but I feel so helpless. There has to be something I can do to help or protect my dad from all the madness. If I go home tomorrow to find out I could have done something, but didn't...

Before I know it, my shoulders are wracking with the sobs I'd been holding back. "Why is she doing this? Why is she so angry—?" I sputter, managing to get a couple of words between whimpers.

"I don't know, but we're not going to solve anything out here. Let's get inside." Wade takes my hand, leading me toward his apartment building.

I can barely contain all of the thoughts fighting for a turn in my head. What if I can't get Abigail to stop? Will she hurt us? *Really* hurt us? Could she—*would she*...kill us?

Wade leads me down the hallway to his apartment, but I'm barely able to focus on staying vertical. All I want to do is sleep. I need to sleep...

Swaying on the spot, I hear Wade take out his keys and kick open his door, but the next thing I know, I'm floating. My hair sways in the movement, but I can't bring myself to open my eyes. Instead, I lean into it, letting it sweep me away.

When my eyes flutter open again, I'm lying beside Wade on his bed. The room is dimly lit by a small table lamp on the other side of the room. He props himself onto his elbow and runs his hand along the side of my face.

"How are you doing?" he whispers, locking his discerning gaze with mine.

"I—" I close my eyes, unable to keep them open for longer than a couple of moments. "I'm not sure. I feel so..."

"It's okay. You're in shock. This has been a lot to deal with. Just rest, okay? You're safe," Wade says quietly as he continues to stroke the side of my face.

The movement is so natural and so comforting, it's all I can do not to fall back to sleep. Somewhere in the recesses of my mind, my anxiety blossoms and my eyes pop back open.

"My dad—"

Wade's eyes soften and his fingertips cease their dance momentarily. "I've called Sheriff Gordon. They're going to go and check in on him. We should be getting a call any time now."

"But what about..." My voice trails off as the memory of Abigail's attack comes rushing back to me. The house is wrecked—absolutely destroyed.

"He's been warned to go in with caution. I gave him as many details as I could about what happened. If your dad's in there, they'll find him."

Relief floods through my body for the first time and I lean back into the pillow. Wade resumes his soft touch along the side of my face. For the longest time, I rest there, just concentrating on the way his hand feels on my skin.

"Thank you," I whisper, unable to put into words everything I'm really feeling right now. Everything I wish I could say.

Wade snickers softly. "What on earth are you thanking me for?"

I open my eyes, taking in his confused expression. "Everything. Coming back into the house after the last time. Being willing to talk to my dad... Getting me out of the resurrection chamber when Abigail made it nearly impossible. Helping me get out of the house... Letting me stay here..." I say, splaying my hand out and gesturing around the room. "It's more than I deserve."

"Don't be ridiculous," Wade says, scrunching his face.

Slowly, I shift myself to a seated position. "No, I mean it. You didn't have to come back to the house. You don't owe me anything. Especially after—"

Wade sits up, too, taking my hands in his and holding them in the space between us. "Autumn, I will never abandon you. I don't know why you haven't gotten that through your thick head yet."

"Gee—thanks," I say, dropping my gaze to the crumpled blanket between us.

"No, I mean it. I know you're just running scared. I get it. You've been through a lot in a short span of time. Finding out about your gifts, not to mention my lineage and all that goes with it. Then Cat and Colton. The Fetch. Besides, my dad can be damn scary... But I've given things a lot of thought over the past few weeks. I love you and I'm not going anywhere. I will always be here for you. Even if I have to do it from a distance," he says, his eyes pleading with me to understand.

Something inside of me softens and I'm consumed with the desire to let go.

I don't know what's changed. Maybe it's the extreme haunting and very real possibility of facing my own mortality... Or the fact that even though I've tried to keep him away and keep him safe, Wade is still always nearby. Even when I try to keep my distance, he's thrust right back into the middle of things. In essence, it renders my decision to stay apart completely inert.

My eyes fall to his lips, which tug slightly downward. I hadn't noticed until now just how worn his eyes look. He's tired and just as scared as I am.

Bending forward, I lift my right hand, placing it along his jawline. Rubbing my thumb across his lower lip, I can't help but be drawn to him. After all the chaos in my life, all the insanity with my gifts, he's been the one constant. The one person I turn to and the one I know without a doubt that I can trust with my life.

Wade closes his eyes, sighing contently into my hand. "I've missed that," he whispers.

Before I have the sense to question myself, I close the distance between us, pressing my lips to his. Instantly, my body sparks with an intensity I didn't know was hiding under the surface. I've missed him, too. More than I could ever put into words.

Wade sighs into the kiss, but within microseconds, it triggers something in him as well. He wraps his arms around my torso, pulling me on top of him. With a quick twist of his hip, he rolls us over, so I'm pressed beneath his weight. The movement unleashes so much pent-up energy between the two of us, it almost catches me off guard a second time.

With his hands on either side of my face, he presses his lips and body against mine. It stirs every nerve ending to life, and for the first time in weeks, I want nothing more than to feel alive. To be fully and one hundred percent in my body—before it's too late.

There's an impending air of doom that presses against my chest, but I ignore its heaviness and give in to the pleasure of Wade's touch. Sliding my hands underneath his t-shirt, I lift it upward. For a moment, he breaks our kiss to tug it completely over his head. It drops unceremoniously to the floor as he lowers himself back to me. His lips crush down on mine, making my lips buzz and my heartbeat sputter out of control.

My hands slide up and down his back, feeling the contours of his muscles beneath my palms. As they drop to his waist, I tug at his belt, unlatching it. He breaks our kiss, trailing his lips to my jawline and down my neck, sending a fresh wave of shivers coursing through my body.

As I get his belt unbuckled, he grabs hold of my hands. Excitement and passion flush his face, but he peers at me with caution hidden in his eyes. "Are you sure? I don't—"

His words trigger an internal check, but I realize I've never been more certain of anything before.

Holding myself very still, I smile. "I'm sure, *Angel*."

The lines of loneliness and weariness practically vanish as the most beautiful smile graces his lips and brightens his face. It's the invitation he must have been waiting for as he bends forward again, kissing me with dizzying effect. His hands slowly trail downward. A soft moan escapes my lips and involuntarily, I arch my back.

He takes it for the invitation it is, dropping his hands to my jeans, and unbuttoning them. He shifts to the side and in a couple of swift movements, my jeans slide off. Tossing them over the edge, he bends forward again, lifting my shirt and exposing my belly to his kisses. His lips graze the side of my ribcage, my belly button, and trails to my hipbone.

I sit up, tugging my shirt off completely and unhooking my bra. His breath hitches as he kneels back, watching me.

"You are so beautiful," he whispers. His pupils are wide, covering up any hint of silver he may have hidden in his irises.

Smiling, I reach out for him, urging him forward. He kicks off his shoes and socks, and shimmies out of his jeans, letting them tumble off the edge of the bed. Lowering himself down on top of me, the heat between our bodies builds with the skin-on-skin contact. Once again, his lips find mine as he tips his hips forward. I open my legs, wrapping them around his waist, and wishing I'd taken off the last shred of clothing I have on. I want to be consumed by him. All of him.

I need to escape reality and be completely absorbed in him.

As if reading my mind, he trails his lips from my face to my neck, then down to my clavicle. Goosebumps instantly rush across my skin, and everything tightens in anticipation of where he may head next. His lips find the most sensitive places of my torso, but his hands gently tug at my panties. I tip my hips so I can finally be rid of them.

When they're shed, my fingertips circle the band at his boxers, pulling at them and sliding them down his legs. A deep growl erupts from his chest when we're both freed of our confines. He lowers himself down, pressing his pulsating body against mine. The movement makes my breath hitch and my entire body tingle in anticipation. Gently, he rolls his hips, sending sparks of pleasure through every nerve center from head to toe.

My hands fly to the back of his neck, pulling his beautiful face to mine. His tongue skates against my lips, parting them. In response, I open my legs wide and tip back. With a shudder, he takes my offering.

My body pulsates, moving in rhythm with his as we intertwine. His hands, mouth, hips all move in sync, making it impossible to maintain any kind of composure. All I can think about is how much I want him, need him, miss him...

For a while, I lose myself completely. Any sense of time or space suspends itself as I give over fully to Wade. Our breath, bodies, and even heartbeats each come into alignment, matching the other's.

Release washes over me, followed immediately by Wade. For the longest time, we don't move. We just stay there, entangled with each other, allowing the moment of bliss to ride. When our breathing returns to normal, Wade drops to the bed, pulling me close.

Resting my head on his bare chest, I close my eyes in contentment. His scent tickles my nose and I can't help but smile. Of all the times and places...of all the circumstances, this may not have been ideal timing. But it was still perfect, nonetheless.

With each rise and fall of his chest, I'm lulled into a sense of peace and tranquility I didn't have even hours before. Yet...slowly, the anxiety snakes its way back in.

Visions of my father trapped in the rubble of the house invade my mind. I see him hurt and bloodied. Or crying out for help... Then, they morph into Wade being taken from me—forced into a life as an Angel of Death because his earthly life came to an early, abrupt end. All because he was close to me. Because I let him back in.

My heartbeat begins to race again, but this time, for all the wrong reasons.

CHAPTER 13
PARANORMAL ACTIVITY

My eyes fly open to the sound of Wade's ringtone. Somewhere between my anxiety and bliss, I must have drifted off to sleep.

Mid-morning light peeks through the horizontal slats from the window blinds, casting strange shadows across Wade's torso as he sits up in bed.

"Hello?" he says gruffly, shifting his gaze to me and smiling. His eyes take on a distant quality as he concentrates on the conversation from the other end. As he listens, he reaches out, stroking the side of my arm. After a few moments, he nods and says, "Okay, thank you. I appreciate it, Sheriff."

Wade ends the call, setting his phone on the nightstand and sliding himself under the covers beside me.

"What did Sheriff Gordon have to say?" I ask, unable to take my eyes off him.

Reaching out, Wade gently pushes a strand of my hair behind my ear. "No one came to the door last night when they checked in on your dad. But a unit went out again this morning."

My heart constricts and I say, "And?"

"Good news. James was there this morning and let the officers in. From the sounds of things, your dad is fine and there's already a crew in there working on cleanup," Wade says, smiling. "They said it just looked like ordinary remodeling work from what they could tell. So maybe the supernatural stuff wasn't as bad as it seemed when we were in the middle of it."

"Maybe?" I say, shuddering back the memories from last night's haunting.

Wade's hand trails down my shoulder, and rests on my forearm.

I exhale slowly, allowing the sense of relief to cleanse away some of my worry. "Did they talk to my dad, then?"

Wade shakes his head. "No, they only spoke with James."

My eyebrows tug in as some of the panic returns. "How do they know my dad's okay?"

"Evidently, James was given the order to call in the construction team by your dad," Wade says. "We can go to the manor and ask him some questions if you want."

I nod. "That might be a good idea."

Raising my right hand, I trail my fingertips across Wade's broad chest. The past twenty-four hours have been a bizarre jumble of emotions. None of which are easily discernible.

"What are you thinking about?" Wade asks, his piercing eyes seeing right through me.

"Nothing..." my voice trails off, but my words don't really reflect my truth. I shake my head and sigh. "No, that's not true. It's just... Does it seem odd to you how often my dad has been gone? He leaves James in charge a lot," I say, running my fingertips through the curls of hair on Wade's chest.

His forehead creases. "A little. But I figure..." His expression tightens as he chooses his words. Then, with a soft smile, he continues, "I mean, and please don't take this the wrong way, but...maybe he's found someone? A woman he really likes and he's scared to tell you about her. I mean, you grew up with your Mom, so maybe he thinks you'll have a problem with it. Could that be possible?"

My eyebrows flicker upward as I consider this new possibility. I hadn't even thought about my dad as someone who would want to date, let alone someone who's already found a new girlfriend. Mom never really dated when I was a kid and if she did, she hid it from me pretty well. But perhaps that explains my dad's bizarre reaction to meeting Wade. Maybe he wants to tell me the truth and meeting Wade triggers his own guilt or worry?

"Should I confront him about it then? You know, let him know that he can tell me..." I say, biting my lower lip.

"I don't know. Honestly, based on what you've told me, he seems pretty set in his ways. I suppose it's bound to happen when you mostly live alone like that. It's probably best to get him to open up a little slower. Maybe drop some hints, but let him come to you when he's ready," Wade offers.

Taking a deep breath, I nod. There's a lot of sense to that. In all fairness, I don't know my dad all that well. We've never had much of an opportunity to grow very close, even in the past year.

Rolling over, I slide my legs over the edge of the bed,

letting the blanket drop to my waist. Wade pushes forward, sitting up right behind me. He shifts my hair to the side, gently kissing the place where my neck meets my shoulder.

A shiver courses through my body and I lean into him, sighing contently. Things are crazy and messed up. And absolutely none of the serious problems with our relationship have changed between us. He's still an angel in waiting and I'm still *me*... But I'm just not strong enough to keep fighting this. Sometimes the heart wants what it wants. That's gonna need to be enough for now.

Somehow, I need to find a way to keep him safe—*and* for us to stay together.

Bending down, I grab my clothing from the floor. I tug on my panties and slide my bra back on. Twisting around, I kneel on the edge of the bed, and reach out for Wade. I place my right hand on his jawline as I bend in and plant a soft kiss on his lips.

He sighs into me, his breath warm and sweet against my lips. As I pull back, a dreamy smile paints his face in a way I haven't seen in so long. Even in all of this mess, it lifts my spirits.

"Well, Mr. Hoffman, we should get dressed and do some digging. I don't know about you, but I need for this haunting stuff to end and I could use your help. Are you up for it?" I ask, tugging on my jeans and zipping them back up.

"With you, I am up for just about anything," Wade says, smirking.

Color creeps into my cheeks and I shake my head, chuckling under my breath. "Not what I was getting at, but that, too..."

Wade beams at me as I pull my shirt on. When he's watched me get completely dressed, he begrudgingly gets out of bed to do the same. I sit on the edge of the bed, watching the way his muscles move as he slides back into his clothing, one piece at a time.

I wish I could see into the future. I wish I could know without a shadow of a doubt whether or not being together is the right move or the wrong one. Suddenly, a thought pops into my head. I chew on my lower lip, surprised it hadn't come to me before. I might not be psychic, but I know a couple of people who are. Some, in fact, who are extremely powerful.

It might be wise to reach out to Dominic and Diana to see if they can pick up on anything. It would at least give me some peace of mind...or help me put an end to things indefinitely.

"Do you want a bite to eat before we go into full-on research mode?" Wade asks, walking around the bed and wrapping his arms around me.

I lean into him and close my eyes. "That would be lovely. I'm starving, actually."

"As you wish," Wade says, with a hint of a grin in his tone. He takes my hand, leading me over to his tiny kitchen area. "Have a seat, my lady. I will whip you up something to eat. With plenty of coffee, of course."

I sit on the bar stool and lean against the breakfast bar. Wade sets to work, grabbing pans and shoving a tiny coffeemaker carafe under the faucet to fill up.

"Bacon and eggs okay? It's kinda all I have at the moment," Wade says, sheepishly.

"That would be great. Do you want me to help?" I say, grinning back. I'm really more of a Pop-Tarts and Red Bull kinda gal, but I'd never turn down an actual cooked breakfast, either. I learned that pretty quick with Mom.

"Of course not. Sit, relax for a moment. I can handle this," he says, shooing me with his hands and darting back and forth in the tiny kitchen space. He gets the coffeemaker going, grabs eggs and bacon, and soon the room smells more like a diner than a guy's apartment. Which, I have to admit, is a not-so-subtle change for the better.

"So, I was thinking this morning..." Wade says, handing me a cup of coffee. "Well, at least before the phone call, that is."

I take the mug, immediately pulling it to my nose. It smells like heaven. "Thank you," I whisper.

"I was thinking, with all of the haunting stuff going on at the manor, maybe you should..." he straightens his shoulders and puffs up his chest a bit. "I'd like for you to stay here with me," he says, his tone light as he taps the edge of the counter with his fingertips.

It's really a question hidden in a request.

I hold my breath, surprised by the sentiment.

"I mean, if you don't want to..." he says, his eyebrows tugging in.

"No, I'm just a little surprised," I counter, shaking my head. "But that makes a lot of sense, actually."

"It does, doesn't it?" He grins, turning back to the bacon and flipping it over.

"Wade, do you think there's a way to help Abigail cross over? She's been dead for so long, I'm worried that maybe..." My eyes fall to the mug of coffee. "Maybe her time has come and gone. Is that why she's still stuck here? Is that why she's so angry?"

Wade slides the eggs and bacon onto plates and walks around the counter with one in each hand. Handing me one and taking the seat beside me, he shakes his head. "I don't have a good answer for you on that one. I wish I did. It's something I can definitely bring up with my dad."

I smile weakly. His dad and I aren't on the best of terms and I doubt he'll offer much in the way of help.

"But are you absolutely certain it's Abigail causing all of these problems?" Wade asks, picking up his fork and staring at it.

"At this point, I don't know much of anything. But I remember when all of this first started, she came at me like I was meant to help her somehow."

He takes a bite of his eggs but shakes his head. "I just keep going back around to...if she's been in the manor so long, why would she start getting violent about things now? You've worked together as a team. Why couldn't she just ask you again for what she really wants? Something about it doesn't make any sense."

"So, if it's not Abigail, what do you think is going on?" I ask, picking up my slice of bacon and biting off the end.

"We already know how powerful you are. Your powers have developed quickly, and I just wonder... What if other energies are being drawn to you?"

"What, like a magnet?" I ask, considering.

"Maybe?" he shrugs. "I'm thinking it might not be a bad idea to start with a cleansing of the home first. Bust out the sage and lemongrass. Put up some new wards, cast a few spells that keep out spirits that specifically don't belong there. Then you'll know for sure what you're dealing with. If it keeps happening afterward, then you know it's gotta be Abigail. Right?"

"That's a very smart idea, Mr. Hoffman," I say, tipping my head. "Then, if it stops, problem solved. If it doesn't... we know I have to move on to more drastic measures. Let's stop and get the supplies we need before we head to the manor."

Wade nods, taking another bite of his breakfast.

These new thoughts coil around my mind, releasing a torrent of unwanted anxiety. There's still so little I know about being a necromancer and postmortem medium. I've barely scratched the surface with my studies at the academy and I highly doubt any of them are prepared for someone like me, anyway.

What if this horrible haunting activity is because I haven't learned to control my abilities? Am I becoming some sort of lightning rod for unwanted paranormal activity?

CHAPTER 14
BANISHMENT & PROTECTION

After a quick stop to pick up supplies for the banishing and warding spells, we find ourselves taking the final turn down my long driveway. As the multicolored trees blur by, a swell of dread threatens to consume me.

What if this doesn't work? What if it only pisses off the angry spirit—*Abigail or otherwise*—that's haunting the manor?

Shuddering away the uneasiness, my gaze extends beyond the cab of the Impala and I focus on the beauty of the scenery. Fall has always been my favorite time of year, but the ghostly malevolence and thinning of the veil associated with the season are hitting a little too close to home. *Literally*.

Wade pulls the car around to the front entry. A few construction vehicles litter the driveway, and men walk in and out of the building, just as the sheriff had said. I hop out and Wade grabs the supplies from the back seat.

"Think they'll care if it smells like sage?" Wade asks, a twinkle in his eyes.

"After the mess in there, I doubt anything could faze them," I say, raising a knowing eyebrow.

"Fair point."

Wade closes the door to the back seat and walks around the car. Together, we head up the stone steps to the gaping entryway. The door to the manor is wide open as workers come in and out like bees. Not a single one of them seems like they have time to spare a glance in our direction.

"Talk about dedicated," I mutter, shooting Wade a sideways glance.

He nods, reaching for my hand. As we enter the building, I stand back, viewing the space in utter astonishment. With the exception of portions of the staircase still being replaced, the majority of the damage has been completely erased by their hard work.

"Holy shit, that's incredible," I say, blinking back my surprise.

Wade nods, his mouth agape. "I'll say. It's almost as if nothing ever went down. Another few hours and you'd never even know."

"Right?" I whisper, meandering through the workers as I make my way to the kitchen.

Just as expected, James is hard at work, a mop in hand. He stops, brushing the sweat on his forehead aside with the back of his hand. "Ah, Ms. Blackwood. So good to see you."

"Autumn," I say out of habit. It's been a year now and he still hasn't taken to my first name. It's doubtful at this point he ever will.

James tips his head and turns to Wade. "Mr. Hoffman, I presume?"

Wade sets the bag down on the counter and walks over, extending a hand. "I am. Nice to meet you, James. I've heard a lot about you."

"The pleasure is mine," James says, shaking Wade's hand. Then, he turns to me with a knowing gaze. "So, the manor was in quite the disarray this morning."

"Yeah, understatement," I say, nodding. "Have you seen my dad? Did he tell you what happened?"

"I did see your father this morning. I believe he's somewhere on the grounds," James says, his features tight as he swaps his gaze between me and Wade. There's an uneasy air about him, like there's more he wants to say, but he's unsure if he can in front of Wade.

"Wade, do you think you could bring our stuff to the bedroom? I'll meet you there in just a second," I say, turning to Wade. Thankfully, he takes the hint gracefully.

"Sure thing," Wade says, grabbing the bag and walking to the doorway. He turns back before he exits and says, "It really was nice to meet you."

When he's left the room, I turn back to James, unsure how exactly to start the conversation I want to have with him.

"Ms. Blackwood," James begins, setting the mop aside and propping it against the wall. "I appreciate your ability to sense my nuance. It's a gift your father also shares."

"No problem. I guess I have a few things I'd like to speak with you about as well," I say, chewing on my lower lip. "You can go first. What's on your mind?"

"Well, as I'm sure you're aware, this...redecorating, so to speak, was pretty extensive. In all of my years here, I've never witnessed anything quite like it," he says, as if treading softly.

My pulse begins to race and it's all I can do not to gape at him. "So, things like this have happened before, though?"

"Oh, yes. This is a very haunted location. There's history here. However, there have been extensive wards put in place to keep the manor in a state of relative peace. I'm concerned..." his voice drops off as he flits his gaze to the window. "I'm concerned there may be a failing in those wards as of late."

I take a deep breath, nodding. "Yeah, that's an understatement. And I'd have to agree—"

"Ms. Blackwood," he begins slowly, his eyebrows tugging down.

"Autumn," I repeat.

His warm brown eyes lift to meet mine and he nods. "Autumn, I am concerned for your father. Do talk to him. Make sure he's okay."

Alarm bells suddenly ring in my head and I step forward. "Did he get hurt?"

"No, he appeared in fine condition when we spoke, but...he just seemed a bit more agitated than normal." James shrugs, considering. "Granted, the house's state was quite enough to be upset over."

"Okay, of course. I'll see if I can find him and have a word," I say, nodding.

"Excellent," James says, smiling. He reaches again for the mop and pulls it in close.

"Wade and I are actually here to reset some of the wards. With any luck, things will be better after today," I say, trying to sound more sure than I feel. It's the first time

I've done any such spellcasting, and, in all honesty, it's still theoretical in my mind.

"Very good," he says, tipping his head.

I take a few steps toward the doorway and turn back to him. "Thanks for telling me. About my dad, that is. I appreciate it."

"Of course."

I shoot him a final smile and walk out. Making my way past the flurry of activity in the rest of the house, my thoughts are drawn back to my dad. I've been worried about him for a while and now James is, too. It makes me uneasy.

When I get to my bedroom, I find Wade organizing the contents of our stash across the foot of my bed.

He looks up at me as I walk in. "Everything okay?"

I screw up my face with my conflicting thoughts. "Yes? No? Ugh, I don't know." I sit on the edge of the bed. "James said he's concerned about my dad and it's got me even more worried about him now."

"What did James say?" Wade asks, stepping around the bed and taking a seat beside me.

"Well, besides the obvious concern about the house— he said my dad's been off. Agitated. Well, we knew that already. I'm worried... Do you think he's upset that we're together? I mean, your dad is. Maybe mine is too," I say, voicing a concern I hadn't realized was there until it slipped from my mouth.

Wade's forehead crumples and he shakes his head. "I doubt that's it. As far as I'm aware, the issue is one-sided."

"Hmmm..."

"What did James say about the house?" Wade asks, placing a hand on my knee.

I take a deep breath and exhale. "He said he's never seen this level of destruction before. The house is a magnet for ghosts, for obvious reasons, but it should be warded. He's concerned the wards are failing."

"All the more reason to get these castings done," Wade says, nodding to himself and standing back up. "I have everything laid out to do the banishing first. Then, we'll need to set runes at strategic locations of the house. I have a compass in there that should help us map those out. Unless of course, you want to get your dad involved. He might be able to help us cut down the time it'll take to locate them."

I consider his words, weighing them heavily. On one hand, it makes sense, but after the reaction he had to Wade the last time, the last thing I want to do is upset him further.

"No, I think we can handle this ourselves. Let's give him some time to get centered. This has been a weird couple of days," I say, reaching for the sage. "If we run into him, we can reassess based on how he reacts. Otherwise, let's give him some space."

"If that's what you want," Wade says, nodding. He gathers up the conch shell, mortar and pestle, and the herbs we retrieved. Setting them on my desk, he places the sage, lemongrass, and lavender in the mortar and begins to mash it together. Under his breath, he mutters words I can't quite make out.

From the bed, I grab the coarse-grain salt and the small, ornate metal bowl. I pour some of the salt into my hand, blessing it with white light before dropping it into the bowl. The granules hit the metal, ringing out in a magical sound that makes the hair on my arms rise. Next,

I open the small bottle of purified water we picked up and pour it into the bowl. With a swish of the bowl, the water dissolves the salt before my eyes. I grab the bowl of water and the white pillar candle still waiting for its purpose, and walk over to Wade.

"Don't forget to word things carefully. You don't want to kick Abigail out by accident," Wade warns, stepping aside.

I nod, placing the candle on the desk beside the mixture. I light it quickly, then recite the incantation, still fresh in my memory from one of my course books.

"As this candle burns, its flame purifies our home. It acts as our cage, binding and banishing *unwelcome* spirits and energies from Blackwood Manor. When the flame is spent, and the smudging is done, they will be cast from this space. Now and forever."

As I finish, the flame reacts, rising higher into the air.

Wade nods, bending down and releasing the contents from the mortar into the abalone shell. Lighting the smudge, it crackles as flames consume the leaves. He blows it out and instantly, it fills the room with the heavy aroma of sage, lavender, and sweetgrass. "It's begun. Okay, you take the smudge and I'll take the salt. We need to smudge every room in this place, so this could take a while."

I pick up the conch shell and a large feather, guiding the smoke to the four corners of the room. "By the four elements, I banish any unwelcome spirits or energies from this space." I walk the room counter-clockwise, the motion of banishment, to help dislodge the unwelcome energies and spirits.

Wade walks behind me, dipping his fingertips in the

water and spritzing it into the four corners. As we finish this one space, the room feels lighter—brighter, even.

We continue from my bedroom to the resurrection chamber, then throughout the rest of the house. One by one, we banish any unwanted energies from the house. The whole process takes nearly an hour to complete, but by the time we make it back to where we started—my bedroom—the house feels like a heavy burden has been lifted. Even some of the workers seem to have noticed, because two of them even said hello and smiled. But throughout the experience, we didn't have a single sighting of my dad.

The embers of the smudging contents are nearly completely burnt out as I place the shell on my desk.

Wade holds the water bowl close and nods to the candle. "Now, it's time to release any of the energies it trapped. Then we can set up the wards."

I exhale slowly, staring at the candle. Its flame flickers back and forth, dancing as if it's any other ordinary flame. Bending in, I blow out the candle.

A shockwave of energy escapes with it as whatever unwelcome energies are cast out of the house and beyond its border.

"Okay, now we're on the clock. We've got an hour to reset the wards," I mutter, gathering four stones from the bed and heading for the doorway.

"And if we miss it, we get to wait a whole month until the next full moon," Wade says, shifting his eyebrows up. He keeps hold of the saltwater and follows me.

I continue down the hallway to the doorway we used last winter when his grandpa had become a revenant. It's the last time I used it, and instantly I'm reminded of the terrifying moments of that day.

When we walk outside, we're greeted by the sweet smell of rain filtering through dying leaves. Drizzle lingers in the air, blanketing us as soon as we walk beyond the shielding of the house.

Glancing down, Wade takes the compass out from his pocket. "Okay, we'll want to start in the north and work clockwise from there." He finds north and starts walking. "I don't suppose you have any idea where the boundary of the property is?"

I shake my head. "Not even the remotest. We'll just need to wing it and do our best." Unfortunately, our property is vast, so finding the four corners to place the stones could prove difficult. Especially if we only have an hour to do it in.

Finding north takes a little bit of time, but we finally walk as far out into the woods as I dare.

"Let's place the ward here. We still have the other three to maintain," I say, dropping to my knees and inscribing the first stone with the Nordic runes for protection and calling upon the element of earth.

As I place the stone on the ground, Wade sprinkles the saltwater across it.

"By the element of earth, I ward thee. Guard this space from all ill will and any unwelcome energies that may wish to bring us harm," I say, still touching the stone. When the words are done, the runes light up, glowing like hot embers.

Pleased by the result, I stand up and brush off my knees.

I shoot a sideways smile to Wade, who returns the

sentiment. "On to east," he says, sweeping his hand out in front of him.

Nodding, I walk in the direction he pointed. We walk in silence, keeping the manor in eyeshot as best we can while we find our next corner. The rainy weather seeps into my clothing, making me shiver in the chill of the fall air. It certainly helps with urging us along to finish this quickly, so we can get back inside.

Finding the east and south corners takes longer than I anticipated, mostly because I wanted to get us as wide a circumference around the manor as possible. By the time we're on the last corner, Wade and I are practically running through the trees to get to the western corner to seal the circle.

"We've got about ten minutes to drop the last stone or we'll have to wait until the next full moon," Wade says, picking up speed.

"Ugh," I groan, rushing forward to keep up. My feet slosh inside my Nikes and I'm already daydreaming about a nice, hot bath.

A sudden flash of movement in the underbrush to my left catches my eye. At first, it looks animalistic, like perhaps a bear making its way through the dense trees. That alone is enough to pull me up short. But the more I focus on it, the more human it becomes. It stands upright on two legs, then turns to face me as if it senses my presence.

"Wade, stop. Don't move," I say, crouching down and freezing.

Wade rushes back, dropping down beside me. "What is it?" he says, his eyes wide as he looks over my shoulder. "What do you see?"

"There's someone out there," I say, standing to a low crouch and weaving my way in and out of trees.

"Autumn, the wards—" Wade says, rushing after me. "This is not the time. It might be out on that side of the circle for a reason."

I look down as Wade tugs on my sleeve, trying to get me to stop. Blinking back my surprise, I shake my head. "Of course, you're right. Let's finish this."

Looking back over my shoulder, the dark figure is gone, anyway.

Strengthening my resolve, I turn back around to hunt for the western corner. However, I find myself stumbling backward as the dark figure comes barreling toward us at an unnatural speed. Its features are half human, half something else. And one-hundred percent pissed off.

Its voice is a strange disturbance in the air, like it speaks across different dimensions, each one slightly out of sync. "GET OUT!" it wails.

CHAPTER 15
AGAINST THE CLOCK

I land hard on my backside and the final stone for the ward tumbles from my hand. Somehow, Wade holds his ground, managing to stay on his feet as the creature looms directly in front of us.

A disturbingly oppressive energy commands the space, pulling away any sense of peace and tranquility held in my body. Instead, it feels as though dread is the fuel that feeds it, making it stronger. Or perhaps, it's all it knows. Regardless, it crushes down on me, making it incredibly difficult to breathe.

Wade rushes to my side, bending down and reaching for the stone. When he has it, he extends his arm and holds out a hand for me to grab onto.

"Come on, Autumn, we need to finish this," he commands with a strange level of authority and calmness I can't even muster.

How is he not scared out of his mind?

I take his hand, pulling myself up, but I can't remove my gaze from the creature's grotesque features. Its skin is a flakey, opaque gray, and its eyes are bottomless black pools, lacking any sense of empathy. My legs tremble and it takes an enormous amount of effort just to stay upright. The creature's fury slams against me, as it circles the two of us, not even touching the ground.

"She thinks she can defy it. Thinks she can escape fate. The *audacity*," it spits in the same strange, distorted way.

"What is it? What can you see?" Wade asks as I press myself against him, following the movements of the creature as it continues around us.

Understanding sweeps through me. *He can't see it.*

"It's a..." My voice quivers and I can't seem to get my brain to form words. And even if I could, I have no words to describe what it is. I've never seen anything like it before.

"Get out," the creature repeats, continuing its circumference around us.

The hairs all over my body stand on end as absolute terror takes hold of me. What will it do to us? Can it hurt us? I freeze, unable to make any movement, even if I wanted to.

"You cannot stop this," it says, lunging forward at me. "It can *never* be stopped. Should have known. Should always have known."

Shaking uncontrollably, I squeak, "What can't be stopped? Wh-why are you doing this?"

As if the simple question itself infuriates it, the creature's fists close and its arms tighten against its body. All around us, tree branches snap from their source and fly through the air as if caught in a tornado's current.

"Cursed. *Damned*...it is her fate," the creature mocks. "It has *always* been her fate. She cannot escape it."

The ground beneath our feet rumbles and small shrub-bery, trees, rocks, and dirt dislodge themselves. They rise into the air, joining the branches already swimming around us in a wide, undulating circle.

Flecks of sand and stone whiz past us, making their way to the cyclone and peppering my face and body. Wade and I each raise an arm, shielding our eyes.

"We need to finish the ward. Whatever the entity is, it has to be cast out fully," Wade says, thrusting the stone into the front pocket of my jeans. "It has to be you, Dru. This is *your* home."

Terrified, I shake my head. The final location is far on the other side of the creature, at the edge of the pond. There's no way I could make it without being attacked or hit by the cyclone of trees. Our time is almost up and I have no way to stop this.

The creature is right. I can't stop this. I'm completely useless.

Reaching around to me, Wade grabs my shoulders and shakes my gaze free from the creature. "Autumn, look. Look at me," he cries out, his silver eyes wide. "You have to run. Get the stone in place and finish the damn ward. It's the only way to expel it. We won't be safe otherwise."

"I can't," I whimper, shaking my head. The level of repugnance coming from the creature is some next-level shit. I'd rather stay right where I am than risk increasing the vehemence of its anger. There's no telling what it will do to us.

"You have to. We only have minutes left. Run, *run*," he says, trying to urge me forward.

My feet, on the other hand, feel like lead weights have

replaced them. I barely move a muscle and Wade lets out an exasperated gasp.

"Dammit," he curses. His hands fly to his hair as he spins in the spot, watching the cyclone of greenery building in intensity.

"She cannot stop what's coming. No one can," the creature's warped speech rings out.

The items caught up in the orchestration of the creature begin to crisscross in front of us, getting closer and closer. Despite the intensity of the vortex, the creature flits in and out of materialization, showing up in one place, then a moment later, in a slightly different location. It's almost as if it can't quite maintain its grip on reality.

"She must know, she must *understand*," it repeats, as if talking to itself rather than to anyone in particular. "She must learn she is not in control. Never in control."

The level of anger in the creature's energy rises another notch and the branches and shrubbery are no longer held back in a cyclone. Instead, they hurl themselves in our direction and new additions are wrenched from the trees to join in.

The smaller trees and brambles reach us first, clashing against my skin, cutting open my sleeve and jeans, and assailing my face. I cry out, groping at my arms as one of the enormous tree branches is heaved directly at us.

Wade ducks, groping for my hand to move with him, but my reaction speed is still too slow. I'm struck across the shoulder and face by one of the massive branches. The force of it knocks me backward and the landing claims all the air in my lungs. My vision blurs and bright white and blue stars explode behind my eyelids as I sputter to take in oxygen.

"Autumn, oh my god, Autumn, are you okay?" Wade cries out somewhere to my right. His words seem so far away, but I swear I feel his hand on my face. "Autumn, please, please, be okay."

My eyes flutter open and blinding pain erupts from the right side of my body and face. Warm, sticky liquid pools in my eye, and I wipe at it, trying to see. When I pull my hand back, it's covered in crimson.

"Dammit, I'm so sorry, Dru. I should have..." Wade's voice trails off as the color drains from his face. His face is a smattering of cuts and blood. He ducks another round of branches, dropping his head to my chest.

Momentarily, relief floods through me, and I let my eyes rest.

Yes, this is comfortable. I could stay like this...

Unfortunately, the longer my eyes stay closed, it creates a dizzying effect, as the world is spinning and swirling beneath me. When I open my eyes again, I'm no longer on the ground. Instead, I'm in Wade's arms, my body draped and dangling from his outstretched grip.

His eyes are locked on the water beyond the creature. I can vaguely remember something significant about it, but I'm not certain what. Oddly enough, behind him, the vortex of tree limbs and shrubbery abruptly stop. Everything drops to the ground, as if simply let go.

"She hurts. She can't escape it. She bleeds the thread," the creature screams, its voice echoing across multiple layers of time and space. "The thread leaks from her veins. It is nearly unraveled."

The creature's words don't sound gleeful; instead, they sound just as terrifying as the energy it exudes.

"Time is running out. Time is running out," it says,

flashing in and out of being. "She must understand. But *he* must get out."

Suddenly, Wade gurgles, and stumbles on the ground. As he drops to his knees, I tumble to the ground, rolling across the debris and uprooted grass. He gropes for his throat, just as he had inside the house, as the creature flickers into existence before us, one arm outstretched and fist closed.

"He must go. He must get out. He draws attention," the creature says, its black eyes and ashen face locked on Wade with an expression of pure loathing.

"Let him go," I scream, abruptly coming to my senses. As if this one act was the button that releases my fear, I rise to my feet and rush at it with my arms outstretched.

It will *not* hurt him. I won't let this happen again.

I don't know what I was expecting would happen, but as I go to tackle it, my body falls straight through it and I land hard on all fours on the other side. Bending over, I heave, unable to shake the way its energy was a potent mixture of terror, fury...*and desperation*.

It wants something so desperately, and it's willing to do anything and everything to make it happen. In that instant, I almost feel sorry for it. *Almost*.

The creature screams, clutching at its chest. It drops Wade and flickers momentarily out of existence. A second later, he's a yard or so away.

On the other side of the creature, the vortex of pain and terror lift from my being like a blanket being ripped away. Instantly, my head clears and I remember why I'm here. I remember what it was we were trying to do. The stone in my pocket practically burns against my hip and I shake any last sense of dread.

Almost afraid to look back at Wade, I scramble from my hands and knees and climb to my feet. The tendrils of the creature's energy reach out behind me, trying to pull me back into its cage, but its strength has been diminished in all of the force it's already expelled.

I ignore it, locking my eyes on the water's edge.

I can make it.

Rushing forward, I run as fast as I can to the pond. My lungs feel like they're about to explode, but when I get there, an intense desire to ensure the ward extends as far as it can succumbs me. I race out further, running onto the dock. I come to a halt on the last plank, and pull the smooth stone from my jeans.

For the briefest of moments, I stare at the stone in the palm of my hand, praying Wade's right. That this is the one thing we need to expel the creature.

"By the element of water, I ward thee. Guard this space from all ill will and any unwelcome energies that may wish to bring us harm," I cry out as loudly as I can muster.

Without any further hesitation, I skip the stone out across the pond as far as I can. It glows brightly as it skips along the surface of the water and quietly slips into its depths.

As it submerges, I hold my breath, waiting for something—*anything*—to happen.

At first, all is quiet. Even the creature behind me seems mesmerized, wondering what will happen next. Just when I think I'm royally screwed, or that we've gone past our time, a shockwave of energy bursts from the center of the house outward. It practically knocks me off my feet and into the pond, but I manage to stay upright by sheer will. All around us, a crystalline dome arcs overhead, beginning along the lines connecting each of the four stones. As quickly as it arose, the imagery of it begins to fade, even though the ward is beginning to take hold.

Twisting around, the malevolent creature rushes at me, but its energy dissipates like a balloon being deflated.

"*The Inflexible One* will not be held at bay," it screeches, its voice magnified and distorted. "They're coming for you. They're *all* coming for you."

Then, as if the creature's energy gives up completely, it explodes in a plume of vapor, dissolving before my eyes.

CHAPTER 16

HIS TIME HAS COME

I barely remember Wade's arrival on the dock, or how we somehow managed to find our way back inside the manor. Everything is a blur of colors, movements, and sound.

All I can focus on now is that Wade has run me a tepid bath and has demanded I get in. His hands run across my hair as he slowly pours the water over it. As he does, the cool liquid slowly turns rust-colored, tainted by the blood from my scalp.

"That branch really did a number on your head," Wade whispers, worry bleeding into his tone. "I'm so sorry, Autumn. I should have protected you. I should have done more..."

I flit my gaze from the plume of red spreading in the water to his torn expression. Small cuts criss-cross his face, but they're all superficial. Still, they tarnish his beautiful face.

I raise my hand, tracing one of the cuts on his chin. "It wasn't your fault," I say, trying not to let the dizziness spiraling in my brain pull me under. "That...creature was..." I close my eyes, pinching the bridge of my nose in the hopes it will help me stay focused.

"I know," he says, taking my hand in his and kissing my knuckles. "That was intense. What matters is you were able to cast it out." He lets my hands drop back into the water as he continues the soothing motion of rinsing out my hair.

I close my eyes, focusing on the way the water trickles through my hair, making my scalp tingle with coolness.

"You're lucky, though. It doesn't look like you'll need stitches. But we'll need to keep an eye on you to make sure you don't have a concussion," he murmurs in my ear.

"Mmmm," I nod, unable to form any more words.

"I'm nearly done here and we can get you in bed to rest. The first twenty-four hours are pretty critical after a head injury," he says, going into medic-mode.

"Yes, Doctor Hoffman," I say, grinning up at him sleepily.

He chuckles, bending in and kissing my temple. "That's the spirit."

After what seems like forever, Wade finishes rinsing the blood from my head and body and helps me to step out of the bath. His hands are sturdy and comforting, and I can see why he makes such a good PCA for the elderly. He'd make a fantastic doctor, too, if he ever wanted to pretend he was human.

Once I dry off and get dressed in my pajamas, he helps me climb in bed. My body's starting to accentuate the pain from all of the bumps and bruises, and it's pretty clear I'm going to be in a world of hurt tomorrow.

I pull the blanket up close, tucking it under my chin and laying on my side.

Wade drops down beside me, resting on the top of the covers as he faces my direction. His discerning silver eyes sweep my face as he traces the side of my cheek with the side of his index finger.

"You know, it's a good thing you thought to throw the stone into the water. I'd lost our saltwater in all the commotion. That pond must be sacred water," Wade whispers.

My eyebrows tug in. His words only halfway make sense in my brain. "Huh, I hadn't even thought about that. I just followed my instincts."

"Good instincts, if you ask me," he says, grinning. "Are you hungry? Do you need anything?"

I wiggle my head into the pillow. "No, I'm just sleepy."

Wade props himself up on his elbow and kisses my forehead. "Okay, get some rest. We'll stay here tonight, since it looks like the wards worked. But I'm going to hop into the shower super-fast so I can clean myself up. I'll only be a few minutes."

"Okay," I whisper, closing my eyes.

He kisses me on my forehead, his breath warm against my skin. The bed groans as he exits it, but he runs his warm hand down the side of my arm before he leaves the room. I sigh into the motion and drift into the darkness beyond.

The inflexible one?

The words permeate the recesses of my mind and for some reason, I can't quite shake them away.

Who said them? What do they mean?

Suddenly, the cylindrical room in the center of the catacombs comes into view, as if it's the center stage of a play and the curtain was just pulled back. I squint into the darkness, trying to make something else—*anything*—out.

Just when I think I'm all alone, Abigail emerges from one of the tunnels. Her dress sways heavily against the dirt floor, drawing my eyes with the trails it leaves behind.

"I apologize for my absence. My energy has been very much afflicted by the presence lingering in the manor. I had hoped to bind him long enough to relay my concerns to you. Alas, it was I who was bound in his stead. Please forgive me," she says, her Colonial accent tinging her words as she walks up beside me.

I look at her, confused. Her words tumble at me like a dust devil, spiraling around, but never quite gaining enough impact to be effective.

"I'm not sure I—" I begin.

"There is much we need to discuss, and in great haste. You see, I have been grievously distressed. I am afraid my words have fallen upon deaf ears and there is much I need to relay. Your body is in need of repairs, allowing your mind to slip beyond the veil. I am hopeful this will be the most effective means to communicate at present. My wish is that our communication will linger after you awaken," she says, her expression sorrowful.

Apprehension spreads through my solar plexus and I hold my breath, waiting for what might come from her lips next.

"I had yearned for a better way to express this most dreadful news," she says, wringing her hands and taking a few steps from me. "Yet, I find myself without the means to do so. I must press upon you the difficult decision you will soon be presented. It will not be a task undertaken lightly, but it is most important it be dealt with without delay."

My shoulders tighten and I'm certain I don't want to know what's on the other side of this comment. But I know it's coming whether I like it or not.

"*His time has come*, and we need you to be strong. Stronger than ever you could imagine. This will not rest until he's safe inside these walls," she says, holding her arms wide. Abigail's voice drifts off, floating through the ether as she slips from my dream and into the darkness of the catacombs.

I wake up with a start.

Moonlight floods in through my bedroom window. I stare at it, trying to understand why the shape of the window is somehow different than I remember. Slowly, the memory of all the destruction filters into my mind. My bedroom had been decimated by the malevolent spirit and like someone snapped their fingers, it's been repaired.

Are there magical construction workers?

The thought creeps into my mind, and after everything that happened here less than forty-eight hours ago, I'm certain there has to be. How else can you explain such a turnaround?

On the other side of the moonlight, something moves in the darkness. Blood pulses in my ears and I clutch the blanket close, unable to move. My breath drops into shallow gulps of air as I struggle with myself. I should move—I need to *move*. Yet somehow, I'm paralyzed, unable to escape the confines of the bed.

The movement transforms into a shadowy figure and as it comes closer, it takes the shape of a man. My mouth opens to scream, but I snap it shut when I realize I know the man.

"Dad?" I whisper. The confines of fear fall away as if ropes binding me were suddenly cut loose. "What are you doing in here?"

He walks up, one side of his face lit by the moonlight. The other half is shielded in darkness. However, the smile on his face is evident as he looks down upon me.

My eyebrows tug in and I shift in an attempt to sit up. Behind me, Wade groans, and rolls over, wrapping his arm around my shoulder. He tugs me closer to him and I drop back into the bed.

I flitted my gaze back to Dad. His expression has switched from contentment to agitation as he stares at the place where Wade's arm rests. As if fighting with himself, his head flicks back and forth quickly, switching between happiness and irritation. Without warning, he stops, facing the doorway to the resurrection chamber.

I bolt upright in bed, following his gaze. In the shadows beyond the foot of my bed, Abigail is hunched over, her hair partly obscuring her face. Her lips move quickly, as if muttering something just out of earshot.

"What's going on?" I say in a frantic whisper, trying to remain calm as my body begins to tremble. "Why are you both in here?"

Wade shifts slightly, running his hand along my arm. "Lay back down, Autumn. You need your rest," he says, sleepily.

I clutch his hand, leaning on him for emotional support. I don't dare move a muscle, and I'm unable to take my eyes off of the way Abigail's hunched form looks like it could attack us at any time.

"Dad, Abigail is—" the words catch in my throat as I turn back to him. No longer fighting with himself, the side of his face once highlighted by the moonlight looks as though the skin is rotting off. His eye is missing and a wide-open socket stares back at me.

The room fills with a high-pitched scream as I scramble backward. My back slams against the headboard and the movement pushes Wade clear to the other side of the bed. Within a fraction of a second, he's out of the bed, searching for the lamp.

"Autumn, what is it? Why are you screaming?" He says, reaching for the chain on the lamp, but it refuses to turn on.

I shake my head, my wide eyes unable to divert from the horrors of my father's face.

"This has to be a dream. I'm still dreaming... I have to be dreaming..." I swallow hard, fighting back tears, and squeak, "*Please be a dream.*"

"Autumn, what is it? Talk to me," Wade says, jumping back on the bed, and kneeling right beside me. He pulls my face from my dad, forcing me to look at him.

"I...I..." I stutter, unable to form words.

My chin quivers, and I tear my gaze from Wade. Suddenly, my dad is inches from my face. A wave of intense cold seeps from his being as his breath hits my skin, making me shiver in terror.

As if no longer able to restrain himself, he gropes for my arms, tugging me in close. His frigid touch is worse than his breath. It seeps into me at soul level, making my body freeze and my heart ache.

"You must denounce it. You must denounce it all," he says, his words coming out in slow, deliberate sentences.

I shake my head, afraid to move much else. "What are you talking about?"

"Promise me," he yells, gripping me tighter. His frozen fingertips bite my skin and I cry out in pain.

"I promise. I promise," I say, unsure what it is I'm even agreeing to.

"I was wrong. So, so wrong. You must denounce our legacy and leave this place. Leave Blackwood Manor and forget about all of this. You need to go now—" he says, his desperate words vibrating in the air as they begin to distort, echoing after each other.

My eyes widen and my fingertips fly to my mouth as a horrific knowing emerges. "No, no, no..." I say, shaking my head, unable to stop the tears from forming. "No..."

"They're coming for you. They're *all* coming for you..." he says, repeating the words from outside. The words from a vengeful creature hell-bent on hurting me. Or so I thought.

"We need to get out of here..." Wade says, gathering our clothing into his arms beside me. "Autumn, we need to go."

"Yes, *go*—" Dad practically screams in my face. "Before fate forces you to join me in death."

CHAPTER 17
TO WHOM THIS HOUSE BELONGS

No matter what I do, I can't stop my screams from coming. It's like they're a part of the home's essence now. They won't go away. Not now—not ever. They'll bleed into its very existence, haunting anyone who dares to become a part of the Blackwood legacy.

Hot tears stream down my face and I blink them back, refusing to let them cloud my vision. I can't look away. As much as I want to, I can't pry my eyes from my dad's decomposing specter.

Wade pulls me into his arms, trying his best to calm me down. He rocks the two of us back and forth gently on the bed. But I can't calm down. Nothing will ever feel calm again. My world has just been tipped on its head.

The room suddenly tilts and I bend over, lurching bile and water all over the floor.

This can't be happening...

"It's okay, Autumn," Wade coos in my ear, stroking my hair, oblivious to the horrors staring back at us. If he knew, he wouldn't be saying that. If he knew, he'd be running in the opposite direction.

I shake my head, unable to put words to any of it. My brain is a blur of colors, emotions, and sounds. That's it.

"I tried to keep you safe. I tried to protect you," my dad says. I've almost gotten used to the way his words sound more like an anomaly than anything else. "You have to trust me. I did this all for you. Repent. Repent everything, or they'll take you, too..." he pleads frantically.

"No, no, no," I repeat, shaking my head as Wade and I rock back and forth. "Can't be true. This can't be..."

Nothing about this makes sense.

I close my eyes, no longer able to take in the horrible way my father's face looks like it's melting against the bone.

Plummeting into the surreality, my mind whirls through all of the recent interactions with him, trying to make sense out of this.

I have to be dreaming. Please, tell me I'm still dreaming. He can't be dead. He *can't be*. He was just here. They said he was okay. He told them to start work on the house. That's what James said...

"Autumn, it's okay. It's okay," Wade repeats, rocking me and stroking the back of my head.

"No, no, it's not," I sputter, unable to keep my body from trembling. I glance at Wade, and once again, tears blur my vision, making it impossible to see his features clearly. "Not okay. Nothing's okay."

His eyes look so sympathetic, but he doesn't understand. How can he? I don't understand.

"Talk to me. What's happening? What do you see?" he

asks, never stopping our continual rocking. "I can't help you if you don't talk to me."

I chance another glance at dad. The rotting face of my father leans forward, its gaping eye sockets staring into my soul.

"He reeks," Dad snarls. "In league with them. They're all in league." The intensity of his anger make me sick to my stomach.

I bend forward, heaving again, but nothing comes up.

"He draws attention," Dad continues, raising a skeletal finger at Wade. "He's a beacon for them. Your time will be cut short. Shorter, even. He must *go*—"

"What are you talking about? *Who* them?" I squeal, trying to force his words into something that makes sense. "This isn't Wade's fault."

"My fault?" Wade says, shock in his tone. For a moment, he stops trying to console me and sweeps his gaze around the room. "What is?"

"He's a beacon," Dad says, ignoring me. "Don't you understand, Autumn? No good..."

He lunges his ghostly body at us, arms wide and gnarly fingers ready to attack. I squelch another scream, flinching and covering my face with my arms, anticipating his blow.

However, nothing makes impact. After a few seconds, I pull my arms back and look up. As if an invisible wall somehow separates us, Dad slams against the air inches from my face, unable to connect beyond it. His face flits through confusion, anger, and frustration as he pounds against it.

"What is this?" He twists around, searching for the source of whatever magic has blocked him from us. "No, it can't be," he fires into the room. "You were locked away. You were under control."

I follow his horrified gaze to Abigail, who is still standing in the shadows, muttering quietly. Her head remains bent, but as he curses at her, she slowly raises her gaze. Power emanates from her, lighting the edges of her being, and it even makes me stop in my tracks. I've never seen anything quite like it. For the first time since I knew I could see her, she actually looks like a ghost.

"You knew this could not go on forever. Your time has come to an end, Lyle," Abigail says, stepping from the shadows and into the moonlight. As if the moon itself lends her power, the edges of her dress, arms, and even her hair glows brighter. "The treachery you bring upon this house cannot endure when it is cast into the light. Autumn has seen you for what you really are. You will harm them no longer. I will not allow it."

"How *dare* you? This is *my* house. You can't do this to me," the remains of my father fire back. What little skin clinging to his skull scrunches and peels back in odd ways as he laments her. It makes my skin crawl and my heart feel completely hollowed out.

Abigail's voice booms out, an unearthly sound that shakes the windows on their frames and the decorations of the room. It echoes straight through me, right down to my bones. "Do not speak of *'to whom this house belongs.'* Child, you are but a speck in the existence of time, as we all are. Yet, even in such deliverance, this home was mine long before you were a fleeting thought upon your parents' minds." She takes another deliberate step forward, her eyes blazing and jaw set.

"What's happened to you?" I say, my words barely a whisper, as I watch my father snarl in anger.

He turns to me, his face contorting between anger and concern—as if he's somehow fighting with himself.

"Do not trouble yourself searching for validation. Your father is too far gone," Abigail says, turning to me. Her face is full concern, but the light surrounding her illuminates her hair, making it look as though she's underwater with the way her hair flies around her.

"I don't understand—" I begin.

Abigail raises a hand to me. "There will be a time to explain all. Now is not this time."

She no sooner says the words before my dad flies at her. However, whatever binding she put him under holds, enclosing him in a cylindrical space and preventing him from getting to her. Abigail doesn't even blink, she stands her ground, tipping her chin in defiance of him.

"This cage won't hold me. I've grown powerful. Far more powerful than even you," he says, writhing against the invisible wall. His fists pound the edges, rippling the air the way as stone ripples the water.

The room quakes, rattling the new window and dropping a picture frame from the wall. It crashes to the floor, shattering the glass in tiny shards across the carpet. A fleeting moment of concern flashes through Abigail's face.

"Autumn, we should leave. Get somewhere safe," Wade mutters, trying to pull me from the bed.

I shake my head, fighting off his groping hands. "No, I can't. I need to—"

Abigail throws her shoulders back, widening her stance. Then, she raises her right arm out in front of her body. "I think you shall find this to be a fallacy you cling to." She turns her gaze to me momentarily. When we lock eyes, she frowns apologetically.

Then, in a swift movement, she turns back to my father and closes her fist.

Dad's arms tighten in on himself, as if bound by some sort of invisible rope. He writhes against the energy, fighting for all he's worth. "Impossible," he spits. "What are you doing to me?"

"Something I should have done long ago," she says, cutting him off. Her arm remains out in front of her, and she turns back to me. "This is not how you should have learned of the truth. I am grievously sorry, Autumn. Truly, I am. His spirit must be contained, and then I will be back. There is much to discuss so he can be laid to rest."

"No—" Dad screeches, flailing against his invisible restraints. However, he's no match for whatever Abigail has done to him.

I cover my mouth, holding back another scream at his tormented cries.

Then, with a final glance, my direction and true sorrow hidden in the depths of her features, Abigail inhales a deep breath and closes her eyes. Before I can even blink, they both vanish, leaving a gaping wound in the center of my heart and soul.

CHAPTER 18
STAGES OF GRIEF

I crumble into a ball on the bed, unable to stay upright anymore. Pulling my pillow in close, I bury my face into its soft fabric. The subtle scent of fabric softener lingers from the last time James must have washed the bedding. I focus on it, rather than anything I've witnessed in the past twenty-four hours. I can't. *I won't.*

None of it can be real. Because if it is...

Wade positions himself right beside me and drapes a strong arm over my shoulder. He doesn't try to console me with words anymore. Instead, he just stays next to me, smoothing out my hair and kissing the top of my shoulder.

Every part of me is numb—even the places Wade tries to revive with his kisses.

For a while, my mind goes completely blank, devoid of any and all thoughts, as I stare out into the darkness of the bedroom. Not even the moon dares enter the space anymore. It's moved on through the night sky, illuminating the courtyard instead. I stare at the edges of the trees and the way the moonlight makes them look like they're glowing.

As soon as the thought of her name appears in my mind, it opens the floodgates waiting to release their deluge. Where is Abigail now? Shouldn't she have come back? Explained herself to me? She promised me more answers.

Fear grips me in the middle of my stomach and I'm suddenly not so sure I want her to come back. If she does, it means...

My dad's dead.

The thought doesn't make sense, no matter how many times it pops into my mind.

How can he be dead? What happened? *When* did it happen?

Abigail told him she was doing something she should have done long ago...

My eyes widen as a new terrifying thought emerges.

If he's...*dead*...how long has it been?

Dad's mysterious "trips" and time away from the manor start to make more sense when put in this new light. All of his interactions have been to me directly or through messages. Until tonight, he was never in the same room with Wade. I never even got to introduce the two of them.

I swallow hard, unable to shake this horrible ring of truth.

Oh my god, if my dad's dead...if he's *been* dead—how did I not know?

You're a postmortem medium, Autumn. You see dead people.

My heart constricts and my face crumples.

Stupid voice inside my head. What does she know?

But it's true. Ghosts look as real to me as any other person. Who knows just how many ghosts I've seen and interacted with, thinking they were alive. It's no wonder I didn't believe in them. Hell, until Abigail walked through my dad's bedroom door, I didn't even truly believe she was one—regardless of her dated clothing and hairstyle.

Wade continues to stroke my hair or my arm, refusing to let sleep consume him. We have that in common. Nighttime slowly changes into the inklings of morning as we both lie there, staring out the window. My mind, as much as I try to ignore it, continues to spiral into dissent as it does its own thing—trying to fathom how any of this could be happening.

The memory of following Abigail into Dad's bedroom sweeps past the screen of my mind and again, I stop to consider. Any time I have been in his room, it's never looked slept in—or *lived* in. Not really. Thick dust blanketed the flat surfaces and the room felt almost shuttered in.

Why?

Surely James would have noticed as well? I mean, he even washes *my* sheets, for crying out loud.

Suddenly, I sit up in bed, making Wade jump in surprise.

"What is it? What's wrong?" he says, instantly alarmed. His eyes scan the room quickly, as if he'll somehow be able to see anything.

"Why would James lie to me?" I say, unable to hide my irritation.

Anger swirls into clarity and I hold onto it, letting it burn brighter. It sears away some of the emotions I don't want to deal with, helping me to think more clearly.

I seethe with a deep loathing for a man who's done his best to seem kind and understanding. But it's all been a lie. He's been keeping things from me—from everyone. The only question is...*why?*

"How dare he?" I say through gritted teeth.

Wade lifts an eyebrow, gazing at me inquisitively. "Autumn, talk to me. What are you talking about?"

My face tightens and flushes with agitation. "James—this is all his fault."

"Hold up, what's his fault?" Wade says, his silver irises flashing in the dawn's rising light. "You haven't explained what the hell is going on. Did you have a bad dream? Or—?"

I turn to him, his face full of confusion and concern. I open my mouth to say the words, but I can't seem to spit them out.

Shaking my head, I say, "I don't know what the hell happened. I just know I need to talk to James. He has to be in on this."

Wade sighs, running a hand across his face. "Autumn, you're not making any damn sense. Maybe we should bring you into the hospital. I'm concerned about your head injury." He raises a hand, reaching out to touch the spot where the tree branch hit, but I swipe his hand away.

"I'm not crazy," I say, indignantly.

"That's not what I—"

I throw back the blankets of the bed and stand up. "My dad's dead and it's all James' fault. He—"

Wade jumps out of bed after me. "Whoa, whoa, whoa. Hold up there. What did you just say?"

"You heard me," I spit back.

His eyes survey me carefully, and he takes a tentative step forward. "How do you know your dad is dead?"

"Because..." I swallow hard, unable to believe I'm saying any of this out loud, "he's the one who's been haunting the manor."

"He—wait. *What?*" Wade says, pulling up short and shaking his head as if it will dislodge something that makes sense. He stares at me with the most confused expression I've ever seen on his face. I definitely know the feeling.

My gaze falls to the space between us and I let out a sigh. "He...came to me last night. I don't know why, but he was watching us sleep. When I saw him, he started spouting off things," I say, running my hands through my hair and taking a step back. Pacing back and forth, I try to push back the memories, but they're embedded in my mind now. "The more I think about it, the more I think he's been gone a while. Maybe this whole time."

"Holy shit." Wade steps forward, reaching out for my arm. "That's intense. What did he say, Dru?"

I look up, fighting back the tears that are threatening to emerge. "He said I need to leave the manor. That he's been trying to protect me, but *they* will find me... and..." I cut off, fighting back the sob caught in my throat, "and you're like a beacon. Whatever the hell that means."

Wade's face crumples. "What in the hell do I have to do with this?"

I shake my head, crying out, "*I don't know.* I don't understand any of this. It's all completely fucked and I'm just—"

"Okay, okay..." Wade interjects, reaching out and pulling me into his arms. "We'll figure this out together.

There has to be an explanation for all of this. Maybe you were just dreaming?"

I shake my head, fighting the tears blurring my vision. "I keep trying to convince myself of that."

His scrutiny is intense, and he finally whispers, "But it wasn't, was it?"

There's no way I can bring myself to say it out loud, so I simply shake my head.

"Dammit, Dru. I'm so sorry," he says, pulling me to him.

I lean my head against his chest, wishing I could take back the past twenty-four hours. Erase it all, like it never existed.

"I just can't believe James would lie to me about all of this. The next time I see him..."

Wade pulls us apart. His eyes shine with a new level of empathy, but skepticism filters into their edges. "Autumn, you have to realize none of this is James' fault. Whatever this is, it's something much bigger than him. Unless, of course, he was involved, but I somehow doubt that."

"But he had to have known. How could he not? He's been lying to me—" I say, still trying to hold onto the anger. It's the only thing right now that feels real.

"How did *you* not know?" Wade asks, cutting me off. "You're the postmortem medium, after all. And if he's been gone a while..."

I bite back my initial response.

He's right. And it's not like I hadn't thought the same thing earlier.

"It doesn't matter. I need to know how much James knows. I need to know how my dad's been communicating with him," I say, clenching my teeth.

"Fair enough," Wade nods. "And I'll be right beside you when you question him. But, you gotta keep in mind, there is some next-level crazy shit happening in this house. I mean, even crazy for us. You know? If your dad is dead, then it means something is *seriously* wrong. We need to find out what it is and how to fix it."

"What do you mean?" I say, gawking at him.

"Well, I'm no expert, not yet—but this isn't a typical haunting. How long have you been interacting with him? A year? More?"

I nod. "I guess. So what?"

"The dead typically go two ways—they get reaped, or they stick around. If they stick around, they're usually echoes of the person they were. Like Abigail—she's been here for centuries and still has some semblance of herself."

"Yeah, but we thought she was the one who was doing all of this at first, remember? I thought she was angry and was starting to take it out on me for not helping her."

Wade raises his eyebrows. "True. But I have to admit, that didn't really make a helluva lot of sense to me. Especially after..."

I glance up at his narrow eyes. "After what?"

"That day in the study. Whatever tried to strangle me —it felt masculine. But it didn't make sense at all. I guess it makes more sense now," he says, frowning.

"Why didn't you tell me?" I say, covering my mouth.

Wade shrugs. "I didn't think it made sense. Besides, it's not like I could see who or what was doing it."

Agony courses through me and hot tears slip from my eyelids. "I couldn't even see him. It's like—" I pause, thinking back. "—It's like he didn't want me to know."

"Or maybe there's a different answer," Wade says,

reaching out for me. He pulls my hands into his. "If it was your dad, maybe it took a lot of energy to manifest so forcefully. I'll bet he had to choose. Or maybe there was no choice at all."

"What do you mean? No choice?" I say, swiping at my cheek.

"Maybe he's been running solely on instinct. You said he thinks I'm a beacon, right? He's obviously trying to protect you from something. The question is—what?"

"Do you think it's your dad?" I ask, widening my eyes. "I mean, that he's protecting me from."

Wade shakes his head. "I don't think so. The Angels of Death have strict rules. They don't come for anyone until they've died. Part of the reason we're not supposed to—" He looks down, screwing his face up. "The reason I'm not supposed to be with you has to do with what Angels of Death perceive as a circumventing of Natural Law. At least, as far as I understand it."

My head is swimming with everything I've learned today. Exhaustion threatens to consume me, so I sit down on the edge of the bed, staring blankly out the window.

"Autumn, you look like you could pass out any second. It's been a long night and neither one of us has slept at all. Let me hold you. You need rest so we can face whatever's next," Wade says, sitting down beside me and placing his left hand on my thigh. "It's barely six o'clock. There's not much you can do unless Abigail comes back—or the police station opens up. I mean, if you plan on contacting them. You know?"

I sigh deeply and nod. I don't know what the best move is right now. I just feel so...numb. The anger I felt moments ago has already begun to drain my energy and even if I wanted to stay up, I can feel my edges fraying and sleep beckoning me into its embrace.

"All right. Let's try to sleep a couple of hours. Then we can decide what to do from there," I say, unable to fight off the fatigue any longer.

Wade pulls back the blankets and we curl in together. After a few minutes, the gentle rhythm of Wade's breathing helps me to relax and I submit to the darkness.

Once again, I walk the dark tunnels of the catacombs in anticipation. There's something very important I need to do. Everything is pitch black, but somehow I know my way around and the direction I'm heading, as if a compass has been embedded inside my mind.

Suddenly no longer alone, I can feel Abigail's presence walking beside me. Though the tunnel remains dark, I'm acutely aware of her, as if I can see her in my mind's eye. We walk in silence for a few moments. It's not entirely uncomfortable, but there's an agitated energy lingering in the air between us.

I'm here for a reason.

Abigail takes my hand, pressing her cool, unearthly palm against mine. Suddenly, we're no longer in the catacombs, but somewhere outside.

"There is much I should have been truthful about," Abigail says, her voice soft.

I'm oddly aware of my state—a strange sort of lucid dream. While I'm sure this place exists, I'm also aware it's all happening inside my mind. The only thing I don't know is whether I'm in control, or if Abigail is.

I stare down at the scattered evidence of a circle—one that vaguely tugs at my memories, though I can't place why. It's off in the recesses of the dreamworld and no matter how I try to focus on it, it slips through the cracks of my mind.

While the circle is evident, it has seen the seasons come and go. How many is hard to distinguish. Inside are the remnants of a ritual—salt, water, candles—as well as a tattered red string. It's almost exactly like the ones I've been finding, but this one has been faded in time's weathering gaze.

Abigail stares down at the circle, her eyebrows tugging inward as she frowns at the contents within. Then she turns slightly to the left, her eyes landing on a small pile of leaves and brambles. No words are necessary as I instinctively follow her gaze.

At first, it appears like any other part of the forest. But there, slightly obscured by nature and time itself, are the remains of a human body.

CHAPTER 19
ANSWERS WITHIN

N o matter what I do, I can't stop staring at the tufts of clothing and bone jutting out from under the brambles. As much as I want to deny what I'm seeing, I know this is no ordinary dream.

"The void is far easier to cross in the space between sleep and wakefulness," Abigail says, somehow reading my mind. "I must do what I can to reserve my energy. It isn't easy to contain..." she eyes me with a hint of sympathy. "Your father has grown very strong."

At first, her words fall on a hazy mind. I stare at her, trying to pull them into cohesion. Then, I look from her to the body of bones and decay, and the truth comes rushing up at me.

I stare with wide eyes. "Is this—?" I can't seem to find the strength to finish the question.

"I am so grievously sorry, Autumn. I should have warned you from the moment you arrived. But I was selfish. I could sense upon you the strength you possess and I wanted to encourage its growth," Abigail whispers, her sorrowful eyes falling to the circle. "I had hoped..."

"This whole time? He's been gone this whole time?" I sputter, biting back tears.

Abigail swallows hard and nods. "When it happened, it wasn't evident at first that there was anything amiss. I had no way of knowing how his death came upon him, but when he remained, I had assumed it was a choice he'd made to stay behind. That there was unfinished business he wanted to attend to. When you arrived—that reinforced those assumptions. But when things started to become more...hostile, I began to look for other answers."

"Didn't you ask him what happened?" I say, trying to hold back the agitation building inside me.

"At first, I tried. However, he barely acknowledged my existence. It was as though, even in death, his diluted abilities somehow refused to open up. It happens at times when departed do not wish to believe they have passed and they close off all that would challenge this belief," she says, beginning to walk the circle, counterclockwise.

I follow her, leaving behind the remains of my father. "What happened to him? Was it some sort of ritual gone wrong?" I ask, pointing at the evidence in front of us.

Abigail's eyebrows tug in. "Perhaps? I have tried to piece together what it was he may have been attempting with this ritual, but I am not certain what his intentions were."

"So, why are you showing me this?"

Abigail stops walking and turns to me. Her dress floats across the leaves, scattering them in a colorful array in the movement. I stare at them, mesmerized by it.

"You must find this circle and bring his remains to the catacombs. His unrest and active violence is because he has not had a proper burial. Spirits, no matter how benevolent in life, will deteriorate into a Lemure if they are not properly interred," she says, raising a hand and suggesting the bones beyond.

I shudder. The idea of moving my father's body makes me feel sick.

"What about the authorities? Shouldn't I let the police handle—"

"We have run out of time for that. Had I known his body was not handled, I never..." Her voice trails off. "He must be dealt with as soon as possible. He's far too strong and I fear that if this is not dealt with in haste—"

"You won't be able to keep him under control," I say, nodding to myself.

"Precisely."

"Shit," I mutter, walking away. "I don't even know where this place is. How will I find it?"

When I turn around, Abigail is already beside me. "Within the catacombs, there is a location spell. It is best to utilize the innate talents of others for it, though. Lean on the Gilbert family, they are strong in elemental magick."

I shake my head. "They're not even in town."

"Call upon them to return," she fires back, indignance flashing through her features. "It matters not what they have done in the past. This is of vital importance."

"I—okay. Yeah." I nod, suddenly feeling so foolish.

"There is one final thing to attend to..." Abigail says, walking up to me.

"Great," I mutter. "What is it?"

Abigail's face falters, but she straightens her shoulders. "I feel whatever your father was attending to—it may be tied back to our family. Although he may have been dreadfully wrong in his approach." She eyes his remains.

"What do you mean?"

She inhales softly. "Within the study, there is a journal hidden amongst the many books. Your father would often write in it and before he..." She blinks at me with wide, green eyes. "Before he deteriorated, he had planned on showing it to you. I would often hear him arguing with himself about the matter in his early stages."

"What's in it? What does it say?" I ask, trying to ignore the strange, unsettling feeling suddenly making a home in my midsection.

"Of that, I do not know. But I am certain it held great significance. I am hopeful it may explain his odd behavior before his demise—or perhaps the ritual he had been attempting," she whispers. "Knowing this could help us to understand how he met his untimely death and, more importantly, how we can protect you."

My eyes flicker open and I exhale slowly, staring at the ceiling of my bedroom. The room vibrates with the high energy of midday, and I roll over. I pick up my phone from the nightstand and groan.

12:13 p.m.

Despite obviously having fallen asleep, I don't feel any more rested than I did before. Beside me, Wade continues to breathe in a soft rhythm, clearly getting better sleep than me. I close my eyes, trying to will myself back to sleep, but no matter how long I lay there, I can't seem to find my way back to a restful state.

I slip my legs over the side of the bed, easing myself out as gently as possible. Wade needs his rest as much as I do and if he's actually able to get some sleep, I'll be damned if I'm gonna wake him up.

Besides, I need answers.

I remember every moment of my dream with Abigail as though it happened moments ago. There's no hazy confusion or feeling like I'm grasping onto something that wasn't real. There were very real, very specific directions she laid out.

Lucid dreaming isn't something I've really studied much, but if I had to take a guess on what just happened, I'd wager that's what it was. But if I'm to really know for sure—I need to find that journal Abigail was talking about. If the journal is real, I'm almost a hundred percent sure the rest will be as well.

I walk over to my dresser, opening a drawer as quietly as possible. I reach for a fresh pair of jeans and tug them on. Then I tiptoe out of my bedroom and into the hallway.

My heart is heavy and my head feels as though it's gone through a pressure cooker. Everything is a strange blur of unwanted events—from what happened outside, to the revelation about my dad... As much as I want it all to be a horrible nightmare, I know better.

I walk the long hallway, slowly making my way to the grand staircase. The delicate carpet tickles at my bare feet, and it's the only thing keeping me grounded. I feel like I could float away—detaching entirely from this crazy, mixed-up world. As I approach the staircase, I reach out, floating my fingertips above the railing's intricate wood-working. I stare at it a moment, not quite ready to ascend the stairs and face things.

They certainly don't put the same level of craftsman-ship into things like this anymore. For the briefest of moments, I stand there, half-admiring the newly fixed staircase and half saddened by the lapse of artistry in modern architecture. I don't know why it matters—maybe because it's something my dad loved, and now...

I close my eyes, refusing to give in to the emotions

playing at the edges of my mind. If I do, I'll succumb and I won't be any good to anyone. Taking a deep breath, I hold it in my lungs and exhale slowly.

"Come on, Autumn. It's now or never," I whisper. Opening my eyes, I head up the steps, keeping my eyes locked on the door of the study.

When I make it to the second story landing, I head straight to the study doors and push them open. The room is bright and airy—nowhere near the dark and oppressive space I remember from the last visit to this room. All of the shattered lightbulbs and glass have been cleaned up and the space is utterly pristine.

My gaze flits over the countless bookshelves. There are hundreds—if not thousands of books here.

I walk over to them, running my fingertips along the books' spines as I read their titles aloud. With the sheer number of them here, the last thing I want to do is go through each and every single one of them. But if I can't find what I'm looking for, I may not have a choice.

After I've gone through the entire left-hand side of the room and come up completely empty-handed, I sigh and walk over to the window. From this vantage point, the view of the courtyard and pond is truly unparalleled. Even from the ends of the house, there is so much beauty to behold from the autumn trees and flowers bursting with color.

Halloween is just a couple of weeks away—typically my favorite holiday—and all I can think about is how this day of the dead will never be the same for me.

Turning back around, I stare at the shelves, letting my gaze take it all in.

If I were my dad, writing in an important journal,

where would I have kept it? Stepping forward, I take a seat at his large mahogany desk. There are no books on the desk at all, only a small calendar, clock, and a few pictures —of me and Mom.

I pick up the one of Mom, holding it close.

God, I'll have to tell Mom about all of this... Swallowing hard, I put the picture down and shudder. I'm so not ready for that conversation.

Shifting back in the chair, I pull out the drawers, but each is filled with files of various papers and documents. Nothing that looks like a journal. I tug open the thin drawer in the middle of the desk, just above my legs. Inside, there is an assortment of pens, paper—and a small leather-bound journal.

"So, not with the books, then," I whisper to myself, pulling it out of the drawer.

My pulse thunders in my ears and I can't help but feel that going through this journal would be an invasion of privacy. Especially if this is all just a big mistake. What if my dad isn't—

I can't bring myself to think the final word. Instead, I flip it open to the first page and all of my worries vanish. On the very first page is a dedication.

To my dearest Autumn.
May this guide you to the answers within.

I pull my chair in closer, exhaling slowly. This is it. If the dream with Abigail is true, if it was really a lucid dream, there should be some important details in here. Things that should help me fit the pieces together and hopefully make sense out of all this senselessness.

I turn to the first page, hopeful there will be some enlightenment coming my way. Yet, no matter what lies in these pages, there's just two questions I need answered above all others.

If everything is true, what was my father doing with that ritual in the woods?

And most importantly, *how* did he die?

CHAPTER 20
A CURSED LEGACY

I clutch at the pages of the journal, unable to loosen my grip for fear the book will vanish before my eyes. I hope like hell it will clue me in on what Dad was doing and where I can find his remains. The last thing I want to do is bring Cat and Colton into all of this. Especially if I don't have to.

Taking a deep breath, I read the first few entries. They're all pretty simple and there's nothing of value in terms of information about his whereabouts or plans. But they're still sweet and make my heart hurt. Most of them revolve around wishing me well, missing me and my mom, and hoping one day I will understand why they did what they did. The idea of him sitting down to write these pages brings tears to my eyes, but I know I can't linger on them right now. I need more to go on so I can put him to rest.

Further in, his words begin to tighten, finding a purpose and resonating with me on a deeper level. The hairs on my arms stand on end and I know I'm on the right track.

Autumn,

If you've been reading the pages before now, I'm sure at this point, it's pretty damn clear our family has a messed-up past. We have a lot to be thankful for, but in my opinion, even more to atone for. After your accident, I had hoped to save you from this life. I never knew just how bad it could be until then. Always looking over your shoulder, always wondering when your time would come due. Even without the kind of powers you and other family members possess, I know the day will come when the Inflexible One will require another sacrifice and it will have to come from me. When I'm gone, I worry about what will happen to you. Your memories may or may not come back and I know even if they do, you're still not prepared to take on what lies ahead. The protections we had put in place are only bound to you as long as I'm alive. What happens if they come calling sooner rather than later? Your mother doesn't want to hear it, but I need assurances you'll be protected—be taught to protect yourself when I no longer can. In all honesty, I worry that there's no way around this. Only time will tell. At least I can take solace in the fact that should it happen, you will be called home. Windhaven Academy is prepared to do what it must to teach you and keep you safe. It's the best I can do for now.

Dad

Atone for? Sacrifice?

My eyebrows tug in and my heartbeat thumps loudly in my ears. I clearly skipped ahead a bit too far. Pinching the bridge of my nose, I try to calm my nerves. I need to find information about what Dad was doing. Even in his lucid, human state, he's brought up the Inflexible One. I don't know who this person is, but I'm getting the distinct impression if I don't figure it out, there are far worse things coming for me.

Turning the page, I read the next entry.

Autumn,

I've begun to see the signs again. For the longest time, I had hoped that perhaps the Moirai had forgotten us. Or perhaps they had been sated by our desire to bind your gifts. But today, I found a red thread outside my bedroom door. At first, I didn't think much of it, but it caught my eye. The moment I picked it up, I knew exactly what it was. There was power emanating from it that even I could feel and it was exactly like the ones I'd seen before your accident. I hope you never have to go through this sort of terror, my sweet girl. It's time I put an end to this. The only question is...how?

I promise you, I'll find a way.
Dad

I stare at the entry, my eyes locked on one word. *Moirai.*

Goosebumps flash across my skin and a creepy sense of deja vu envelops me. Wade and I were so close when we did our presentation weeks ago, practically tiptoeing around information tied directly to my own life.

The Moirai are the Three Fates—supernatural sisters who choose a person's lifespan and, more importantly, when and how they die. One sister spins the thread of life, one measures it, and the final sister cuts the thread.

But why would they be after my family?

Shaking my head, I read it again and this time, something different stands out. Suddenly, images of my own findings tumble through my mind. Red threads have been following me since I moved to Windhaven—at grave sites and other locations. I had no idea they were really tied to something more. Something far bigger...

But what?

A terrible feeling twists in the pit of my being. This is what my dad was doing when he died. He was trying to appease the Fates somehow. *And lost.*

Terror washes over me and I drop my gaze to the journal. I can only hope he explains why. I flip to the last entry, searching for anything to help me illuminate the path ahead or give me an idea of the whereabouts his body. The final entry is longer than the rest and I hold my breath, reading his final words.

Autumn,

This could very well be my last entry. If it is, you should know there are certain things in this world that have been stacked against our family for generations. Our family's powers aren't normal. Conventional supernatural wisdom believes necromancy to simply be another ability, like shapeshifting or turning water into wine. Only, far more unique and rare. However, when you look closely at the lineage of necromancers, you will find they are all tied back to a single bloodline. Ours.

In our family grimoire, you will find family history if you ask it to reveal those secrets. The grimoire is more than a simple spellbook; it's also an account of our legacy. But in case you have not discovered it, I will paraphrase here, because you need to know. Necromancy was a gift from the old gods. It was given to our family as a means to resurrect Apollo's son, Asclepius. Before then, the ability didn't exist. Originally, it was meant only for this purpose. It was never meant to continue onward. But once touched by a god, the effects can linger. Through the ages, the gift remained. At first, it was under the strict rule that it only be wielded by our family. So, no one else was allowed to attempt the magick of resurrection—at least, not without great cost —and, of course, it could only be used at the discretion of the Moirai.

Then, more rules were established. We could only perform resurrections when the loss of the soul was sudden and unexpected —and when it would put the balance of things in peril. Then finally, and most importantly, we could never try to circumvent our own deaths.

The Moirai allowed our family to wield this power of life and death, under the pretense that we were to maintain the natural order of things. In essence, we were relegated to keepers of the dead. It became our job to protect the souls of the supernatural, entombing them in the catacombs within our grounds.

For centuries, everything went as planned. All of that changed with our ancestors, Abigail and Warren. Now, we have all been paying the price for their transgressions.

I stop reading, shaken by this revelation. What on earth did Abigail and Warren do?

Irritation rises through me like a pot beginning to boil.

Clearly, she must have known this. Has she been using me all along?

I drop my gaze back to the page.

Abigail was asked to perform a resurrection on a child who was dying of cancer. Rather than refuse the request, because the death was neither sudden nor unexpected, she went ahead and did it anyway. Abigail allowed her personal feelings for the child to cloud her vision, probably because the girl was a close family friend—a Gilbert. I wish I had the gift to speak to Abigail so I could know for sure why she did it.

What I do know is, regardless, the action triggered a series of horrible events that have rocked our family tree ever since. Angered, the Inflexible One, also known as Aisa, cut Abigail's cord in penance for this transgression. She died instantly and fell from the second-floor landing of our home. Accounts in newspapers say that she committed suicide because beside her body, they found tattered red rope. But Warren's personal testimonies on record say she was in mid-sentence with him when she suddenly went blank. Then, before her body even hit the ground, her ghost was beside him.

Distraught and confused, he did the unthinkable. He tried to resurrect her.

He'd seen her perform the ritual enough times and evidently, he thought he could do it. Of course, he ignored all of the rules.

This was ultimately a mistake on two counts. He was not a necromancer, for starters. Secondly, in the attempt, he was breaking one of the sacred rules. He was trying to circumvent her death. A death determined by none other than one of the Fates.

The rest has been etched into family lore. Repeated from generation to generation—so we all know what is coming for us. This is what your mother and I hoped to save you from...

From that point forward, Abigail was cursed—never being allowed the relief of being delivered by the Angel of Death and crossing into the light. A statue was erected in the center of our driveway, hoping to encourage the Angel of Death to return for her. But I believe her presence still haunts this manor. Warren, on the other hand, was destined to deteriorate into madness; living and dying alone, despite having children to care for.

From then on, each generation of Blackwoods must pay a price to the Moirai. A price that is only paid with their life. When there are multiple children in a generation, it could be any one of them. The Moirai don't care—men, women, necromancer, medium, or mundane human... They accept them all. We don't know when it will come. For some, it's middle age. For others, it's in childhood. It's all at the discretion of the Inflexible One. We only know none of our family lives beyond the age of forty-seven.

We also know the time for one of us is coming when red threads appear. The more frayed they are, the more we have to worry. When I saw them during your childhood, I thought the Moirai was coming for me. I never dreamt they would come for you first. Before then, it was unheard of.

I've spent the last decade searching for a way to make amends. To break the family's cursed legacy and appease the Moirai so they will relinquish their vendetta on our family. Finally, after years hunting, I believe I may have found what I've been searching for. There is an obscure ritual from the Temple of Apollo that is supposed to allow me to open a gateway to the Moirai's realm.

I'm going to beg for forgiveness and, if that fails, I have a backup plan. I will offer up my own life then and there, in order to save yours. To save any other descendants from a life of fear.

But if it goes wrong, and it might, it could be up to you to carry the torch and end this curse.

However, let's hope it doesn't come to that.

I love you, Autumn. With all of my heart.

Forever and infinities.

Dad

xxx

. . .

Tears brim in my lids, blurring the words at the end as I try to read them.

So, it's what I thought. He was trying to contact the Fates—and from what I can tell, they killed him for it and left his body to rot in the woods, knowing full well he'd deteriorate into a Lemure without a proper burial.

My anger swells, fueling a hatred for the Fates beyond anything I've ever known. I want to see them suffer—make them hurt as much as I do right now, in this moment.

To top it all off, Dad knew things might go wrong and he was willing to offer himself to save the rest of us.

Slamming the book shut, I fight back the sob clawing its way up my chest.

Abigail and Warren are intertwined in all of this, and have been from the very beginning. If it hadn't been for them, my dad would still be alive. But now, I have to find his body and make sure he's finally laid to rest so he can't do any more damage. And I still have no idea where to look.

Guess I'll be needing some additional help after all.

CHAPTER 21
WHAT KIND OF CHOICES ARE THESE?

I stand up, clutching the journal in my left hand as I walk toward the doorway. As much as I hate to admit it, I need to make a plan for how to find my dad's remains. That means waking up Wade.

Despite the impending vibe of doom, I have to admit there's an odd sense of peace in finding out some of this information. Pieces of this strange puzzle I've been surrounded by are beginning to lock into place. My life and this gift of mine are starting to make more sense. All the little nuances and frayed edges.

Before I can even reach the landing, an envelope drops from the journal and flutters to the floor. I bend down and pick it up, turning it over to have a closer look. It's addressed to my mom and even has a stamp on it. Cramming the journal under my arm, I run my fingertips along the seam. It was never sealed properly, so I flick it open and peer at the contents.

Inside is a folded piece of paper. I pause for a moment, unsure if I should even be looking over a letter that's not meant for me. Somewhere in the back of my mind, the angel on my shoulder reminds me it's supposed to be a felony to open someone else's mail. But the devil on the other side justifies it since it was never officially sealed—or even mailed.

I bite my lip, fighting internally until I pull it out and gently unfold it. The letter is dated August 1 of last year— mere weeks before I got my letter from Windhaven Academy.

My pulse races as I scan the letter meant for my mom.

My Dearest Andrea,

I wish I were writing you with better news. Perhaps I'm wrong, and things will go far better than I anticipate. But I'm not holding my breath.

I know I had promised you I would do whatever I could to keep Autumn safe. Believe me, I intend to do everything in my power to keep that promise. However, you should know, the Moirai have been back, calling for a sacrifice. I don't intend to be caught off guard this time. Especially if they were again to come for Autumn.

I have found a spell that allows me to summon Aisa. It needs to be done on the eve of the full moon and I believe I have found ley lines on the property that will be conducive to the attempt.

At the next full moon, I will cast the spell and beg Aisa to reconsider. If that doesn't work, I will take more drastic measures. I truly hope it doesn't come to that.

However, should things fail, I want you to know that I will not leave Autumn unprotected. I've set a fail-safe, triggering a paid scholarship to the Windhaven Academy. If she gets an acceptance letter, it means the Moirai have taken me. It's not the news we have longed for, but it might be what has been fated from the beginning. (Yes, pun intended. I have to keep my humor about me while I can.)

Andrea, I know we wanted to keep Autumn away from all of this for as long as we could. But it's possible our time is up. If this ends up being the case, she will need to understand her gifts and the legacy we hand over to her. She will need to return to the manor and I hope that you will return with her. This house needs to feel the light and love of both of you. Autumn will also need someone who can help her to understand why we did what we did. Learning how to master her gifts—learning about my family—it's the only way she'll be able to defend herself against the curse.

I hope this works, Sweetheart, I really do. My deepest desire is that the Moirai will hear me and turn a blind eye to Autumn and the Blackwood Family. But if it doesn't, this curse will end with her. One way or another.

I love you always.

Lyle

My fingertips press against my mouth and I swallow hard. Regardless of the distance of time and space, it's clear from this letter that my dad loved me—*and my mother*—very dearly. Even to the very end. He was trying to protect me and he wanted to keep whatever promises he'd made to my mother.

Tears blur the page from my view as I realize this is why Mom has hated the supernatural world. It's meant more than cool parlor tricks. It's buried deep in family curses and a legacy entrenched in death.

My heart breaks for my dad, knowing he lived out his last days alone—without the love and companionship of those he cared most for. And in no small part, he was doing it all for me. To protect me and give me a chance to fight off some curse against the Moirai.

And at what cost?

His love? *His life?*

Sorrow sweeps through me, and I wish I could put an end to all of this, but I also know I can't go in half-cocked. If the Moirai killed my dad, they're not going to even think twice about me.

No, first I need to help put my dad to rest. Then, I'll find a way to end this curse, or die trying.

"Autumn, there you are," Wade says from the bottom of the stairs. His voice pulls me from my thoughts and I blink back in surprise. "Whatcha been doing? I was getting worried."

The letter is still clutched in my hand and I glance at it, then silently hold it out. Wade's dark eyebrows knit together as he bounds up the stairs, two at a time.

When he reaches the landing, he shoots me a questioning glance, but accepts the letter. Glancing down, he reads it. With each passing moment, his face darkens.

I fiddle with my fingertips as I pace back and forth in front of him.

"Where did you find this?" Wade asks, lifting his silver gaze to mine when he's finished.

"In this," I say, pulling the journal from under my arm and handing it to him as well. "It's my dad's journal."

Wade takes it, looking up with confusion painted across his face. "How did you—?"

"Abigail," I say, cutting off his question. "She said the only way to help my dad is to find his body and get him to the catacombs. But she felt there was information in here that might help us find out what he was doing before he died."

"Well, she was right about that part," Wade says, lifting his eyebrows high.

"Yeah, but there's still nothing about where. Just a vague mention about ley lines."

With the journal and letter clutched in his right hand, Wade steps forward, wrapping his arms around me. "Autumn, I'm so sorry. This whole thing is so fucked up."

I lean into him, but I can't find it in me to relax. As much as I'd like to be a normal person, dealing with my father's death and grieving in my own way and in my own time, I can't. I have far bigger things to worry about. My dad's not just dead; he's in a progressive transformation as a Lemure and there's only so much time before he finds a way to overcome Abigail again.

And on top of it, I have a horrifying fight for my own life coming. One that begins with a family curse and ends in death. Either the Moirai—or my own.

But before I can worry about any of that, I need to find my dad's remains and let him rest in peace.

I need to find his bones.

There's no more time for falling apart.

"We need to find my dad," I say, pulling back from Wade.

He nods. "All right. What do we do? Do you have a plan?"

"Abigail wants me to call the twins," I begin.

Wade backs up, shaking his head. "No, nu-huh. No way. We cannot bring that guy back into the mix of things. Not after what he did this winter."

"Wade, I really don't think we have a choice. She said

there's a spell in the grimoire and they're the best ones to—"

"Ask that guy, Dominic whatever," Wade offers, his eyes blazing.

I snicker. "I thought you didn't like him either."

"I don't. But at least he's not trying to steal you away from me."

I wince.

Wade runs his free hand through his dark hair and steps away from me. "Look, Dominic helped us find my grandpa and the entrance to the catacombs. He's got skills in this area and we didn't need a spell to do it. That's all I'm saying. Let's see what he can do."

I bite on my lower lip. He has a point. If we can use Dominic's skills to find my dad, it would be a lot faster than having to get the twins here from wherever the hell Diana Hawthorne has them.

Besides, how would that even go down. My first call to Cat since she left is to ask for a favor of epic proportions.

"Okay, fine," I say. Pulling my cell phone from my pocket, I dial Dominic's number. Wade's right. He's just as powerful at finding lost things and a helluva lot less complicated than the twins.

I step away from Wade, clutching the phone to my ear as I wait.

"Hello?" Dom says, picking up the other end of the line.

"Hey, Dominic. It's Autumn."

"Yeah, I know. What do you need this time?" he says, his voice thick with sarcasm.

Taking a deep breath, I swallow hard. How do I put everything into words? If I say it all out loud—and to someone who didn't see it all go down, it makes it all so real.

"I could really use your help," I finally say, walking over to the railing and placing my free hand on it. My gaze sweeps the entrance space, traveling to the windows and the autumn-painted trees beyond.

He snickers. "Oh yeah? Well, I'm shocked. What, not enough mojo to come in here, guns a blazing and—" he pauses for a beat, then audibly gasps. "Shit. I'm sorry, Autumn. I didn't—"

I sigh, pinching the bridge of my nose. "Why are you sorry?"

"I just picked up on what happened. I should've realized before I started speaking..." he says, his voice softening. "What can I do?"

"Look, I need you to help me find my father's..." I close my eyes, my voice choking out. "I need to find my dad. It's a long story and I don't really want to get into it right now. Will you help me?"

"Of course," he says.

His sudden compliance is somewhat heartening, but it's alarming at the same time. On a typical day Dom is all about what's good for him. To have him care about anyone else for a change feels...weird.

"Thanks. I really appreciate it," I say, glancing over at Wade's expectant gaze.

"Where do you think your, er, *dad* is?" Dom says, tiptoeing around the word as much as I did.

"I'm not entirely sure. They—I mean, *he*—could be anywhere. I'm not even sure I know the first place to start. All I know is it has something to do with ley lines," I say, scratching my forehead as I think.

"All right, what do you need me to do?" Dominic says.

"Can you come over?"

"On my way," he says, hanging up the phone before I have the chance to say good-bye.

I pull the phone back, staring at the wallpaper of my phone in surprise.

"He's on his way," I say, shoving my phone back into my pocket.

Wade takes a deep breath. "This will work better. Dominic can be a bit of a dick, but he's come through when we needed him, surprisingly enough."

I nod, but there's a gnawing sense of foreboding that tickles at the back of my mind. Abigail specifically said to use the Gilberts, and I'm defying that request.

God, I hope I'm making the right choice.

CHAPTER 22
SUMMONING THE FORGOTTEN

The resurrection chamber feels like an ominous place to go right now. Had I not known my dad had been dead for over a year, I would have been getting this space ready to bring him back. Or at the very least gearing up to try. Now, the best I can do is put his body to rest so his soul can be at peace.

But even if it were possible to bring him back, which I'm pretty damn certain it's not, I'd be defying all of the rules of the Moirai anyway. Who knows what kind of hell I'd be bringing down on myself and anyone who might be unfortunate enough to help me.

It's not a risk I'm willing to take.

"All right, I'm going in to consult the grimoire," I say, handing Wade my phone. "This won't take long."

"Tell me again how this works," he says, clutching my phone in his hand. His eyes are deep, dark pools of concern and I wish I could do something to quell his fears. But they're the same ones I have.

"I'm going to astral-project—at least, I think that's

what it is. It's faster than trying to physically maneuver the tunnels in the catacombs," I say, reaching for his hand and giving it a squeeze.

I take in a slow, steady breath and sit down on the floor. I cross my legs, like I plan to do a meditation, and rest my back against the stone wall. The quasi-cool stones make me shiver, but I know what's waiting on the other side brings a whole new level of chill.

"And you're absolutely sure you can do this?" Wade asks, squatting beside me.

"I am," I say, nodding. "I've done it before, remember? If Dominic arrives before I'm out, just wait for me. Don't do anything until I'm back. Okay?"

Wade nods. "I wouldn't dream of it." He bends in, placing his free hand along my jawline. Bending in, he brushes his lips against mine. Then, as he backs away, he winks at me. "Now, go do your thing, Dr. Strange."

I smile, shaking my head at the reference. "Let's hope there's more chance for this working out, than there was for the Avengers. Here goes nothing," I say, hoping I look more confident than I actually feel.

Closing my eyes, I settle into the energy around me. There's an intense level of anxiety rolling through me and I have to actively push it aside so I can focus enough to reach the astral plane. I stretch my neck and place my hands on my knees.

After a few moments, the energy settles and my body feels as though it's sinking into the dirt floor beneath me. Despite my eyes being closed, colors burst beneath my lids. Bright, energetic signatures that vibrate around the edges of each item in this space. Suddenly, I pull back from myself, able to see the room in a whole new way. I stand up, but this time, I can tell I must not be connected to my body anymore, yet I'm somehow still bound by the rules of gravity.

Unlike in the physical realm, where the stones are all still in place on the wall, the stones I removed last semester remain cast on the ground. It's like they're the ghostly remnants of a different time and place. I suppose technically, they are.

Taking a deep breath, which doesn't even feel like it reaches my lungs, I bend down and walk through the hole. Somehow, the frigid cold from the catacombs rushes at me. Shivering into the darkness, I keep my eyes closed and my senses open.

It's strange how I can interact in this space, almost as though I'm doing it in my physical body. But this time, I know I'm not.

I follow the distance of the tunnel, mesmerized by the vibrating colors. They're even more prominent than before. I don't know if it means something, or if I'm simply getting better at concentrating. I just hope it's not an ominous sign.

When I reach the end of the tunnel and cross the threshold into the circular chamber, the ethereal torches along the walls ignite, lighting the space with an eerie glow behind my lids. I open my eyes, taking in the space. Each tunnel leading to various grave sites fades into the darkness beyond, but in the center of the room, the stone pedestal rises from the floor, revealing the grimoire. It's like it was ready and waiting.

"Abigail?" I call out, hoping she's nearby and can guide me to the spell we need. However, I also know she's doing her best to restrain my father's malevolent energy.

When she doesn't answer, I walk up to the grimoire, confident that even without her, I can find the answers I need. She wouldn't have told me where to look if I didn't have the ability to do it on my own.

I run my fingertips along the edges of the ancient-looking tome, feeling the reverence and mystical energy vibrating beneath my touch. Even though this book exists in a different realm, it's imbued with a magical essence and it demands respect. Straightening my shoulders, I slowly flip open the book. I turn the pages with utter care, knowing how ancient it must be. Even if the book's pages themselves aren't real, I refuse to be the one who damages them with assumptions.

The paper is thin under my touch, and each page is handcrafted, written in a delicate scrollwork that is made in ink—and something else. Gold? Blood? All of the above?

The first few pages are familiar, showing me aspects of things I already know—things I've either learned or searched in the grimoire before. But nothing that stands out in terms of a location spell for my dad's remains.

I narrow my gaze.

"Where are you?" I whisper to myself as I turn the pages.

Then, I remember something from my dad's journal. He mentioned the grimoire can show me things about our family history—if I ask it. Perhaps it works the same way with spells?

Gingerly, I turn to a set of blank pages. Placing my hands over the top of the splayed paper, I close my eyes and try to clear my mind of anything but what I need from it.

"All right, grimoire—I need a spell to help locate my dad's...."—I swallow hard—"*body*. We need to stop his Lemure. Help me find a spell that will locate him."

Keeping my eyes closed for a moment, I let the energy from my thoughts flow down through my arms and out my hands. In my mind's eye, there are all sorts of colors, as my intentions slide through the energy centers of my body. In a strange way, it's as if I've plugged my arms into some sort of an energetic outlet, only I'm the energy source and the book is what's being charged.

When the information flow feels like it's pulling itself back, my eyes flit open. I stare in awe as the pages beneath my hands begin to fill themselves in. Removing my hands from the paper, I can't help but smile. There's so much about this world of magic that never ceases to amaze me. The world of fiction isn't all that far off.

Leaning in, I read the heading on the top of the first page. It's written in bold calligraphy, with delicate embellishments of gold and red and reads:

LEMURES.

Biting my lip, I begin to read.

Lemures, also known as Shades, are the restless spirits of the dead who were, for one reason or another, never afforded a proper burial by the living. They have not been interred into a tomb, grave, or other sacred location. Because of this, it has opened their spirit to the malevolent forces within the physical realm. Demons will seek their light out, seeking to destroy them. Should that happen, their soul becomes trapped on the earthly plane and slowly descends into a spiritual form of madness. As it tries to hold onto a sense of self, a Lemure might be able to last years before manifesting its own malevolent tendencies.

Lemures will often become attached to specific people, places, or things and will lash out at anyone who might wish to affect the items of their fixation. Their level of haunting may range on a spectrum from benign to indistinguishable from that of a poltergeist.

Should their remains not be properly buried, ultimately, their madness will even destroy those they are most attached to.

For those seeking to stop a Lemure, it's important to know that very often their remains will be difficult to locate, particularly since it can be months, weeks, or even years before their madness catches up and their hauntings turn violent. By then, their body may be ravaged by time.

You can say that again. On both counts.

I shake my head, continuing on to the next section.

In order to fully vanquish a Lemure, it is imperative their hauntings are dealt with at the root. A simple seance or spell to cast out a spirit will only anger a Lemure. Instead, their remains must be located and burned in the Flames of Eternity.

I inhale sharply. *Flames of Eternity.*

There's only one person I know with the power to summon flames—normal ones or otherwise.

I run my fingertips across my lips, suddenly able to see why Abigail wanted the Gilberts involved.

"Shit," I mutter, reaching for my cell phone. But as my hand hits my pocket, I realize I can't call her—I'm not even in the real world. Instead, I continue reading.

Without this elemental magic in play, the spark of their eternal essence—their soul—cannot be released and will not be reaped. Finally, their ashes must be properly interred and funeral rites be given.

The other page has another delicate heading that reads:

Summoning Spell for the Forgotten

The following location spell must be cast by a biomancer with the deep-rooted power to connect to earth energies. This allows them to bypass the spirit interference of the Lemure so they can connect with the earthly remains alone.

It's important to note that no ordinary witch will have the power to summon the location for the remains of a Lemure. It is especially important that a psychic witch not perform this spell. Their spirit energy will be too strong and will actively block any attempts to locate their body. As such, a Lemure grows in power, lashing out and actively seeking to destroy anyone who might wish to get in its way.

I look up, shaking my head.

I'm completely wasting Dominic's time. If he tries to

do anything, he could be putting himself, and everyone else, in danger.

"Dammit," I say, quickly studying the spell and committing it to memory.

The summoning spell requires something physical that's directly tied to my dad. Like a picture, or some other likeness. The rest is all up to the biomancer's intentions and summoning. Which, of course, would be Colton.

I should have listened to Abigail from the start.

Now I need to make it back to my body quickly so I can call it all off. As much as Wade and I wanted to avoid pulling the twins in, it looks like we're going to need them both to make this happen. And if we're going to make it work, we're going to need to act fast.

"Thank you," I whisper, sort of to the grimoire and sort of to the catacombs in general as I close the book.

As I step away from the pedestal, the flames begin to go out, one at a time. I walk to the tunnel entrance, which brings me back to the resurrection chamber, and close my eyes. Immediately, I sense the rest of the space go dark.

I wait a moment, allowing my extrasensory vision to catch up. When the bright colors spring to life, I don't waste any time. I race forward, willing myself to get to the other end—and to my body faster.

Somehow, before I even reach the end of the tunnel, I'm thrust back into my body and I lurch forward with a jerk. I gasp for air, as if it's the first time I've ever done so.

As I regain my awareness, though, the world is spinning in and out of view. Sand spirals around the resurrection chamber in a vortex and the entire space hums with an energy that makes my skin crawl and stomach lurch.

Oh god, I'm too late.

CHAPTER 23
INTO THE VORTEX

At first, I can't make anything out—it's all a blur of sand as it cyclones around the room. The velocity of it makes it damn near impossible to get out, as the granules thrash across my arms and face. Any light from the torches on the walls has been extinguished and all that remains is the dying light from the window beyond the stairs.

"What in the hell?" I shriek, shielding my eyes.

Wade is suddenly at my side. "Thank god. We gotta find a way to get out of here."

"What happened?" I say, trying to get to my feet.

Wade groans. "Dominic. What else? He wouldn't listen to me. I told him you wanted us to wait to do anything until you were back to yourself. But of course, that guy thinks he always knows better than everyone else."

"Great," I mutter, looking around the space but unable to make anything out farther than a foot or so in front of me.

"Yeah, I don't know what was going on in his head,"

Wade says, shielding his eyes with his forearm as he peers into the vortex of sand and stone. "He tried to summon your dad's location and it—I don't even know what the hell happened, to be honest."

"He gave my dad a power boost," I say, running my hand along my forehead. "Is he still here? Dominic, I mean?"

Wade ducks a stone the size of his fist, pulling me down with him so we're both in a crouch. It whizzes by, careening around with the rest of the cyclone. "I think so? When stuff started to rumble and the dirt started this whole thing, he took off for the stairs, though. *Coward*."

"It was the right instinct," I say, yanking the collar of my t-shirt up to cover my nose and mouth.

He does the same and shrugs. "I guess."

"You should have done the same," I say, biting my lip.

"Like hell. I'm not about to leave you here, unprotected," Wade says, looking incensed.

My thoughts tumble around, spinning at the same speed as the cyclone of sand. I'm not sure how to make it out of here and if my dad's taken control of the house, nowhere is going to be safe. Especially if he's managed to trap Abigail again.

My heart thumps loudly in my chest as I realize just how dire this situation really is. Especially for Wade. He shouldn't be here, and if his father realizes we're still together...or worse, if he gets himself killed...

I cover my mouth in horror.

"Oh my god. Wade, we need to get you out of here," I sputter.

Wade's silver gaze widens as he makes a face. "We *both* need to get the hell outta here."

"No, I mean, if you were to get hurt..." I say, reaching out for him. "Or worse..."

"Hey, hey, look at me," Wade says, grabbing hold of my arms and making me turn to face him. "We are in all of this together. There's absolutely no other place I'd rather be right now. I'm not gonna die—and neither are you. Do you hear me?"

I nod, unable to stop the sheer panic consuming every fiber of my being. If something happens to Wade, I would never be able to forgive myself.

"We're gonna get out of this mess, I promise you," he says, gazing round the room. "There's nowhere that's protected other than beneath the stairs, from what I can tell. But good luck getting up them right now."

Suddenly, the room begins to rumble, as if the stones holding up the walls are getting ready to catapult themselves at us.

"Shit's getting way worse. We need an exit strategy. How do we stop your dad?" Wade says, eyeing the walls. "What did the grimoire say?"

I shake my head. "For starters—not to mess with a location spell if you're not a biomancer. Otherwise, this would happen," I say, ducking a stone as it hits the wall behind me. Smaller chunks of sand and debris pepper the top of my head as it explodes on impact.

Wade's silver eyes are wide as he brushes off my hair and says, "Figures. Dammit. I'm sorry, Dru. I tried to stop Dominic, but you know what a stubborn jackass he can be. He went into a tirade about how I should stay out of this."

I cast him a knowing look. "He was probably right about that."

"Don't you start, too," he says, casting me a warning look.

"It doesn't matter now. We need to get the Gilberts here as fast as possible. Do you still have my phone?" I say, holding out my hand.

"Well, yeah. But what do the twins have to do with this?" Wade asks, digging my phone out of his pocket and handing it to me.

"Colton's a biomancer, remember?"

"Shit," Wade says, rolling his eyes.

"But that's not all. We need Cat, too. My dad's remains need to be burned in something called the Fires of Eternity, or his soul can't be released to..." my eyebrows tug inward and my shoulders drop, "*your dad*. Shit, Wade—you can't be here. If he finds out..."

"Look, we'll deal with that bridge when we cross it. Right now, the priority is getting out of here in one piece. Call the twins," Wade says, shaking his head. "I'll give you some cover."

Again the room rumbles and I nod quickly, kneeling down. The faster I do this, the better. Wade kneels as well, taking off his coat and holding it around us like a cloak of protection.

Taking a deep breath, I punch Cat's name and start silently praying she'll answer the phone. It's been so long since we last talked and with everything that happened last semester between Colton and the revenants—and her and her Fetch—I haven't even known what to say.

The phone starts ringing and I hold my breath, waiting for her to pick up. After four rings, her voicemail picks up.

"Dammit," I spit, hitting the redial.

"No answer?" Wade asks, being thrust forward as something hits him from behind.

I shake my head, clutching the phone to my ear. Again, it goes to voice mail. Immediately, I dial Colton instead. His phone also goes to voice mail.

I exhale in exasperation. "Neither of them are answering me."

"Then we need to figure out how to get out of this mess on our own. I think if we can edge along the wall, we might be able to make it to the underside of the stairs," Wade says, tipping his head toward the open slats letting in our only source of light.

"Then what? It's not like we'll be able to fit through them," I mutter. The sandstorm spirals around, peeling back layers of rock and mortar from the wall that holds the other side of the stairs up.

"Maybe we can peel back one of the treads. It might give us some room to get out. If nothing else, it looks like the wall is blocking the sand a bit better than this damn coat. Come on," he says, nodding toward the stairs.

Getting up into a crouched position, I shield the side of my face with my right arm and start almost duckwalking toward the stairs. Wade does the same, continuing to hold his leather jacket up to protect us.

Sand pelts the other side of his jacket. The sound is reminiscent of rain falling on the roof or hitting the edge of a windowsill. Larger stones buried in the walls crumble and pull into the cyclone, as if being drawn to the center of a black hole.

I race forward, practically diving into the small alcove in order to be shielded beneath the stairs.

"That was close," I breathe, turning around to face Wade.

Just as I face him, a stone the size of his head dislodges from the wall beside him. It hits him in the shoulder, pushing him off balance. He stumbles backward a couple of steps. Another rock, much larger than the first, and already caught in the vortex, cycles around, catching him in the back of the head.

I blink back my horror and dismay. But before I can even reach out for him or call his name, his eyes dim. His expression doesn't even change.

Then, as if in slow motion, his knees buckle beneath him. In the longest of seconds ever, his arms fall to his side, and he lets loose his jacket. It's scooped up by the sandstorm behind him, instantly consumed by it. The dark strands of hair across Wade's forehead flutter wildly, almost as if he's just on a joyride in a convertible, as he drops to the ground.

Rushing forward, I somehow manage to grab onto his upper body, hoisting him up before he can fall face-first into the dirt. With all the strength I can muster, I yank him backward, dragging him into the tiny space beneath the stairs.

My body trembles as I try to gently set him down on his back. Placing a hand behind his head, I support his neck as I lay him flat. Removing my shaky hand, I fight the urge to hurl. My hand is totally covered in crimson, and a small pool of blood begins to spread across the sand beneath his head.

A guttural cry escapes my lips as I scramble to find a pulse on his neck. My fingers slip and slide against his skin and my hands quake too much to get a good read.

"Wade, stay with me—" I say, barely holding back my sobs. "I'll get you help. I swear, I'll get you help."

The typical flush of color that would be splashed across his cheeks is fading and even his lips take on an odd whitish tinge. I bend forward, clutching him to my body as I instinctively rock back and forth.

My worst nightmare is coming to pass.

"Wade," I repeat, over and over. Tears stream from my eyes, mixing with the sand and grit covering my face, but I can't bring myself to care.

Beyond the small wall, the stones and sand continue to circle, ripping away years of history from this space, but all I can worry about is Wade and whether or not he's okay. And if he's not—then the fucking cyclone better just scoop me up now, because I'm done. *End me now.*

"Stop—" I wail, wishing there was some way to get through to my father. Some way to make him understand what he's doing and just make him stop.

Instead of slowing down, it's as though the sound of my pain pisses him off more. The walls of the resurrection chamber rumble with a thundering roar that's deafening. Bowing my head and pulling myself over Wade, I cover him, refusing to let anything else hurt him without going through me first.

All around us the stones rattle like they're about to collapse the room completely, and I almost welcome it. The wall giving us a momentary shield of cover crushes in on itself, flying apart rock by rock as it gets sucked into the vortex in the room. A few of the stairs that were attached to it fly off, joining the chaos. The remaining stairs dangle from the supporting wall like wobbly teeth, ready to pop out at a moment's notice.

Unable to hold back my sobs, I cover my face in Wade's neck. Sandalwood and soap mix with the potent, sickly stench of blood. Though I'm not willing to face the end, I hold my breath, waiting to be swept away with the cyclone of sand and stone.

I never should have given in and brought him back into my world. This was always going to happen. One way or another, Wade was going to die because of me.

He knew it, *I knew it*...even his dad knew it. Being around me brought him into my family's curse.

I should have trusted my instincts and let him go. It would have kept him safe.

Now it's a horrifying mistake I'll have to live with for the rest of my life.

What in the hell was I thinking?

CHAPTER 24
TICK TOCK

The floorboards from the room above groan, snapping the beams and buckling a handful of them inward. It's only a matter of time before the upper level collapses completely. My body quakes uncontrollably as I cling to Wade, wishing this was over. If the Moirai want to wipe out the Blackwood family so badly, *just do it already*.

I'm ready to die. At least I'll be with Wade.

Suddenly, the raging wind and cacophony beyond comes to a complete halt and the room goes deafeningly silent. Too terrified to look up, I clutch Wade closer, rocking with his body for fear of what might be on the other side of my eyelids.

Are the Fates here to accept my challenge? What will they do with us?

Footsteps creak on the stairs above us and my head snaps up. Opening my eyes, it's as if the entire room has been put on pause. Every rock, board, nail, and granule of sand is suspended in mid-rotation. Even Wade's jacket floats at an odd angle in the mixture of it, almost as if it's suspended in water.

My ears still ring from the commotion, but I swear I hear movement and voices, but I can't be sure. I watch the ceiling above me, waiting for the shoe to drop. Or at the very least, the craziness to resume. There's no way the Lemure would stop for the fun of it.

"This looks like a death trap. Are you sure the stairs are secure?" a male voice says from somewhere above me.

"For godsake, he's got this. Would you just go?" An air of irritation filters from a second, female voice.

Narrowing my gaze, I hold my breath and wait.

Two sets of feet make their way down the steps, each one descending with a little bit of caution. Clutching Wade close, my heart pounds in my ears.

A rush of relief sweeps over me and I collapse back into Wade as Dominic and Cat round the bottom of the rickety steps. Cat's eyes brighten when she sees me, but she twists back toward the stairs.

"They're here—" Cat calls out.

Dominic races forward, dropping to his knees beside me. As he takes in the situation with Wade, his face goes ashen, but he doesn't say a word. His eyebrows just tip up in the middle in a silent question.

"Is he okay?" Cat asks, her eyes full of worry. Gently, she reaches out and runs her hand along my upper arm.

I look from Wade, back to her, tears blurring my vision. I shake my head. "I don't...I'm not sure."

Cat settles back onto her feet, releasing a slow breath.

"Come on, we need to get you both out of here. Colton's not gonna be able to hold all of this back for long," Dominic says, jumping into action. As he stands, he reaches out a hand for me to latch onto.

As smoothly as possible, I release my grip on Wade, allowing Dominic and Cat to pull me to my feet. My body aches and my legs feel like they're going to give out at any moment.

"Are you hurt?" Cat asks, her dark eyes full of concern. Her hair looks different from when I last saw her, braided in dreadlocks and tied into a sophisticated-looking ponytail.

I shake my head, unable to get my brain to form any more words.

"Can you make it up the stairs on your own? Cat and I can manage Wade," Dominic says, his white eyebrows tugging inward.

"I'm not leaving him," I say, jutting out my chin defiantly. My body continues to shake uncontrollably, but I reach for him.

Cat grabs hold of my arms and forces me to look her in the eyes. "You're too shook up, Autumn. Let us help you. Okay? We got this. I promise."

I glance back at Wade's pale face. He needs help, and fast. He's not going to get it bleeding on the floor of the resurrection chamber. "Okay." I nod.

Dominic grabs my hand, leading me over to the edge of the stairs. "Stay to the wall side. Colton's promised me he's got them steady, but no reason to test that theory."

My eyes follow the steps up to the small door at the top. Most of them look like they're barely hanging on.

Suddenly, Diana Hawthorne crouches in the doorway. "Well, what in the hell are you waiting for? We don't have all damn day. Come on, guys. Clock's ticking." She holds out a hand as if I could reach it from where I'm standing.

I nod, leaning against the stone wall as I begin my ascent. The stairs feel oddly secure despite not being attached to anything that supports them on the one side. But the steps with the missing treads are a pain. Cat and Dominic follow me, taking their time and maneuvering with care. Dominic has his arms locked beneath Wade's as he carries his upper body, while Cat carries his feet. My legs are wobbly, but I push myself through until I reach the doorway. Diana latches a firm grasp around my forearm as I extend my hand to her.

She pulls me into my bedroom, which looks again like it's been tipped on end. There's broken glass, wood, and items scattered all over the place. My bed is cattywampus, resting on its side against the window seat, and there's an enormous crack down the wall behind me.

To my left, Colton stands completely still, his arms raised out in front of him and fingers splayed. His eyes are a bright, glowing white, without a single hint of the normal deep brown.

"Coming through," Dominic calls out behind me.

I step out of the way, rushing over to Wade as they enter the room with him.

"We need to get out of this house. The manifestation is only being held back by Colton. As soon as he lets go, the Lemure will resume its destruction," Diana says, tipping her head toward the door. "Let's get the hell outta here and assess everything when we're at a safe distance."

Dominic nods his head and starts walking toward the door. Cat keeps up the pace, making sure to keep Wade's body somewhat level.

"Autumn, follow them. Colt and I will take up the rear. He has to pull his power back very slowly so we can all make it out with the least disruption," Diana says, raising an arm and pointing to the door.

Trembling, I nod my head and do as she says. Everywhere I look, things are smashed and strewn across the floor. It's as if all of the previous construction work and cleanup has been completely erased. Rushing to catch up, I walk beside Wade's body, holding onto his right arm as it drapes over his torso. My eyes are drawn again to the sickly color of his complexion, and I hold back a sob.

Please don't be...

I shut down the thought, darting ahead of Dominic, so I can open the front door. I step over a broken vase and pry the door back. Dominic treads carefully, making sure not to trip or drop Wade's upper body. Whenever possible, he pushes debris out of the way so Cat has an easier time focusing on the path ahead.

Once they go through, I leave the door open wide and follow after them.

The man who was with Diana last semester—Blake, I think his name is—gawks at us as we rush out of the building. His arms open wide as his dark, penetrating eyes look straight through the three of us, searching for something else.

As Diana and Colton make their slow exit from the building, he races past us and up the steps toward them.

"What in the actual fuck, woman?" he sputters, wrapping his arms around Diana. "Why can't you just stick to our plan?"

She chuckles softly, pulling back from his embrace. "I

don't know what you were so worried about. It's not like I can die, Blake," she says, patting him on the chest.

"Regardless, I can. I just about had a heart attack out here," Blake shoots back.

"So dramatic," Diana says, running a hand along his jawline.

My eyes widen and I stop to gape at them. "Wait, what? You're immortal?"

"Later," Diana says, placing her hand on my shoulder as she walks on by and heads to the black SUV parked on the drive.

"Autumn, can you get the door?" Dominic calls out, tipping his chin to the back door of his red Honda Civic.

I scramble around them, pulling the door open and rushing around to the other side. Sliding into the backseat, I help take Wade's body. Half pulling him across, Dominic helps Cat feed him into the back seat so he rests across my lap.

The irony of this situation isn't lost on me.

Shuddering away my trepidation, I run my hand over his forehead.

"I'm here, Wade. I'm right here," I whisper.

Once Wade's fully inside, Cat closes the door and races over to the black SUV. She opens the back door and reaches for Colton, whose eyes are still white and face expressionless. Her hands guide him to the seat and Colt disappears inside.

Dominic, on the other hand, hops into the driver's seat and starts the engine. Leaning out of the window, Blake does some sort of hand signal to follow them and he gets inside. When everyone has taken a seat, the black SUV spins its tires, propelling the vehicle forward.

As they do, the front door to the house slams shut. The stained-glass windows along the outer edge shatter, speckling the ground with multicolored glass.

"Go, go," I cry out, knowing just what my dad's capable of doing—even outside the manor.

Dominic doesn't waste a moment. He puts his foot down and the Civic jolts forward as he races after the others. The smell of burned rubber filters through the air, thankfully taking over the smell of blood momentarily.

Exhaling a jagged breath, I blink back tears as I run my fingertips across Wade's forehead repeatedly, pushing back any stray hair.

"How is he?" Dominic asks, his tone painted with worry.

I look up, catching his gaze in the rear-view mirror.

Shaking my head, I say, "I don't know."

"Is he—"

"I said I don't know," I say, louder this time. "My hands are shaking too much to find a pulse."

"Sorry, it's just that..." Dominic slams the butt of his hand on the steering wheel. "This is all my fault. Dammit, I'm so sorry, Autumn. I really am."

Anger wells up inside me and I fire back. "You should be. He asked you to wait for me, but you didn't listen."

"Do you honestly think I don't know that?" he says, gripping the steering wheel tighter. "I thought he was just being overprotective. I thought I knew what I was doing."

"Yeah, well, your arrogance may have gotten him killed," I spit, ignoring the tears that distort my vision. "I know you wanted him out of the picture, but this—"

"It wasn't like that and you know it," Dominic says through gritted teeth.

"Sure as hell seems like it now," I say, swiping the tears from my cheeks.

Dominic snorts, shaking his head. "Whatever. You don't get it."

I roll my eyes, casting my gaze out over the driveway.

Right now, the only thing I know is my dad is dead and my boyfriend might be next.

The trees blur by, and the only think I can think about is what happens if Wade is dead? Could I resurrect him the way I did with Cat? How would I know for sure? Wouldn't I see his spirit leave his body the way I did with Cat? What would happen next? Will his dad come for him?

Will I ever see him again?

CHAPTER 25
WHAT IS IT GOOD FOR?

The end of the driveway comes into view a few yards away. I close my eyes, relieved to be leaving my family's domain behind so we can focus on Wade.

But I no sooner let the emotion roll through me than the trees around us begin to sway heavily. Dominic tightens his grip on the steering wheel, shifting in his seat to sit up straighter.

"Christ, the wind—" he mutters.

My eyes widen as I look out into the wooded area. Everything from the trees to the underbrush moves like a hurricane is coming to town.

"That's no ordinary wind," I warn, my voice creeping upward into a screech. "Go, Dominic, floor it—"

Ahead of us, the black SUV also picks up speed. They must have noticed the change. Small trees and bushes start to uproot themselves as they get swept up into the angry force that is my dad. A tree branch cracks apart from one of the large oak trees along the right edge of the driveway.

It lands feet in front of the SUV, but Blake somehow manages to dodge out of its way, narrowly avoiding it as the SUV off-roads into the grass and keeps going.

My eyes widen in horror as I stare out into the sea of trees literally uprooting themselves.

"Hold on tight," Dominic says, swerving to avoid a large branch.

The second our tires leave the driveway, a birch tree on the left dislodges itself from the ground and contorts at a strange angle like it's ready to catch us. Dominic veers us back onto the driveway and floors it.

The SUV hits the road, taking a quick turn to the left. As it disappears from sight, another tree uproots beside us. I don't even have time to figure out what it is before the branches of it slam into the side of the car, smashing the windows on my side and veering us wildly off course. I dust the glass chunks away from Wade, ignoring the rest of them scattered across the seat and lodged into my hair.

The car careens into the woods, barely managing to miss being smashed by a falling willow. I brace my hand on the ceiling of the car as underbrush, branches, and small trees whip at the edges of the vehicle, smashing against the windshield and windows.

Dominic somehow manages to stay in control, maneuvering us through the chaos with a strange sense of proficiency. We burst through the trees, practically driving on two wheels as we hit the ditch, then make it out onto the road.

The moment we get beyond the border of my property, the wind dies and the trees return to normal.

Exhaling a jagged breath, I lean my head back and close my eyes.

"That was close," Dominic says. "Remind me to never piss off your family again, would ya?"

My eyes flitter open and I snicker.

The SUV takes a quick left ahead of us and Dominic speeds up.

"Where are they going? Wade needs the doctor—" I cry, my voice squeaking out.

Dominic shakes his head. "I trust them. I go where they go."

"Oh, now you trust people? That's just great, Dominic. Wish you would have trusted me before you fucked everything up," I say, unable to hold back the utter despair surging through me.

Dominic winces, but he stays the course, taking a sharp turn after the others.

Seething, I drop my gaze to Wade. His blood is everywhere; on me, the car. Even Dominic is covered in it. My heart constricts and I run a trembling hand along his face.

Wade's head rolls to the side and he groans. Relief washes over me as he lifts a hand weakly to the side of his head.

"Oh my god, thank you," I say, dropping down to him and peppering his face with kisses. "Thank you, thank you, thank you."

"What haaa—" he mumbles, struggling to open his eyes.

"You're hurt," I say, fighting back tears of joy.

"Tell me something I don't know," he chuckles, grimacing as he tries to sit up.

"Don't move. You need to keep still," I say, holding him close so he can't get up.

He relaxes into my arms. Slowly, some of the color returns to his cheeks, but his lips are still incredibly pale.

"You scared the hell out of me, Wade."

"What happened?"

"You were trying to reenact my concussion in the woods," I say, erupting in a relieved half-laugh, half-sob.

"That explains the pounding in my head," he says, reaching his hand back and staring at the fresh blood on his fingers. His eyes roll slightly at the sight of it, and he drops his hand to his chest. "Excellent. Battered and bloody. Two for two."

The car rolls to a stop beside the SUV. Glancing up, I see that we're beside a modest-size home. It's built in a similar fashion to my own, but not nearly as large.

"We're at Cat and Colton's?" I ask, confused.

"We need to regroup. This was the closest," Dominic says, putting the car in park and shutting off the engine. He opens his door and gets out. Then, the backdoor swings open and he leans in. "Come on, Sleeping Beauty."

Wade makes a face and gives him the finger.

Dominic just laughs it off. "Think you can manage to get yourself out? Or do you need more assistance?" He extends a hand, not even waiting for an answer.

"I got it," Wade says, struggling to sit up.

With a little nudge, I help to push him upright. When he's in a seated position, Dominic helps him out of the vehicle. Twisting to my own door, I try to get it open, but it won't budge. I even try putting my shoulder into it, but it's no use. Instead, I scoot across the seat, following Wade.

Once outside of the vehicle, I quickly understand why.

Dominic's Civic is a mess. The entire passenger side looks like it was crumpled by the Hulk.

Dominic sets Wade down on the front steps of the wraparound porch, then walks over to me. He picks a glass chunk from my hair and tosses it into the trees.

"Does this make us even now?" he says, smirking.

I quirk an eyebrow, confused.

"I know you were pretty pissed about your paint job," he says, scrunching his nose and scratching at the back of his head.

"Yeah, I was. But for the record," I begin, pointing at his vehicle, "you're the one who let the genie out of the bottle. This wouldn't have happened if you had just waited."

"Yeah, well, I guess there's that," he chuckles, scratching his head.

I glance back at Wade. Diana, Blake, and the twins have gotten out of the vehicle. Colton has managed to take a seat next to Wade, who looks utterly incensed. Colton reaches around to the back of Wade's head, but he bats Colt's hands away.

Walking up to them, I sputter, "What are you doing?"

"He needs help," Colt says, turning to face me.

There's a new sense of confidence rolling off of him, and it makes me pull up short. The Colton from a couple of months ago could barely look me in the eye, let alone speak with such determination.

Wade winces, leaning back on the steps slightly as he props himself up on his elbows. His eyes flutter a bit, rolling to the back of his head.

"Oh, would you stop being such a baby? Let him help you," Diana says, dropping into a squat in front of them.

Shooting Colton a sideways glance, Wade doesn't say anything to him but nods his approval.

"What's going on?" I ask, stepping forward.

Diana holds up a hand. "Just watch."

Colton leans in, raising his hands and placing them on either side of Wade's head. Then Colt closes his eyes, his chin dropping down in concentration. Wade closes his eyes as well. I'm not sure if it's in concentration or exhaustion. Probably both.

Colton blows out a slow exhale. As he does, the space between his hands glows a bluish-green color. The color expands outward from his palms until the light practically obscures Wade's entire head from view. Raising my right arm, I shield my eyes as I try to keep watching.

After a few moments, the color pulls back, as if sucked into the center of Colt's palms.

"Remember to ground yourself," Diana urges, setting a hand on Colton's knee. "Cat, can you grab him some water?"

Cat nods, racing up the steps and inside.

Colton's eyes remain closed as he breathes slow and steady, almost as if he's in some form of meditation.

Wade, on the other hand, sits up straighter. His eyes are bright, and his normal color is slowly returning.

"What in the hell did you do to me? That was..."—Wade raises his hand to the back of his head—"*amazing*."

Diana twists around, looking directly at me as she raises an eyebrow, "Quick on the uptake, this one."

"He healed you," Cat says, walking out the front door with a tall glass of water in her hand. She holds it out for Colton as she runs her free hand over the top of his cropped hair.

"Thanks," he mutters, taking the glass with his eyes still closed.

"That's a thing?" I ask, confused. "I didn't know that was a thing."

Blake chuckles, leaning against the SUV.

Diana stands up, walking over to me. "Turns out, a biomancer's earth connection is best used to heal. Colt's been working on the ability, but practice on this scale has been a little light. Not that any of us are complaining."

"Definitely not," Cat says, her eyes wide as she shakes her head.

Wade pulls his hand back, staring at it. It's still covered in slightly dried blood, but there's no fresh blood at all. Slowly, he turns to Colton, his mouth slightly agape.

"I..." Wade's eyebrows tug inward. "I don't know what to say."

"Pretty sure a *thank you* wouldn't go amiss," Dominic chuckles.

Wade's gaze flits to Dominic, but he returns it to Colton. "Thank you."

Colton shrugs. "It was nothing."

"Eh, you're doing it again," Diana says, shooting him a severe look. "Knock that shit off."

Colton's eyes widen and he nods.

"What's he doing?" I ask.

"Acting like a little mouse. He's one of the most powerful biomancers in the world, thanks to his god energy. There's no reason to hide—"

"His what now?" Wade says, slowly pushing himself to a stand.

Cat walks down the steps, then leans against the railing. "We're Gemini Twins, remember?"

"What does that have to do with god energy?" I ask, reaching for Wade's hand and pulling him close. I wrap my arms around him, keeping my gaze fixed on Cat.

"Gemini Twins are created when one child is conceived by a human—and the other by a god," Diana says. Before I can open my mouth to say anything else, she raises a hand to stop me. "Yes, before you ask, dual conception happens pretty much at the same time."

"That's some imagery I won't be able to get out of my head," Wade mutters.

"Go Mrs. Gilbert," Dominic says, clearly impressed. "Rawr."

Colt's hand flies to the back of his neck. "Can we not talk about our conception?" he says, standing up.

A woman sharing a remarkable resemblance to Cat walks out the front door, wiping her hands on an apron as she does so. "Did I hear someone say my name?"

"Mrs. G.," Dominic says, beaming. He practically races up the stairs with his arms open wide.

"Dominic," Mrs. Gilbert says, matching his stance and embracing him on the porch. Her smile is wide and her dark eyes sparkle with mischievousness. "It's been a while. So good to see you, dear. How's your grandma?"

Dominic pulls back a bit, his lips pressed tight. He shrugs slightly, then says, "She's been better. You know how it is."

Mrs. Gilbert nods knowingly, patting him on the shoulder as she steps out to the top of the stairs. She reaches out for Colton, kissing the top of his head as he stands a couple of steps below her.

Diana grins, walking up the steps next, with Blake

following closely behind. One after the other, they give her a hug until all that's left is Wade and me.

"Autumn," Mrs. Gilbert says with a hint of reverence in her tone. "It's so good to see you, dear."

I smile back and wave awkwardly. Even though I feel like I should know her, and I guess I may have as a kid, I just don't remember.

"This is Wade, Autumn's boyfriend," Cat says, sweeping a hand out toward him.

Mrs. Gilbert's eyes take him in, assessing his situation. "You all right, sweetie?"

Wade lowers his chin, chuckling under his breath. "Yeah, I am now, thanks to Colton."

Mrs. Gilbert grins broadly, patting his shoulder.

"I don't mean to cut this reunion and introduction short," Diana says, choosing her words delicately. "But we have a situation that needs to be dealt with."

"What can I do to help?" Mrs. Gilbert asks, her face suddenly serious.

"I'm afraid it's going to be a matter for the twins," Diana says.

As if this makes total sense, the twins' mom simply nods.

Diana turns to me, her face the epitome of resolve. "You consulted your grimoire on how to help your dad. Care to get everyone else caught up to speed?"

CHAPTER 26

IN HIS LIKENESS

For the most part, Diana is stoic as I tell the group everything I know about my dad's death. But I can tell none of it surprises her.

I explain why he died, how he became a Lemure, and why we need a biomancer like Colton to find his body and a fire starter like Cat to finish everything off. As I mention the Moirai, Diana and Wade exchange a significant glance, but neither of them says a word.

Throughout the entire conversation, each of them stares at me with rapt attention. Even Mrs. Gilbert doesn't move a muscle. However, her dark eyes cloud with tears as she waits, listening until everything I know is now in their hands.

"Well, what are we waiting for?" Dominic says, standing up and brushing off the front of his jeans. "Let's get to work."

"Hold up there, cupcake," Diana says, patting Dominic on the chest. "We need to get clear on our roles and take things one step at a time." She shoots him a knowing glance.

"Yes, ma'am," he mutters, shrinking back and sitting down.

"Good god, call me ma'am again and we're gonna have some problems," Diana says, shuddering. "It's also getting dark. We need to decide if we're going to press on tonight or—"

"This can't wait any longer," I interject. After everything I've experienced and now know, the last thing I want for my father is to allow his torment to continue.

Diana turns to me, her expression thoughtful. "All right. Does the spell require anything specific? Or is Colton free to locate the remains as he sees fit?"

I drop my shoulders, tipping my chin to the sky. "Shit. In the rush to get out, I didn't even think. We need something of my dad's. The grimoire mentioned something that's tied to him or shares his likeness."

"I think I can help with that," Mrs. Gilbert says, twisting around and heading inside before any of us has time to respond.

"Mom keeps everything," Cat says, smiling as she rolls her eyes.

Colton nods in agreement. "She really does."

After a couple of minutes, Mrs. Gilbert walks out, extending a framed photograph to me. "Will this do?"

It's a small, four-by-six-inch photo surrounded by a rustic-looking wooden frame. The picture is old, at least fourteen or fifteen years by the looks of it. My mom, dad, and I are huddled together on the left-hand side of the shot and the Gilberts are huddled on the right. Everyone looks so...*happy*.

I run my index finger over my face, staring at it. Even though I know there's still time I'm missing from my childhood, it's strange to see photos of me when I don't remember being there. I don't remember my time with the twins—or having ever met Mrs. Gilbert before now.

Sighing to myself, I stare at my parents' faces. They both look oblivious to the pain lying ahead as they huddle together, holding onto me and each other.

I look up to everyone's expectant gaze.

Clearing my throat, I say, "I—uh, I think it will do. One way to find out, I guess." I hold the photo out to Colton, letting him take it from me.

Diana tips her head. "Agreed." Turning to Colton, she adds, "Are you up to giving this a try?"

Colton walks down the remaining steps from the porch and walks to Diana. "Wouldn't be here if I wasn't."

Diana beams, patting him on the shoulder like a proud parent. Mrs. Gilbert clasps her hands in front of her chest, smiling softly.

It must be so weird for her, having the twins whisked away and staying with Diana.

"So, there's no incantation or anything? I'm just…free to locate him?" Colton asks, staring at the photo.

I nod. "There was no incantation. It said it was in the hands of the biomancer."

"Good," he says, walking out into the middle of the driveway. "That will make this a little easier."

"Don't forget to lay the foundation of protection, like we've talked about," Diana says, eyeing Colton.

He nods, turning to his sister. "Cat, can you grab me the salt? That should be all we need."

"On it," she says, bounding up the steps and heading into the recesses of the house.

I bite my lower lip and reach for Wade's hand. "Thank you, guys. All of you. I..." my gaze falls to the grass at my feet and I shake my head. "I wouldn't have been able to do this without all of you."

Wade leans into me, nudging me with his shoulder. "That makes two of us."

"That's what friends are for," Dominic says, standing up and shooting him a smirk.

Colton nods, smiling in our direction.

There's a strange duality of emotions fighting for dominance inside me. On one hand, there's a profound sense of sadness and heartache clutching at my chest. On the other hand, I'm also filled with gratitude. After last semester, I would never have thought I'd be standing here, feeling as close to each of these people as I do right now.

Cat bursts out of the door, and in her hands is a large jar of sea salt. "Will this be enough, Colt?"

He nods and walks over to a clear patch of dirt on the driveway. Kneeling down, he sets the photo a couple of inches in front of him. Cat follows him, opening the jar of salt. She walks around him in a clockwise motion, pouring the salt in a circle of protection.

Each of us follows them, standing just outside the circle and watching them set to work. When the contents of the jar are gone and the circle is complete, a small shockwave of white light shoots upward toward the sky like a cylinder of protection.

"Remember, focus on Lyle's physical being. Not who he was as a person," Diana says. "That should help you differentiate the two. You don't want to provoke his Lemure any more than necessary."

Colton's eyes widen, and he takes a deep breath. "You can say that again."

Nodding to herself, Diana takes a step back, with Blake by her side. Her perceptive gaze takes in everything as she sweeps it over the entire scene. It's almost as if she's playing a large game of chess and we're all the game pieces.

In some ways, there's a sense of security in it. I know that with her psychic powers and Colton's biomancy, together we'll find my dad.

A hushed reverence descends through the group of us as Colton lowers his head in concentration. With his hands outstretched to the photo, he begins speaking in a low chant.

Collectively, we hold our breath as he does his thing. At first, it doesn't look like anything is happening, but then white, whispy energy erupts from the palms of his hands. It wraps around the picture frame, sweeping across it the way incense smoke rolls around the objects near it.

"What are you getting?" Cat asks, narrowing her gaze.

Colton shakes his head. "I'm not—it's like it's not connecting to it. The energy is too scattered. There are too many people in this photo."

A sickening feeling settles in the pit of my stomach. I totally jinxed it with my thoughts.

"Well, what about sending Autumn in?" Dominic says.

With the exception of Diana, everyone turns to face him with the same question written across their faces. *Why?*

Dominic looks at us as if it's completely obvious. "Did any of you pay attention to what Autumn said?"

Clearly amused, a slow smirk slides across Diana's features.

When no one replies, Dominic huffs, raising a hand out in front of him. "She said we need something tied to him, or that shares his likeness. Well, I don't know about you, but you don't get much more tied to someone than being their kid."

One by one, they turn to face me.

"Plus, she does kinda share his likeness," Cat says, raising her eyebrows in approval.

"She's practically the spitting image," Mrs. Gilbert chuckles.

I turn to face Diana, hoping to get her consensus. "Will this work?" I ask.

Something hides in the depths of her eyes, but she tips her head. "It would stand to reason."

"But you can't tell?" I say, making a face.

"When the works of gods are involved, even the best psychics in the world will have their limitations. The Moirai, while not gods specifically, have powers many gods have fought over. I find it's best to tread lightly and hope that *fate favors the attempts*," she says, accentuating the final words.

Casting a quick glance at Wade, I drop his hand and walk over to the circle.

Colton brings his hands into prayer position in front of his chest, then tips them forward at the wrist so his fingertips face me. As he pulls his hands apart, the energy of the cylinder of light separates like curtains being drawn back.

Stepping gingerly over the salt, I walk to him. Shifting the photo to the side, I kneel down in front of Colton, taking the photo's place.

"This won't hurt her, will it?" Wade asks. I look up to his worried expression.

Diana shakes her head. "It shouldn't. He's just using her connection to her dad like a scrying tool. Their DNA is linked."

Wade nods, scrunching his lips tight.

Turning back to Colton, I take a deep breath. "What do you need me to do?"

He extends his hands, palms upward. I stare at them for a moment, then slowly reach out, placing my hands in his. As soon as our skin comes into contact, the blue and orange flames erupt. They begin at the place of contact, and spread up my arms.

"Holy shit," Dominic mutters.

Ignoring their mutterings, I close my eyes, not wanting to see the look on Wade's face. Colton's hands tighten around mine and he begins to chant again.

While there's no pain from the fire, there's a deep sense of movement inside me, like he's summoning the very coding in my blood to do his bidding. Shuddering at the thought, I open my eyes to see if it's working.

Colton's head is no longer bent forward, but, instead, raised back up. Just like at the manor, his eyes glow a brilliant, bright white as he stares straight through me.

After a moment, he speaks. His voice has an odd, echoing quality that makes me shiver.

"He's not far. Just beyond the trees," Colton says. Raising his right arm, he points back toward the general direction of my house.

"Can you see his body?" Diana asks.

"Yes," Colton says. "He's on the ley lines, just beyond the ridge."

My insides constrict and I feel queasy. I knew we needed to find his body, but to know it's really there is something totally different.

"Hold up. Are you saying his body is back on the Blackwood property?" Dominic interjects. There's an edge of panic hidden in his tone.

"Yes," Colton repeats.

"Shit," Dominic curses.

Suddenly, the glow in Colton's eyes dims, and he pulls back from whatever sight the spell or his power itself has given him. He blinks the remnants of it away, and his deep-brown eyes take me in.

"I'm so sorry, Autumn," he whispers.

My lips press into a thin line, and I drop my gaze to our connected hands. Pulling back my hands from his, the blue and orange fire extinguishes in a puff. Before I stand up, I chance a sideways glance at Wade. He quickly tries to hide his wounded expression as I exit the circle to stand beside him.

Colton stands up, grabbing the picture frame and stepping over to his mom to hand it to her.

"Well, this is swell," Dom mutters, rolling his eyes and stepping away from the circle. "How do we get to it without being pummeled by Hurricane Lyle?"

"A valid point," I say, nodding. "My dad's too strong. If we go onto the property, his Lemure will attack. He nearly killed Wade. Hell, he nearly killed all of us."

Dominic nods. "We can't just go marching over there to collect his remains. That would be suicide. We need a better plan."

Diana crosses her arms over her chest and quirks an eyebrow, clearly waiting for something.

Dominic makes a face. It's like the two of them are communicating on a completely psychic level.

"Well, we do have a few people in our midst who can't die," Dominic mutters. "Maybe we can use that to our advantage?"

"So, you want to send in the immortals and hope they can clean up the mess? You know they can still get hurt, right?" Blake says, speaking up for the first time. His face is dark as he shakes his head indignantly.

"Hurt, but not dead," Dominic says. He winks as he clicks his tongue and points his index finger at Blake.

Blake lets out an exasperated sigh and walks away from the group.

"What about Colton?" Wade says, tugging his eyebrows in.

"Yes, he's immortal," I say, wondering what he's getting at. "But he can't go alone—"

"No, that's not what I mean." Wade turns to me, taking my hands in his. "Hear me out, okay?"

I narrow my gaze, waiting.

Wade scrunches his face and exhales slowly. "What if Colton summons your dad's remains?"

My mouth pops open, but I can't find the words to refute him. There's a certain amount of sense to the idea.

"After everything that went down last semester, you want to put Colt in the position to use his powers to make another revenant?" Cat says indignantly. "Do you know how hard he's worked to put all of that behind him?"

"Yeah, well, at least this time, he could put the skill to some good. Don't you think?" Wade fires back. "If any of us go onto the property, we're as good as dead. I don't know about you, but I don't want to see any of us die over this. Do you?"

Cat opens her mouth, but snaps it shut after a moment.

"He's right, you know," Diana whispers, speaking up for the first time in all of this.

Everyone turns to her, but no one says a word.

"Colton has powers he's barely begun to explore. He needs to learn how to live with them. Unless he tests the waters, he won't be able to find his center," she says matter-of-factly.

Colton swallows hard, swapping his gaze from me to Diana.

She casts him a stern glance and tips her chin. "You got this, kiddo," she whispers. "This is what you've been working so hard for."

Straightening his shoulders, Colt exhales a slow burst of air. "All right, I'll do it."

Despite being the lesser of the evils, my pulse pounds loudly in my ears.

Even if we can reanimate his remains, which is cringe-worthy on its own, we still have to find a way to get him into the catacombs and finish the interment. That means for sure Cat and I will have to get onto the property.

What if messing with his remains magickally just pisses him off even more? Or somehow gives him even more power? What else could he be capable of?

CHAPTER 27
PUPPET MASTER

The eight of us form a circle on the grass, huddling together to come up with the best plan of action. Even if Colton is able to summon my dad's remains, we still need to follow it up with Cat's ability to direct her element of fire, and I'm the one who will have to help her find her way through the labyrinth of the catacombs.

I glance over at Colton. He looks as apprehensive as the rest of us, shifting his gaze to the ground and kicking at the dirt. It reminds me of the way he was when I first met him, but he's still somehow very different.

"All right, so let me get this straight. Once Colton's able to summon Lyle's remains, he'll go with Cat and Autumn to the catacombs as their protection?" Wade says, his face a blanket of seriousness as he looks to each of our faces.

I nod. "You didn't see it, but what he did was incredible. He was able to put everything on hold, like he pressed the pause button."

Wade's shoulders relax a little bit. "All right. What about the rest of us?"

"There's no reason for anyone else to put themselves in danger," Diana says. "We all stay here, out of the way."

"This is bullshit," Dominic mutters under his breath.

Diana narrows her gaze on him, shaking her head. I swear I hear her mutter, *kids*.

"Dominic's right, though. I don't like the idea of standing back and letting Autumn head into that," Wade says, shaking his head. "Even if she has Colton's protection."

Turning to him, I take his left hand in my right. "Wade, I can't have you come with me. After what happened last time, I'd be so distracted, worrying about you and making sure you're safe. I don't know what I'd do if I lost you. Please, the best thing you can do is stay here. It will help me focus on what I need to do."

His silver eyes bore into mine, trying to will me into submission. "But..." he begins.

I raise a hand to the side of his face, running it along his cheek. "There are no buts. I have to go because I'm the only one who can inter my father. The catacombs are meant for my family. This is my job."

"I can enter the catacombs, remember? Besides, I know the way, too," Wade says, his jaw hardening.

"I know. And if this were any other situation, I would welcome your company. But when things are as hostile as we've seen—I won't risk it," I say, pressing my authority on the matter. "I need you to stay here and stay safe."

Wade reaches up, dropping my hand from his face. His fingertips press against his lips as he turns away from me.

Turning to Colton, I say, "Are you absolutely sure you can do this?"

"Now that we've reached out to your dad's remains, I can sense them. It's almost as if they're an extension of me," he says, his eyes going slightly distant.

"That's your god essence," Diana offers. "Once they've become a part of you, it's hard to let go."

Colton glances her direction, nodding in understanding.

"Do you need anything else from me?" I ask.

Colton's lips tug down as he shakes his head. "No, I don't think so."

"So, assuming you Puppet Master his bones, how do we know when it's safe to head in?" Dominic asks, crossing his arms over his body. He's clearly not happy about being on the bench for this, but he's just as vulnerable as Wade and Blake.

Everyone turns their gaze to Colton. His shoulders tighten and he takes a deep breath to release them.

"Once the remains rise, I'll be able to sense the movement. At least, that's the way it was before. To know for sure if they're doing as they're told, I just need to tune in to him. Honestly, it's just like doing a meditation. We wait until he's outside the catacombs. Then, the three of us will follow," Colton says.

"Hopefully, all of this goes unnoticed by the Lemure. The entrance isn't all that far into the woods between the two properties. Once we get inside, my guess is my dad's power will diminish," I say, chewing on the side of my cheek.

"And what if it doesn't?" Wade asks, lowering his eyebrows.

"Then I'll have no choice but to start my end of the bargain early," Cat says, snapping her fingers together and lighting a fire between them.

"Are you clear on what this Flames of Eternity thing is?" Dominic asks, tipping his head to the side.

Mrs. Gilbert smiles, rubbing a circle on her daughter's upper back. "I can assure you, she does. It's one of Caitlyn's specialties."

"Mom," Cat says, rolling her eyes.

"What?" Mrs. Gilbert says, shrugging. "Don't be so modest. You've worked hard on your gifts through the years."

"Yeah, but I've only used it on the dog," Cat says, scrunching her face. She looks up, her gaze flitting around each of us. "It's a fire that's only meant for the dead. Our dog died, so I got to practice."

"But you executed it perfectly," Mrs. Gilbert says, smiling softly.

Cat grins back, her cheeks filling with color.

"I think we should get started," Diana says, eyeing the sky. "Sun's setting and it'll be dark soon. I don't know about you, but I'd rather have this over before that happens."

"Agreed," Blake says with a nod.

Taking a deep breath, Colton tips his head to the side, then walks over to the circle of salt still evident in the driveway. He raises his gaze to Cat and she nods, prancing up the stairs and heading back inside.

All of my emotions swirl, making it harder to breathe. It's barely been a day since I found out about my dad's death. And here we are, getting ready to raise his bones and turn his body into a revenant. There's something so wrong in all of it.

Slowly, each of us makes our way back to the circle, taking up our previous locations outside of it. A couple of seconds later, Cat comes back with a new jar of salt in her hands.

"Ready?" she asks, making sure to capture Colton's gaze before she begins.

He nods, kneeling down again and placing his hands on his knees. As he closes his eyes, Cat starts laying down a fresh circle of salt. When the tunnel of light erupts, locking him within it, Colton's eyes flick open. The blazing white light consumes his irises, glowing brightly.

For the longest minutes of my life, he sits there like that, completely unmoving. Each of us seems to be holding our breath and ignoring the foreboding and uneasiness swirling around us. The tension continues to build until Colton's body sways slightly from side to side.

Wade leans in and whispers in my ear. "I feel like we should all be holding hands and singing kumbaya or something."

I chuckle softly, letting the lightheartedness of his statement release some of the pressure.

Then, with eyes still white in magickal concentration, Colton's body bolts upright and begins to quake. Sweat breaks out across his forehead and his arms splay out wide. His fingers twitch, contorting at odd angles in the air.

"Colton," Cat gasps, taking a step closer to the circle. Her mother reaches out, grabbing her by the shoulders, pulling her back.

Diana narrows her gaze, holding up a hand. "Give him a minute."

As if suddenly released, Colton bends forward, clutching at the dirt in front of him. When he sits back up on his haunches, blood trickles from his left nostril. It glistens in the dying sunlight as it drops from his lip to the ground.

Mrs. Gilbert cries out, covering her mouth with her hand.

"What's happening to him?" I ask, my pulse hammering in my ears. The question is for anyone who might have an idea, but no one says a word. "Is this normal?"

Diana's concerned gaze matches my own and she shakes her head ominously.

Colton continues to jerk, but his eyes remain white and open wide.

"Someone should help him," I sputter.

Raising a hand toward me, Colton shakes his head. "No, I have him," he says breathlessly. "But there's something—*strong* magick—that doesn't like what I'm doing. It's...difficult."

"Is it my dad's Lemure?" I ask, dropping to my knees beside the circle.

Colton drops his chin to his chest and winces. "No, I don't think so. It's bigger than that. Much, much bigger."

"It's the Moirai," Diana whispers, turning her palms are upward at her side. Despite not being within a circle, her eyes match Colton's in a similar glow. "They've been punishing him for his insolence."

"So, they wanted his soul to be displaced? They wanted to make him a Lemure?" I say, my mouth dropping open.

The more I deal with the Moirai, the more I'm starting to despise them.

Diana turns her white eyes to me. "It appears so. And they have a message for you..."

The wind around us starts to pick up, tousling my hair over my shoulder. I shudder from its coolness, eyeing the treetops suspiciously.

"You know, guys, this is starting to seem like a bad idea," Dominic says, shaking his head and backing away from the circle.

Diana continues to face me, her words coming out slow and deliberate, and completely unlike her. "Until the evils of previous generations are consumed, we are prepared to slaughter the children for the sins of their ancestors. A reckoning is upon you."

Then, Diana's eyes fade in brightness, returning to their calculated and brilliant blue.

I stare at her, unsure what on earth to say to something like that.

"Lyle's remains are on their way to the catacombs. I think I'm past the worst of it now," Colton says softly. His eyelashes flutter and the glow in his eyes also dissipates. As they return to normal, he slumps forward, dropping his head to the ground, breathing hard.

Cat kicks open the circle of salt with the toe of her shoe and enters the space. Dropping down beside her brother, she wraps an arm around him.

"Are you okay, Colt?" she asks, her eyebrows weaving together.

Remaining in the same position, Colton takes a few slow inhalations before finally saying, "I don't know. I feel so...*drained*."

"Please tell me that's something that always happens

after something like this," Wade says, narrowing his gaze. "And that it goes away quickly."

Cat's face scrunches and she shakes her head like that was the dumbest statement ever. Then she huddles in, whispering in Colton's ear. He tries to raise himself back up, but slumps over, his forehead touching the dirt.

Even Diana, who's been the epitome of calm since I met her, looks shaken. Either by Colton or the information relayed through her. Or both.

"Shit, what about the rest of the plan?" Wade says, turning his wide eyes to me. "Do we nix it until he's better?"

Cat lifts her head, staring at each one of us like we attacked Colton personally. "What if this is permanent? I've never seen him like this."

Dominic snorts. "That's the least of our worries. Looks to me like we've drawn the attention of the Moirai." His lips press into a thin line and he flicks his wrists, raising his palms to the sky.

"We can't put the plan on hold," I say, shaking my head. "If anything, it's more important than ever to get this finished *now*."

"But—" Wade begins.

I cut him off with a swipe of my hand. "If we don't, we could risk my dad being trapped forever. Especially if the Moirai are sending me warnings now."

"But if we don't have Colton to keep you safe, how do you propose we go forward?" he asks with panic creeping across his features.

I bite my lip, thinking. "Wade, I hate to ask you this, but what about your dad? If we call him specifically, would he be willing to take my dad's soul without the interment?"

"It won't work," Diana says, turning her blue eyes on me. "Remember, it's the Flame of Eternity that separates him from the ties of this world and cleanses it. The Angel of Death won't want a partial soul."

I walk away from the group, raking my hands through my hair. "Dammit."

Without Colton's protection, how do finish what we started and still keep everyone safe in the process?

CHAPTER 28
DEATH WISH

If Colton is down for the count, no one can rely on his gifts to protect us from the Lemure's destructive power. But I can't let that be the end of it. We've come too far to stop now. There has to be a way to make this work.

My dad's remains are already on their way to the catacombs, and if the Moirai don't want that to happen, who knows what they'd be willing to do? We have to make sure he gets laid to rest. *Tonight.*

"What if we sent in Cat alone?" Dominic suggests, bobbing up and down with anxious energy. "She's immortal now, right?"

Everyone turns to look at Cat, who looks like she's just been told to go on stage without knowing her lines.

"She might be immortal, but she could still get lost. The tunnels of the catacombs are like a maze—and for good reason. They're magickally protected to keep out those not graced by death's gifts," I say, floating my gaze around the group. "If anyone goes in who's not worthy—

they can be lost forever, or find themselves in some form of Purgatory."

The tension that descends is thick, and everyone has the same air of restlessness. We know we have to make a move, but we don't want to make another mistake. Not even Dominic. Nearly losing Wade was bad enough.

"But wasn't Cat in the catacombs last semester?" Wade asks. "Maybe Dominic is onto something here."

"Not exactly. Remember, that was her Fetch. It was just a piece of her that had splintered in her resurrection," I say, flicking my gaze over to her. "Technically, she didn't even have physical form. So..."

"But now that the Fetch is a part of Cat, wouldn't that mean she could still enter?" Colton asks, his jaw hardening. He leans back, pressing the side of his head to the wooden pillar keeping up the porch roof.

My forehead creases. "Both have obviously been touched by death. Cat, because she literally died, and Wade because..." I flick my gaze to him, and he stares back at me with wide eyes. "Well, you know."

"Huh?" Blake says, quirking an eyebrow.

But the rest of them all nod their heads knowingly.

Cat's face scrunches and she walks over to me. Then she reaches out, taking my hands in hers. "I never did get to say sorry for everything that happened. I didn't know I was...*broken*. I never would have done any of those things she—"

"I know," I say, squeezing her hands. "None of that matters right now. What matters is you're here and helping me to set some things right with my dad. So, thank you."

"Always," Cat says, bending forward and wrapping her arms around my neck.

I close my eyes, wrapping my arms around her waist and leaning into her embrace. This semester has been so hard, and I didn't realize just how much I missed her bright, bubbly presence.

"Do you think Abigail is okay? I mean, with the Lemure in charge of things over there, does that mean he's overrun her?" Wade asks as he paces in front of the porch. "And if she's okay... Do you think she could help us? Maybe distract him for us?"

My eyebrows rise, and I step away from Cat. "Honestly, I don't know. She was the one thing holding him back. But I haven't seen her since last night. It's safe to assume he's done something to her."

"How was she able to contain him before?" Diana asks, leaning against the railing of the porch. "From what I understand, a Lemure's energy is a lot to bear. Especially once they get going."

"It is," I say, thinking back to the recent experiences. "I'm not sure what she did, but I think they're on a more level playing field."

"What do you mean?" Wade asks.

"It's like they're on the same energetic plane or some-thing. It's easier to interact with each other than it is with us. Anytime they have to manifest or expend a lot of energy in the physical realm, it tires them out. But when-ever I've astral-projected into the catacombs, Abigail has always seemed more vibrant, more real to me. I don't know. Maybe this just sounds stupid."

"No, I think there's something here we can use," Diana says, her blue eyes going distant.

"If you were to astral-project, would you be able to reach out to Abigail? Connect with her somehow to coordinate a plan?" Cat asks, walking over to the steps and taking a seat.

I walk a few feet away, thinking. "I could try. But even on the best of days, she doesn't always come to me when I summon her. I wish there was just a way I could get through to my dad. Help him realize—" I press my fingertips to my lips as if they just spoke the secret we've been searching for.

Turning around, I catch Diana's eye. Slowly, she smirks at me.

"I could astral-project into the house and summon the Lemure," I say. "He's been trying to maintain his hold on reality to protect me. He might be deteriorating now, but his energy is tied to me. When he realizes I'm there, he'll want to connect. Then we could send Wade and Cat into the catacombs while he's distracted."

Speaking the words out loud sounds even crazier than they sounded in my head.

"I don't know about this, Autumn. How do you know it will work?" Wade asks, clearly not convinced. "I mean, you've never astral-projected from this far away—let alone do something like this."

"What other choice do we have?" I ask. "It may not be the best of plans, but at least it gives us a chance. We can't just sit around here and wait."

"From what you've said, even for a ghost, Abigail is powerful," Dominic says, "But if you're right and the Lemure has overpowered her—what makes you think you stand a chance?"

"Thanks for the vote of confidence, Dom," I spit back.

"It's not that. It's just—" he stands up, scratching at his forehead. "Look, I don't want you to get hurt. The astral realm isn't one to take lightly. I've tried to master it and it can be..." He glances down at the ground. "It has its own set of challenges."

Wade takes a step forward, his voice deep with worry. "Like what?"

"Like, she could get *trapped*," Dominic says, making a face. "If the Lemure gets ahold of her and doesn't let her go—" He shudders away the remainder of the thought.

"What happens then?" Wade presses.

"To us, she becomes a vegetable. But to her consciousness—she's in whatever hell the Lemure can conjure for her," Dominic says grimly.

"Then I make sure that doesn't happen," I say, straightening my shoulders. "My dad needs me. We don't have any other choice. So here's how this is going to go down..." I pause, waiting for everyone's total attention. "The remains will be at the catacombs soon. Colton will let everyone know when they're in place. Cat and Wade, I need you to get them to the central chamber. You're the only ones who can do this besides me. I'll astral-project to draw my dad's attention until I know the remains are safely inside. From what I understand, having the remains in the catacombs should weaken the Lemure enough for me to join you. Then, you wait for me. Everyone else—I want you to stay here. And stay safe."

"How will we know if your distraction is successful?" Wade asks, his jaw set. "I won't leave you to fend for yourself if it's not even working."

He's clearly not happy about my plan.

I lift my gaze, sweeping it from Dominic to Diana.

"We have two powerful psychics here. I'm pretty sure they'll be able to work it out."

Wade's mouth snaps shut. He knows I'm right. Diana was even able to get Cat and Colton back here in the nick of time. She knew they'd be needed before I even did.

Turning to Colton, I ask, "How long do we have?"

Colton closes his eyes and drops his head in concentration. "Minutes maybe. He's almost there."

I nod, brushing off my jeans. "Good. Then, it's time." I step away, looking for a comfortable place to sit. My eyes lock on a set of Adirondack chairs facing the water and take a couple steps toward them.

Wade grabs hold of my wrist, pulling me up short. "Are you really sure about this?"

I look into his scared eyes and exhale. "I'm not sure of anything. But I know I have to make this work. For my dad...and for you. It's our safest bet. I refuse to send you into this unprotected. If astral-projecting might give you a chance, I have to try. Plus, it's a helluva lot safer than if I were to go in this form," I say, sweeping my hands down my sides.

"Not the way Dominic tells it. Besides, I'm not worried about me," Wade says, pressing his lips tightly.

"You should be. This is your one life and I won't let it end early because you chose to be with me. I won't let your dad be right," I say, bending in and brushing my lips to his.

"You seem to forget this is *your* one life, too. I swear, you have some sort of death wish, woman," he says, swallowing hard.

I pause, taking a moment to think about his words. "Maybe you're right. Death does seem to follow me around." Slowly, I look up into his worried eyes and smirk.

"This isn't funny," he mumbles.

"I know," I whisper, holding my chin up.

He places his hands on either side of my face, drawing me to him. His lips press down, making my skin buzz and my pulse quicken. As he pulls back, he whispers, "You better be damn careful."

"I will. Now, go. I need to concentrate. Get Cat and be ready to leave as soon as Colton gives you the signal. I promise, I'll join you as soon as I can," I say, pressing my forehead to his.

He nods, placing one last kiss on my lips before turning away from me.

"All right, ladies and gentlemen, showtime," Dominic says, rubbing his hands together.

I sweep my eyes over the group one final time. Everyone is here for me—for *my family*.

I hope I don't let them down.

Hopefully, it goes the way we want, but if it doesn't, it won't be for lack of trying.

I continue to the Adirondack chairs in the middle of the yard and take a seat, resting back. The view is of the pond, but it's more obscured than my view. There are a lot more trees and plants growing wild between here and the shore. In the distance, though, I can still make out my house.

Taking a deep breath, I lower my shoulders, trying to get into a more relaxed state.

I've only ever done this while inside the resurrection chamber, and never in search of something that could tear me apart.

God, I hope I can reach the part of my dad that's still human.

I hear footsteps come up behind me, crunching in the grass.

Diana kneels down beside my chair and pats my arm. "This is a brave thing you're doing."

"Thanks," I mutter. "I don't feel all that brave."

She locks her piercing blue eyes with mine, holding them until I squirm in the seat. Then, her eyebrows knit together, and she says, "Bravery often masks itself as uncertainty. At least in the beginning. It isn't always easy to do the right thing. Especially when it means advancing through the unknown." Standing back up, she pats my shoulder as she walks away. "Good luck, Autumn. I'll be watching from this side and keeping a close eye on you."

I stare out into the pond, not really looking at it, as I listen to the sound of her footsteps make their way back to the group.

Colton's words, though distant, come to me loud and clear. "He's at the catacombs."

Exhaling slowly, I lean my head back and close my eyes. *It's time.*

CHAPTER 29

SPLINTERING

I inhale slowly, listening to the sounds of my friends chattering behind me as some of them gear up to leave. Their words blend together, then fade out as I focus on the sounds of the pond creatures. Frogs sing at the edge of the water and various birds call out to each other somewhere in the distance. I let their songs settle my nerves and calm my brain until I lift up and out of it all.

My consciousness spreads out, blanketing the space around my body until I completely separate from it. Unlike my other astral attempts back at the house, there's no distinct direction to follow, no pathway to take that will guide me. Instead, I float upward like a balloon no longer tethered by its string.

At first, it's disconcerting, but I can't help but be in awe of the beauty in colors from high in the sky. The view is breathtaking, actually. Not only can I see the pond and my house, but the entire town and the roads leading to and from it like the veins bringing lifeblood to the city.

I'm absolutely dazzled by the synergy of it all. Then, something catches my attention—people walking through the spaces between autumn-painted trees. The movement is curious from this vantage point as they dart in and out of the trees. I watch them for a moment, mesmerized. Something about them is familiar... Before I consciously make the decision to move toward them, I float closer. As I do so, I realize I know all of them. In those seconds, I snap back into the awareness of my mission and why I can fly.

Turning my gaze from my friends, I face Blackwood Manor. The rooftop of my home glimmers in the setting sun and a trail of gold cascades across the pond from the sun behind me.

I need to protect them.

They've begun to move before I've even done my part. What are they thinking?

All I do is think about being inside the manor, and my consciousness condenses in on itself as if being pushed through a funnel and spat back out. I find myself in the manor, standing in the entryway, and facing the grand staircase.

The house rings of emptiness, but somewhere hidden in the shadows, a combination of malevolence and terror lingers in hibernation. With every fiber of my astral being, I know my father is here, *waiting*.

Forgetting I lack form, I walk around the small entry table and eye the shadows as they undulate with anticipation. As I move deeper into the entry, his energy pools together, like a terminator who's been melted down and is starting to reform.

My father isn't the only one I sense, though. Abigail is

also here, but her energy is scattered. It's as though the frequency of her spirit has been put slightly out of phase, or she's tuned into the wrong spirit channel.

I don't know how close the others are to the catacombs, but I do know I need to act quickly.

"Dad?" I call out.

My voice echoes in the large space and I pause, looking around at the walls and wondering if my voice can be heard in the real world, too? Or if it's all happening on the astral plane.

"Autumn?" a voice calls from the staircase. My dad suddenly appears in mid-stride, as if he was walking down the stairs the whole time. "What are you doing here? It's not safe," he says.

"I came to talk to you," I say, taking a few steps toward him before I stop.

There's nothing about him that would suggest he's the entity causing so much pain and damage. Yet, there's an undercurrent of anger, ready to burst out and it makes me step back.

"You shouldn't be here," Dad says, confusion and concern clouding his features. "Things aren't safe here."

"I know," I say, nodding. "That's why I came here to talk to you. I needed to know you were okay."

Dad chuckles softly. It's a strange, feral sound and nothing like the heartfelt laughter I remember.

My pulse begins to race and I take another step back. He edges forward, following me like a predator stalking its prey.

"As you can see, I'm fine," Dad says, holding his hands out wide. "But I'm sure that's not all you needed, now was it?" His face contorts into a grimace and he stretches his neck, clicking it back and forth like his features are a glove he's just tried on.

"Well, I—"

I no sooner start to speak than Dad's specter is within inches of my face. His blue eyes lock with my own and there's a panic unlike anything I've ever seen hidden within them. The Lemure is winning the fight inside him and he's utterly terrified.

A visceral snarl erupts from his mouth and I squelch a scream. Flaring my nostrils and standing my ground, I say, "Don't do this, Dad. This isn't you."

"How would you know what is me? You've barely said two words to me for a decade," he spits back. The venom in his words hit their mark, making my heart hurt and my soul ache.

He's not wrong, and I know somewhere, even within the truest parts of him, this is a thought that's plagued him. Even when he was trying to protect me.

"I know. I'm so sorry. I should have been better at reaching out," I sputter, shaking away the despair welling up inside me. "But I love you. You have to know that."

He scoffs, circling around me. "You know nothing of love. You think you do, but you don't."

If I were in my body, tears would be welling in my eyes at such a frontal attack. I came here to distract him, to keep him occupied so the others could deliver his remains —but I never anticipated a psychological attack.

Even his Lemure fury would be better than this.

"Dad, what have you done to Abigail?" I ask, hoping the switch in tactic will soften his energy. "I feel her here."

As if suddenly appalled, he recoils. "It's all her fault. None of this would have happened if it wasn't for her."

"But what did you do to her?" I press, this time reaching out for him.

He recoils, pulling his hand back as if touching me would burn him. The blue in his eyes deepens, darkening to the point of turning purple as he stares at my hand.

"You should stay away from me," he warns, his face tilting away from mine. "This is not the place for you."

"I know what happened. I'm here to help you," I say, trying to keep my voice calm and steady. "I read your journal."

A flash of insight sweeps across his features, but fades away before it can take root.

"There's nothing left for us. The Blackwood family will end with us," he hisses. "You should have stayed away. I never should have summoned you..." Dad tugs at his hair, pulling large tufts of his strawberry blond strands out. He stares down at his clenched fists, his eyes wide with horror.

"Dad, you're stronger than this. Don't let the Lemure win," I whisper, watching his every move.

His dark eyes tip upward, taking me in for a moment.

I hold my breath, unsure what's going on in his mind. He's so unpredictable, and without knowing what he's truly capable of in this form, worry begins to gnaw at my reserve.

Maybe Wade was right. Maybe this wasn't the best idea after all.

"Dad, please stay calm. I'm trying to help you," I say, holding out my hands. "You can fight this."

An absurd laugh erupts from his lips. "Fight fate? You truly are out of your league."

His fingers fly to his mouth, as if saying the word *fate*

suddenly reminded him about the Moirai. His features writhe in agony, and all at once, his skin melts away from his face. He arches backward at an odd angle, contorting into something dark and grotesque. The shape of his eyes elongates and his skin is replaced by an inky-black film. The joints in his arms and legs twist and grow until he looms over me.

"No, you're mine. I won't let them have you..." the Lemure wails. "They can't have you if they can't find you."

Holding gnarly black hands out in front of him, a ball of red energy grows between his palms. The Lemure mutters under his breath as his focus turns solely on the growing ball of light between his fingers. As it gets bigger, he pulls his hands apart like he's playing some sort of magickal game of cat's cradle.

Without warning, my entire astral being feels like it's being torn apart from the inside out. The room darkens, then shifts in and out of focus as he continues to mutter to himself. I stumble forward, trying to reach out for him, but my feet sink into the ground as if they've melted down and become a part of the floor somehow.

"Dad, please, no—I don't want to stay with you. I need to go back," I cry out, clutching at the air and struggling to maintain my sense of self.

The room spins and it's almost as if everything I am is melting away, deconstructing atom by atom.

"You heard the lady. She said no," someone says from somewhere in the room, though I can't tell where.

The dark figure of the Lemure spins around. With his concentration no longer on the ball of energy, the room comes back into focus. Everything that I am pulls back together, and I'm no longer melting into the floor.

Dominic somehow rushes to me, bringing in a wave of fresh energy and light where only moments ago was utter darkness.

"How—?" I sputter.

"Forget that. We need to get out of here," Dominic says. "Time to pull the plug."

"No, we have to protect the others," I say.

"Others?" The Lemure snarls. Its dark-purple eyes widen, and fury erupts across its quivering body. "What others?" Tipping his nose to the sky like some kind of animal, he sniffs at the air.

"The others need you alive, remember? Time to go," Dominic repeats, tipping his head to the door.

I wave him off, shaking my head. "But what about him?" I stare at the mutated version of my father, unable to stop the well of compassion bubbling up inside me. "Will he be bound to his remains?"

Dominic's eyes reflect the same confusion I feel and he shudders. "I don't know, Autumn. It's not my area of expertise."

Panic spreads through me like wildfire, and I'm struck by total insight. He can't stay separated from his body for this to work. I know what I need to do. I was never meant to simply distract him. I'm meant to bring his soul—*pieces and all*—to the catacombs. This was...

Fate.

The word floats through my mind, chilling me to the very core.

"What others?" The Lemure demands again. Its size expands, darkening the entryway and pulling all of the light with it. "What have you done?"

"Nothing. I didn't mean—" I begin, putting on my best performance and trying to sound as terrified as possible.

"Where are they? How did I not know?" he growls, turning to face Dominic. "They can't come in here and take you away from me. This is *my* home."

The Lemure raises one of his gnarly hands, swinging it back to attack Dominic.

Rushing forward, I grab my Dad's mangled body. Wrapping my arms around his torso, I press my cheek to the Lemure's cold, almost clammy, chest and focus on the love I feel for my dad. How grateful I am that he loved me and my mother as much as he did.

Grateful for his sacrifice—even if it failed.

Then, with my mind centered on just one final wish, everything around me vanishes from view.

CHAPTER 30
ALWAYS BE WITH YOU

When I open my eyes, my dad and I are no longer in the middle of the entryway of the manor. Dominic isn't with us, either. Instead, it's just the two of us. We stand beneath the archway leading into the catacombs' central hub, which glows softly from the torches on the walls. The symbols on the archway twinkle in bright oranges and blues, waiting, as I now know, to see if my dad's soul is worthy.

"What is this place?" Dad asks, his voice a hushed whisper beside me.

I turn to see the distorted and darkened version of the Lemure fade away. He transforms before my eyes, as if there's a plug in the center of his body and someone's pulled the drain. When the last of darkness has faded, his blue eyes fill with wonder as his gaze extends beyond me.

"Welcome to the catacombs, Lyle," Abigail says, stepping out from one of the dark tunnels beyond. "You've waited a long while."

Dad's lips falter, slipping into a frown as his forehead creases. "Abigail, I'm so sorry..."

She waves a hand dismissively. "None of this should be yours to shoulder alone, Lyle. You are but a byproduct of the centuries. Come, it is time to absolve you," Abigail says, waving us into the inner sanctum.

Tilting his head to the side, Dad looks my direction with the question written across his face.

I nod, stepping into the central room as I extend a hand to him. "Come on—it's time for you to rest."

His shoulders stiffen as he looks down at the space separating the inner chamber from the outer tunnel. Lifting his right foot, he crosses the threshold. A deep rumbling starts off low and grows louder. The walls rattle, sifting dust that floats from its crevasses into the room like a blanket of smoke.

Dad steps the rest of the way into the chamber, his eyes glued on the walls around him.

"This is..."—he sighs contently—"*beautiful*."

I narrow my eyes, confused.

Abigail smiles. "I wish dearly to see it as you do."

Dad's eyebrows tip up in the middle as confusion blossoms across his features.

Abigail turns to me, her features softening. "To you and I, we see this place of stone and earth. But I know not what the others behold. Perhaps it's different for each, as there are many accounts."

Turning back to my dad, I reach out for his hand. This time, as I take his spectral appendage, there's no fear hidden in his eyes. He takes it, squeezing gently.

"What do you see?" I ask him.

"It's the most beautiful garden I've ever seen. Flowers,

trees, and animals are everywhere. There's a pond over there," Dad raises his free hand, pointing beyond Abigail. "The swans are circling by a willow tree just over there. I always wanted a willow tree..." His eyes go distant and his chin tips downward. When he looks back up again, he turns to Abigail. "This isn't real? Is it?"

Abigail walks over to him, her dress swaying with her movements but never touching the ground the way it really should.

"For you, it is but the only reality you need to focus on," she whispers, placing a hand along his cheek. "I wish I could have saved you from this untimely passage, grandson."

"That makes two of us," Dad says, shifting his gaze from Abigail to me. Sighing, he walks my direction. "Autumn, I never meant for any of this to happen. I had hoped..."

"It's okay, Dad. I know," I whisper. My chest suddenly feels very heavy, despite having no physical form. The thought makes me pause, curious about how the feelings of physicality can linger so strongly in this form.

Dad's jaw tightens, and his expression darkens—only this time, it's out of concern and not Lemure rage. "I wish I could have protected you from all of this."

"It's not up to you to protect me," I say, shaking my head.

"But it is. Pretty sure it's in the parental handbook," he says, narrowing his gaze.

My eyes widen. "There's a parental handbook?"

Chuckling, Dad's head drops a bit. "No, sweetheart. I wish there was, though. It might have made things a bit easier."

I flit my gaze from my dad to Abigail, who simply watches us thoughtfully.

"What happens now?" Dad asks, turning to Abigail.

"You'll be called home soon," she says. Though she smiles, there's a hint of sorrow hidden in her features.

He nods, as if this makes total sense to him. "How long?"

I turn to Abigail, who lifts her chin and says, "Should the others manage to maneuver the maze, we have but minutes. Your remains have entered the catacombs."

Dad turns to me. "Autumn, there's so much I wish I could say to you."

"It's okay," I say, stepping forward and wrapping my arms around him.

He returns my embrace, holding on so tightly I almost feel like I'm five again.

"Sweetheart, you do need to be careful, though. The Moirai—"

"I know," I say, pulling back from his hug.

His forehead furrows and he tilts his head. "You know?"

"Yeah, thanks to you," I say, trying to keep myself from succumbing to the panic and sadness rising inside of me.

"Promise me you'll be careful. Aisa and her sisters, they're formidable and they won't bend to compromise," Dad says. "It's up to you to break this curse, sweetheart. I wish that weren't the case, but it is."

Footsteps and voices echo into the inner sanctum from not too far away. Some of the pressure that's been building during the wait falls away. Cat and Wade have managed to find their way through the tunnels after all.

I exhale in relief. Wade is carrying my dad's remains in

his arms, but they're covered by a black sheet. I don't know what I'd do if I had to come face to face with what the Moirai have done to him. I want to remember him the way I see him here, now.

Wade steps into the circular chamber, his eyes full of trepidation. "This is the place, right?" he asks, readjusting the load in his arms.

"Don't look at me. I barely remember what happened. It's like a dream and I've been awake too long to keep hold of it," Cat says, shrugging.

"I know the feeling. It took a lot longer to get this far than I thought it would," Wade says. "All of the tunnels started looking the same."

Cat nods. "I think that was the point."

I step away from my dad and Abigail, reaching out to Wade. My hand goes right through his arm and I take a step back. "Oh my god, they can't see us, can they?"

Abigail shakes her head. "Neither of them have the sight."

"How will they know when to summon the Fires of Eternity?" I blurt out, suddenly afraid my entire plan is about to fall apart.

"Of that, I am not certain," Abigail says.

"Is there a way to make contact? How can I reach them?" I say, waving my hand in front of Wade's face. He doesn't even flinch.

"Without the gift to see the dead, it's all but impossible to reach them. These walls do not allow for manifestations," Abigail says, her eyebrows knitting together.

"What are you talking about? Cat's Fetch took over Wade—"

Abigail's face is a stern warning. "And you believe such

an action would be wise? It took the Angel of Death to push her aside."

My gaze drops to the stone floor. "Oh, right."

Suddenly, the circular chamber is flooded by the sound of a ringtone blaring. Cat scrambles, digging her cell phone out of her coat pocket.

She holds the phone up to her ear as she says, "Hello?" For a moment, she holds utterly still. Then, shooting a sideways glance at Wade, she put one hand against her other ear, her eyes narrowing with her focus. "Diana? I—I can barely hear you. What are you saying? You're cutting out."

For a moment, Cat holds very still, her eyes searching the space in front of her as she listens to whatever is being said on the other end of the phone. Then, after what feels like forever, she nods to herself.

"Thanks, Diana. Understood," she says, dropping the phone and hitting the end button.

"What is it? What did she say?" Wade asks, his silver eyes flashing.

"Dominic entered the astral plane to help Autumn. She was... *struggling*. But he says Autumn and the Lemure vanished a few minutes ago. He's not sure what happened to them," Cat says, her eyes reflecting the same worry evident on Wade's face.

"Shit, we never should have let her do this. What if she's trapped, like Dominic said?" Wade says, his voice heavy with worry.

"If she's trapped, it's because of the Lemure. That really leaves us no other choice—we need to burn the remains and hope that it does what we want it to," Cat says, inhaling sharply.

"What if we're wrong?" Wade says, blinking wildly.

"You're not wrong," I say, reaching for him and wishing he could hear me.

Cat's face hardens. "Then we cross that bridge when we get to it. Diana thinks—"

"I don't give a damn what Diana thinks," Wade cries.

"We need to do something. I need to let him know I'm here—that I'm okay," I say, turning back to Abigail.

She shakes her head, holding up a hand.

"We don't have any other choice, Wade. We need to finish this and check in on Autumn. The only way we can help her now is to do what we came here to do," Cat spits back. She holds out her arms, flicking her fingertips at him. "Hand the body over. I can handle the rest."

Wade stares at her for a moment, but tips his head and does as he's asked. The battle to know for sure if I'm okay has won out in his mind.

"You're going to want to take a step back," she warns, her face the epitome of seriousness.

Wade nods, moving backward as he stares at her.

Taking a step back myself, I sigh in relief. I cast a quick glance in Abigail's direction, smiling at her as she merely tips her chin in acknowledgement. It's like she knew he'd cave the whole time.

Cat cradles my dad's bones, still wrapped in the sheet, close to her body. She lowers her chin and closes her eyes. For a few seconds, she does nothing but take deep, deliberate breaths.

Under her breath, she begins to whisper. At first, I can't make out the words, but after the third incantation, her head tips back and her eyes glow with the energy of fire blazing against the darkness of her irises. Fire rolls out of them, growing in intensity, as if her eyes could consume you simply by looking in her direction.

"Fili mi requiem. In ignibus uri. Somnus in aeternum," she chants over and over.

All of a sudden, the fire in her eyes is drowned out by the fire that erupts all over her body, consuming both her and the bundle in her hands. The blaze is so intense I take another huge step back.

"Was this meant to happen?" I cry out, twisting to face Abigail.

She holds out a hand, lifting a single finger and urging me to wait.

The flame changes colors from bright orange to a deep, brilliant crimson. Both Wade and I hold up an arm, shielding our eyes, but refusing to look away.

As the fire dies back, it returns to its original orange and yellow, then settles into the purest white I've ever seen.

"Fili mi requiem. In ignibus uri. Somnus in aeternum," Cat continues to chant until the fire pulls back, settling once again in her eyes.

As it fades completely, not a single part of Cat is singed or burnt, but the bundle of bones that were in her arms scatters to the ground, nothing more than a pile of glowing cinders.

My mouth drops open as I stare at the power and capability of Cat. I knew what she could do with fire, but I had no idea just how impressive she is.

As if an enormous burden is released from his shoulders, my dad sighs.

"Is that...everything?" Wade asks, holding out a hand and helping Cat get to her feet.

She nods. "Everything I can do. I don't know about the interment stuff. We'll need Autumn for all of that."

"Let's go find her, then," Wade says, his face full of determination.

"Agreed," she says, sweeping her hand out and letting him take the lead.

The two of them disappear the way they came, and I'm left alone again with my dad and Abigail. The air is heavy with anticipation as I realize there's still more that needs to be done.

"Why is he still here?" I ask, turning to Abigail. "Shouldn't he have been taken?"

Abigail's thoughtful smile eases my mind. Then, she closes her eyes and slowly raises her arms and her fingertips splay open, almost as if she's about to conduct a symphony. And maybe in a way, she does. With the simple gesture, the embers and ashes rise off the stone floor, floating through the air like glimmering red smoke.

I step away, following their journey into one of the tunnels I haven't been in before. The ashes float through the darkness of the catacombs, illuminating one of the empty stone platforms as they come to a rest. When every last granule is in place, my father's name transcribes itself into the stone above him.

"Hail all gods, goddesses, and protectors of the Temple of the Soul—each who weigh heaven and earth in delicate balance, and in honor of the Fates' grand plan. Oh mighty Death, taker of life, I deliver unto you the body of my father before me. Ashes to ashes, dust to dust, bless him please, so he may slumber in eternal rest," I whisper, remembering the sacred words of interment.

A powerful energy rocks the space, sealing off the tomb; protecting him now...and forever.

I stare at the tomb for a moment, holding my breath, scared to go back into the room and face what I know lies ahead of me. Struggling to hold back tears, I close my eyes, pressing my lips tight and swallowing hard.

Suddenly, Dad is by my side. He rests his cold hand on my shoulder and waits. When I finally turn to face him, his eyes are alight with childish wonder.

"Do you hear that music?" he asks. "It's absolutely..."

"Beautiful?" I say, finishing his thought.

Dad shakes his head slowly. "*Haunting.*" For a moment, his eyes go distant. "But also beautiful, yes."

"Those are the songs of rebirth," Abigail whispers, now beside us.

I shake my head, tears brimming in my eyes. "No, Dad. I'm sorry. I think it's playing just for you."

"I wish you could hear it," he says, still engrossed in the melody.

The tears I'd been trying to hold back slide down my cheeks and I hold back a sob. "I'll hear it one day."

Dad's gaze pulls back into focus, taking me in again. For the longest time, he stares at me with a sense of wonder and confusion shimmering through his expressions. "Why are you crying?" he finally asks.

I wipe at my face, wishing an astral form couldn't feel these emotions that practically tear me apart. "I'm going to miss you so much. I wish..." My words are choked out by the sob that wracks through my body. "I wish we had more time."

Realization forms across my dad's face and he walks up to me.

"I'll always be with you, sweet girl," Dad says, pulling me in close. "I love you, Autumn. Never forget that."

"I love you, Dad. I really do," I say, clutching at the back of his shirt and holding him close.

Suddenly, an inky black cloud billows out into the circular space of the inner sanctum a few yards away. Instantly, I know what this means and I've never been more relieved—and more terrified.

Will he take my dad's soul? Or will he be like the Moirai and hold a grudge against me and my family?

CHAPTER 31
CHIN UP

The Angel of Death steps out of his dark portal, entering the catacombs with a couple of natural strides.

Dad steps forward as if drawn to him like a magnet.

The Angel of Death's silver eyes glimmer in the low light of the catacombs, and he reaches out for my dad as if he's a long-lost friend.

"Lyle Blackwood," he says. "I had wondered if we'd ever cross paths again."

My dad reaches out, wrapping his arms around Wade's dad. After a short embrace, he slaps Wade's dad on the back and steps away. "Good to see you, old friend."

At first, my eyebrows tug inward, but understanding isn't far behind. They knew each other thirty years ago, the last time revenants were raised in this town. It was their combined efforts that eliminated their threat the last time. It makes sense that a friendship of some sort may have grown between them.

"Indeed," he says, nodding his head in agreement. Then

the Angel of Death chuckles. "I had hoped you'd look more like a shriveled old man by the time I saw you again, though."

Dad glances down, opening his hands out wide. "Sorry to disappoint."

"Well, at least you have more gray than I do."

This time, it's Dad's turn to laugh. "Yes, well, it doesn't matter much now, I'd wager."

"Very true," the Angel says. His eyes flit briefly to me, then return to my dad. "Are you ready? Or do you need a moment?"

Looking over his shoulder at me and Abigail, Dad steps away from the Angel of Death.

"I have to go now, sweetheart," Dad whispers, pulling me into a final embrace.

"I know," I whisper into his shirt. Tears again flood my eyes, no matter how hard I try to hold them back.

Abigail keeps her distance, her hands folded gently in front of her.

After a moment, Dad places his hands on my shoulders, pulling me back.

"You're strong, Autumn. I know you'll get through what comes next. Keep a watchful eye. The Moirai are coming, and this is a game we can't win. At least not with the rules as they are. You'll need to be resourceful," he says, turning his gaze to Abigail. "Thank goodness you have some key players on your side."

"She is quite special," Abigail says. "I will do what I can to protect her."

Dad nods his head, shooting her a lopsided smile. "Thank you."

Abigail tips her head.

"It's time, Lyle," Wade's dad says, taking a step toward him. "Walk with me."

Without another word, Dad places a crooked index finger under my chin, lifting it up. Smiling softly, he turns back to the Angel of Death.

"I'm ready," he says.

The two of them walk away from the central chamber, making their way down the tunnel where my father's body now rests. It's almost as if they're just taking a walk in a park, or a garden. And maybe to Dad, they are. Their conversation is light and friendly as they disappear into the darkness.

I swipe at my cheeks, batting at the tears still falling.

Abigail walks over to me, wrapping her arms around me. "I am so sorry, my dear one."

The best I can manage is a guttural sob as I return her embrace.

"I do so wish I could say this was the end of our family's torment. But you must return to your body. You must be prepared for all that lies ahead. The path will not be easy and I make no promises of your success," she whispers.

"Gee, thanks for the vote of confidence," I mutter, stepping back.

"However," she says, holding my gaze. "I am certain that if anyone can break this curse, it will be you."

"How can you be so sure?" I ask, scrunching my face.

"Because you are more powerful than you know."

My eyes flutter open and I'm consumed by darkness. I'm no longer inside the torch-lit catacombs; the sun has set long ago, and the stars twinkle in an inky canopy above me. High in the sky, the full moon's silver light floods the grounds, illuminating the yard.

"Autumn," a soothing voice says from somewhere over my shoulder, "how are you feeling?"

My head lolls to the side as I look into the concerned gaze of Diana.

"I'm...okay. I think," I say, doing a quick inventory. Everything feels like it's in place and coming back down from the crazy ordeal I've just witnessed.

While nothing will ever be the same again, I also know this time around, things could have been a lot worse. But there's a certain amount of peace knowing that my dad's no longer suffering. He's free.

"You did it," Diana smiles, patting my arm. Like a momma bear, there's a sense of pride filtering through her features despite looking like she could be a classmate—not a mentor.

I smile softly and clear my throat. "Yeah, I guess we did."

Glancing to my left, I see Dominic seated in the other Adirondack chair with his hands behind his head. To his left, Colton and Blake stand by with wide, expectant eyes.

"So, looks like you managed to find your way back," Dominic says. "Gotta admit, I'm kinda relieved."

I grin. "Thanks. I'm relieved to be back, too. And..." My forehead scrunches as I search for the words. "*Thank you*. Thank all of you."

My gaze falls on Colton's worried face and I stand up. Walking over to him, I throw my arms around him, barely acknowledging the way my arms burst into the strange blue and orange flames.

"Had you not been able to get my dad's remains to the

catacombs…" I whisper. "None of this would have worked."

"You would have found a way," he says, shooting me a lopsided grin.

I shake my head. "I don't know if I would have. After how hard that was—letting go of my dad—I don't think I would have been able to handle physically being around his remains."

Colton's lips press into a thin line and his chin tips upward. "I'm glad I was at least able to do that much."

"Don't sell yourself short. It was a lot," I say, releasing him.

Twisting around, I search the darkness for Wade and Cat. "Where are the others? Are they not back yet?"

Diana shakes her head. "Not yet, but I'm sure they will be soon."

I nod. "I can't believe this is all over. It feels sorta…"—I pause, trying to find the right word—"*surreal*."

"It's not over yet," Diana says, her face darkening. "Your family has pissed off some entities in high places. Dark days are still coming."

My eyebrows tug in and I frown. "Yeah, I know," I say, tracing my fingertips over my lips.

"Autumn?" Wade's voice filters through the darkness.

I look up, searching for him. The brush rustles as he races through the trees, then breaks into a sprint when he hits the yard. As soon as he reaches me, his warm embrace consumes me and I sink into him, wishing we could stay this way forever.

"Are you all right? You're not hurt?" he asks, pulling back and checking me over.

"I'm fine. Everything's fine—thanks to you both," I say,

reaching out to Cat as she walks up behind Wade. Hugging her as well, I'm so thankful to have them both on my side and in my life.

They've risked so much for me and I don't know how I'll ever repay them. *Any of them.*

I pull back, my gaze floating around the group of misfits standing with me.

This may be my family's fight, but I know now that we're all somehow bound together to fight all of this. I don't know how it will all play out yet, but I do know that I need them.

The porch light flicks on and Mrs. Gilbert walks out, wiping her hands on an apron.

"Come on, everyone. It's late. Time to come inside. I've made up some stew. I'm sure you're starving," she says, standing at the top of the porch stairs.

"Oh, yes, please," Dominic says, bounding up the stairs two at a time.

Mrs. Gilbert chuckles, turning around and following him.

One by one the others all head inside. Wade and I linger, letting them all do their thing.

"I was so scared. I couldn't stop thinking about Dominic's warning," Wade whispers, running the back of his hand along my cheek.

"You didn't have to worry," I say, closing my eyes and leaning into his touch.

As much as I thought I could feel with my astral body, there's still nothing like the actual physical sensations—especially those of his touch.

"Never gonna happen," he whispers.

"I don't even know if an astral form could possess someone," I say.

"Let's hope we never have to find out," he whispers. "Come on, let's get inside."

Nodding, we turn to make our way up the steps.

Suddenly, an inky black cloud forms in the space between the porch steps and the doorway. Wade's dad steps out of it, blocking our way into the Gilberts' house.

"Dad?" Wade says, surprise clear in the simple word.

My heart thrums in my chest and I race up the steps. "My dad—?"

The Angel of Death holds out a hand, stopping me in my tracks. "Your father has ascended. I'm not here for you."

I turn to face Wade with wide eyes. His expression is just as concerned as mine.

"It was a simple request—stay away from the necromancer. Why could you not listen?" Wade's father asks. His eyes flash with concern more than anger, but I can't figure out why.

"You know why," Wade says, reaching for my hand. "I love her—and I'm not going anywhere."

"Please, I need you to reconsider," his dad says, inhaling sharply.

Wade snickers, shaking his head. "No, I don't need to reconsider anything. I'm right where I'm supposed to be." He looks over his shoulder at me, smiling.

I swallow hard, my heart constricting. I love him so much. More than I ever should. But not more than he deserves.

"Wade, I warned you... I tried to reason with you, but you didn't listen," his dad says grimly.

"That's new, how?" Wade chuckles softly.

"This is no laughing matter, Wade. Thanks to your association, the Moirai have turned their attention to our own family. To *you*," he says, pressing his lips tightly.

"No," I breathe, covering my mouth with my fingertips.

"I'm sorry, son. I have no other choice but to release you from your birthright," the Angel of Death says, taking two huge strides toward his son.

Wade stumbles backward, but his father manages to get ahold of him, wrapping his left hand around Wade's upper arm. Crying out in surprise, Wade tries to pull away, but he's no match for his father's strength.

Then, pressing his right hand to Wade's chest, bright orange and white light streams from underneath his father's hand, bursting out in all directions, and escaping through the fabric of Wade's shirt.

The stench of burnt flesh floods the air as Wade scrambles to get away. I wrap my arms around him like a cloak, holding him close, for what little it does. My pulse races and nothing feels safe.

"What did you do?" Wade cries, clutching at his chest. "What is this?"

His father's jaw tightens as he stands firm, his gaze now ice cold. "It's the mark of expulsion."

To Be Continued in the Final Installment of the Windhaven Witches: ***Cursed Legacy***, *Book 4*! Available December 1st, 2020!

NEXT IN THE WINDHAVEN
WITCHES SERIES...

Now that the Moirai are coming for Autumn and Wade, will his expulsion as an Angel of Death put his life on the line?

Find out by reading **Cursed Legacy**, *Book 4 of the Windhaven Witches*! Available December 1st, 2020!

ORDER YOUR COPY NOW!

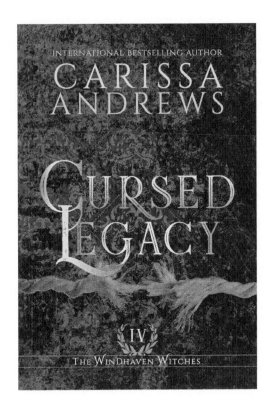

How do you break a family curse set by the Fates themselves?

The Blackwood family curse is closing in on Autumn. No matter where she goes, the tattered red threads of the Moirai follow her. It's only a matter of time and she'll join the early grave of so many Blackwoods before her. What's worse, the curse is expanding and threatening to take more lives.

Expelled from his birthright for loving a necromancer,

Wade is now completely mortal—*and vulnerable*—human. If he dies, there's no coming back because not even Autumn can save him when fate and death conspire.

After an eye-opening revelation, Autumn realizes everything about her crazy, supernatural life has been built on a lie. And that lie is about to wipe out her entire lineage forever. With time running out, will Autumn find a way to appease the Fates and break the curse?

THE WINDHAVEN WITCHES

Secret Legacy *(Sept 15, 2020*)
Soul Legacy *(Oct 6, 2020)*
Haunted Legacy *(Nov 3, 2020)*
Cursed Legacy *(Dec 1, 2020)*

ABOUT THE AUTHOR

Carissa Andrews
Sci-fi/Fantasy is my pen of choice.

 Carissa Andrews is an international bestselling indie author from central Minnesota who writes a combination of science fiction, fantasy, and dystopia. Her plans for 2021 include continuation of her Diana Hawthorne Supernatural Mysteries. As a publishing powerhouse, she keeps sane by chilling with her husband, five kids, and their two insane husky pups, Aztec and Pharaoh.

To find out what Carissa's up to, head over to her website and sign up for her newsletter:
www.carissaandrews.com

facebook.com/authorcarissaandrews

twitter.com/CarissaAndrews

instagram.com/carissa_andrews_mn

amazon.com/author/carissaandrews

bookbub.com/authors/carissa-andrews

goodreads.com/Carissa_Andrews

Printed in Great Britain
by Amazon